Sun on the Wall

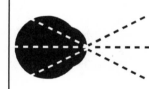

This Large Print Book carries the
Seal of Approval of N.A.V.H.

Sun on the Wall

Wayne D. Overholser

THORNDIKE PRESS
A part of Gale, Cengage Learning

GALE
CENGAGE Learning™

Detroit • New York • San Francisco • New Haven, Conn • Waterville, Maine • London

GALE
CENGAGE Learning™

ALL RIGHTS RESERVED
Thorndike Press® Large Print Western.
The text of this Large Print edition is unabridged.
Other aspects of the book may vary from the original edition.
Set in 16 pt. Plantin.
Printed on permanent paper.

LIBRARY OF CONGRESS CATALOGING-IN-PUBLICATION DATA

Overholser, Wayne D., 1906–1996.
  Sun on the wall / by Wayne D. Overholser. — Large print ed.
    p. cm. — (Thorndike Press large print western)
  ISBN-13: 978-1-4104-2355-9 (alk. paper)
  ISBN-10: 1-4104-2355-7 (alk. paper)
  1. Large type books. 2. Frontier and pioneer life—West
(U.S.)—Fiction. 3. Farmers—Fiction. I. Title.
PS3529.V33S86 2010
813'.54—dc22
                                                  2009048786

Published in 2010 by arrangement with Golden West Literary Agency.

Sun on the Wall

CHAPTER I

Paul Lerner was finishing his second cup of breakfast coffee in the Windsor Hotel dining room when Alex Dolan, editor of the *Rocky Mountain News,* stepped through the door, glanced around until he saw Lerner, then came directly to his table.

Dolan offered his hand, asking, "How's the roving correspondent this morning?"

"Tired." Lerner shook hands and motioned to the chair across the table from him. "Had breakfast?"

Dolan nodded. "I'll have a cup of coffee with you, though. Have any luck in Meeker?"

"No." Lerner signalled the waitress, asked for coffee for Dolan, and went on. "It's the same old story. A little band of Utes come over into Colorado from Utah to hunt. A white man runs into them, gets scared, and takes a shot at them. Then he runs like hell and tells everybody there's an Indian war."

Dolan's coffee came. He reached for the sugar, questioning eyes on Lerner. He asked, "You're free now and looking for another job?"

"I'm free and I'm going to stay free and I am not looking for a job. I had enough riding in the stagecoach to make me feel like I've been through a meat grinder." He started to lift his coffee cup to his mouth, then set it back in the saucer, his eyes narrowing. "Oh no you don't. I don't know what you've got in mind, but I'm not taking the assignment no matter what it is."

"Yes you will," Dolan said. "You're the only man for it. You won't have to even look at a stagecoach. Just get on the train and ride it to Cheyenne."

Lerner shook his head. "No! I'm not hungry yet. When I get hungry, I'll look you up."

"It'll be too late then," Dolan said. "As a matter of fact, I'm not even sure there's a story in what I'm talking about, but I want you to check it out. We like to run historical accounts of the Rocky Mountain region if the source is reliable, and I think this one is."

Dolan paused, watching Lerner, who was lifting his cup to his mouth again, and added, "I'll pay you for your time. If you

8

get a story, I'll pay you for that."

"Why me?" Lerner demanded. "You've got a dozen reporters. Send one of them."

"No, I want you," Dolan said. "This is the kind of thing you specialize in, and you do it well. The average reporter would go to Cheyenne, twist a few arms, bull headfirst into whatever he finds, and wind up in a Cheyenne callaboose. You've got compassion and tact, and if I'm any judge, that's what this job needs."

Dolan paused again, knowing he had to choose his words carefully, then went on. "Besides, you don't have a regular job, so since you freelance, you've got time to work all the angles. You might even get a book out of it. The man I'm talking about had a good deal to do with the Cheyenne Vigilantes."

Anticipation replaced the expression of negative determination on Lerner's face. He had been engrossed in the vigilante organizations in the West for several years and had hoped to write a book about them. Dolan, he knew, was aware of his interest and had baited his trap with that information.

"Well now," Lerner said cautiously, "maybe I would like this job. What am I supposed to do?"

"You're to interview Jim Glenn. He's Mr. Cheyenne himself. I don't know whether they believe in God up there in Wyoming or not, but they sure as hell believe in Jim Glenn. I'm uncertain what you'll do after you see Glenn, but you'll probably interview more people. Of course it's Glenn's story I want, but chances are you'll have to talk to some others to round it out."

Lerner reached into his coat pocket for his pipe and tobacco pouch. "I've heard of Jim Glenn, but I'm a little hazy about him. He's a cripple, isn't he?"

"That's right. He's been in a wheelchair for more than twenty years. He lives alone except for his servants, a man named Ron Ballard and a housekeeper named Ella Evans. He was one of the first settlers in Cheyenne and for a while he had an exciting life. That's the part we want. Then he was shot and got his spine busted up so he's paralyzed from the waist down, but all through these years he's done a lot for Cheyenne. He's given a big chunk of his money away to libraries and hospitals and schools and the like. I've read about the shooting and the trial of the man who did it, but there's a lot that never came out. This is the time to get it."

"Why?"

"His health's failing. Apparently he hasn't got long to live. He's only forty-six, but chronological age doesn't have much to do with it."

Dolan watched Lerner tamp tobacco into his pipe and light it, then went on. "What triggered me on his story was a letter I got from him last week. He said he thought he had something to say and he wants it published in a book or newspaper, or anything else where folks can read it. I knew you had gone to Meeker, but I kept thinking you'd be back any day, so I waited."

Lerner slouched in his chair, pulling on his pipe. This was the kind of assignment he loved, but it wouldn't do to appear too eager. He said casually, "I'll think about it, Alex. I've been looking forward to getting back to Denver and just sitting around and —"

"You're not going to sit around thinking about it very long or I will send one of my men up there," Dolan said sharply. "Now you get up off your behind and pack up and hike over to the depot. If you get a move on, you can catch the morning train that'll put you into Cheyenne by noon. I don't know whether Glenn's alive or not. All I know is that I've waited a week and I'm sure as hell not going to wait another week. Or even another ten minutes."

Lerner saw from the editor's expression that he couldn't play hard-to-get any longer. "All right," he said. "I'm on my way, but what do I use for money?"

Dolan grunted and took his wallet out of his pocket. He counted out fifty dollars and handed the bills to Lerner. "That's expense money." He drew a piece of paper from his wallet. "His address is 2202 Ferguson Street. I copied it down for you. And don't blow that money on a good hand in the first poker game you see."

"I wouldn't think of it," Lerner said blandly as he pocketed the money and the address. Then he asked, "Why did he write to you? There are some good Cheyenne newspapers that would be glad to get his story. The *Daily Sun.* Or the *Daily Leader.* Seems to me I've heard that he's been hard to interview."

"He has," Dolan admitted. "He said in his letter that he hadn't been in any hurry about it because he hadn't thought about dying. I guess he's like most of us, thinking everybody else was going to die but him. Anyhow, he's been going downhill and he decided it was time he did something. He wrote to me because he's heard of me. He said he didn't want to talk to any of the

Cheyenne reporters because they were too close to home and they'd think they knew more about what happened years ago than he did. Some of them were around in those days. Besides, they might slant a story in a way he wouldn't like."

"A prophet is not respected in his home town," Lerner observed. "He's probably right."

"Oh, one more thing," Dolan said as Lerner rose. "He ended his letter by saying the sun was on the wall. I don't know what the hell he was talking about."

"I don't know, either," Lerner said, "but I'll find out."

He left the dining room and hurried along the hall to the stairway, his feet silent on the lush Axminster carpet. He spent only a few minutes in his room packing his shaving gear and a change of clothes into an overnight bag, then took the elevator. He left the hotel by the Larimer Street entrance and ran toward the depot, knowing he had very little time.

He bought a round-trip ticket and sprinted across the depot and on toward the tracks. The train had begun to move as he swung up on the back steps of the rear car. He went inside, panting from his run, and dropped into a seat after stowing his bag in the rack.

He was more tired than he had realized. Every muscle in his body still ached from the jolting he had received when he'd ridden the stagecoach from Rifle to Meeker and back to Rifle. There should be a law against stagecoaches, he thought bitterly.

He tipped his hat forward and put his head back against the red plush seat. Closing his eyes, he thought about the way Jim Glenn had closed his letter: "The sun is on the wall." Lerner had never heard the statement before and it didn't mean any more to him than it had to Dolan. What the hell had Glenn meant?

CHAPTER II

Lerner went directly to the Inter Ocean Hotel in Cheyenne and took a room. The Inter Ocean was older than the Windsor in Denver, having been opened in 1876, but it had been improved in 1884 — only five years ago — with new wallpaper, elegant chandeliers in the lobby, and a twenty-five-foot cherrywood bar. Lerner had stayed here before and knew the rooms were comfortable enough and not at all like the primitive quarters he'd had in Meeker.

He ate dinner and then walked the six blocks from the hotel on the corner of 16th and Capitol to 22nd. He turned to his left and walked one more block to Ferguson and found that he had reached the Glenn house. He could have picked up a cab, but the June day was pleasantly cool with little of the blustery wind that was typical of Cheyenne, so he had enjoyed the walk. And he had needed it to work the kinks out of

15

his legs.

Lerner paused on the corner to study the house. Cheyenne had in the past been called the richest city for its size in the United States. That may or may not have been true, but certainly this section of Ferguson Street had rightly been termed "millionaire's row."

Jim Glenn's house properly belonged with the other fine houses on the street, many of them built by rich cattlemen during the prosperous years before the "big die" and the decline of the price of beef.

The house was designed in Queen Anne Style, with a pointed roof and three tall chimneys. There were two large porches on the Ferguson Street side with several stained-glass windows between them. One of the porches was almost covered by lush vines which had grown up over a trellis to the right of the steps.

An iron fence mounted in cut stone ran along the street sides of the house, which, with its yard and barn, took up a full quarter of the block, as did most of the houses in this part of town.

Lerner smiled as he opened the metal gate, stepped through, closing the gate behind him, then walked up the curving path toward the front door. There were few houses in Denver any finer than these on

Ferguson Street in Cheyenne. Some were larger and more ornate than the Glenn house, but he doubted that many had cost more. He wondered what sort of man Jim Glenn was, or the others, for that matter, who would build houses as ostentatious as these.

He had not quite reached the porch steps when a big man appeared from the shrubbery where he had been working. He moved in front of Lerner, blocking his path, and said in a low, deliberate way, "Mr. Glenn ain't well and he ain't having no visitors."

Lerner was irritated as he wondered why he had come all the way from Denver to see a man who was too ill to receive visitors. He started to turn; then, because the irritation grew and became anger, he asked, "Why did he write to the editor of the *Rocky Mountain News* to send a reporter up here if he's too sick to have visitors?"

"I don't know —" the man began.

"I'm well enough to see him," a man called from the porch. "Let him come in, Ron."

The man moved aside and motioned toward the porch. He mumbled. "I was just following orders," and returned to his work in the shrubbery.

Lerner stepped up onto the porch and saw

17

the man who had called. He sat in a wheel-chair, having been hidden from Lerner by the vines. Now he held out a claw-like hand as he said, "I'm Jim Glenn. I didn't know who you were. Fact is, I almost gave you up because I wrote to Alex Dolan more than a week ago. Our mail service is abominable. I believe it gets worse every year."

"My name's Paul Lerner," Lerner said as he shook hands. "I'm not actually on the *News* staff. I'm a freelance reporter, picking up assignments wherever I can. I was out of town for a week. Dolan waited until I got back because he thought I was particularly suited for this job."

Lerner understood why Jim Glenn was concerned about telling his story now. He looked seventy rather than forty-six. He was so thin that his gray, parchment-like skin seemed to have been pulled tightly over the bones of his face. At one time he must have been a very large and strong man, judging from the size of his bony frame and the big knuckles of his hands, which still had enough strength to give Lerner a firm grip.

His hair was completely white and his voice had the quavery tone of an old man, but his eyes, which were boldly fixed on Lerner's face, were as bright and sharp as a chipmunk's. His mind, Lerner told himself, was as quick and nimble as it had ever been.

"Tell me one thing," Glenn said. "Just why are you particularly suited for the job of interviewing me?"

"Why, I don't know," Lerner said, surprised by the question. "I guess it's mostly that I'm interested in the history of the Rocky Mountain region. I've interviewed a good many pioneers in Colorado, particularly the fifty-niners. I've written their stories largely for the *News,* although I do write for other newspapers, too."

"I see," Glenn said, his eyes narrowing thoughtfully as if he were not sure that Lerner was the man for the job. "Sit down, my friend." He motioned toward a chair. "Would you like something to drink?"

"No thank you," Lerner said.

"Good," Glenn said. "I don't drink any more. I guess I've had too much in my time. The lining of my stomach must be gone. Feels that way when I take a drink these days."

"There's one more thing," Lerner said, "along with the fact that Dolan's regular reporters were probably busy and couldn't be spared. I've been interested in the Vigilante organizations in Denver and the Montana mines, thinking that there was likely some connection. Might be tied in with a lodge, too. This connection might be true with the Cheyenne Vigilantes, although they came a little later. Dolan said you knew a good deal about them."

"A little, my friend, a little." Glenn's gaze had not left Lerner's face, but now he turned his head to look through the network of vines at Ferguson Street and the slowly drifting dust cloud that rose behind a buggy that had just passed. "I'm not sure that I have anything to say that's worth hearing, but I have lived in Cheyenne from almost the first day of its existence . . . I was involved with some of the exciting historical events in the early days. I also believe that those months were filled with interesting personal incidents, but whether my story is worth telling is a decision you'll have to make."

He frowned, his thin lips pressed tightly together. He reached into his coat pocket for a cigar and handed it to Lerner, then took one himself and bit off the end. He raised it to his nose, smelled of it, rolled it between his finger tips, and finally reached for a match.

"Mr. Lerner, I'm not sure you're my man," Glenn said, "although I'll have to settle for you because time has run out for me. I look like an old man, and sitting in this damned chair for more than twenty years is enough to wear any man down to a nubbin. You see, I have already written my story. Now I'm going to leave it up to you as to what happens to it . . . I don't have any idea how well I've done. If you take the job, you'll have to go over it and correct the spelling and punctuation and the like, and maybe improve some of the writing. My housekeeper copied it for me and she writes an adequate hand. Her grammar is good, too, so it may be that when she copied the manuscript, she cleaned up my mistakes. Maybe you won't have to do much with it."

He struck the match, fired his cigar, pulled on it a moment, then went on. "We'd better get one thing straight, Lerner. You've written about the fifty-niners and the excitement of those days that went with their discovery of gold and the vigilante hangings and the Civil War and all of that . . . Now I'm not saying there was no excitement in my first years in early Cheyenne, but I am saying that I had a bigger and better reason for writing about my life than excitement. I'll be damned if I'll let you take all of that out and build up the fighting and screwing and such just to make your story more sensational so you can get a newspaper to buy it."

Lerner's heart sank. He had never run into a situation like this in which his story was already written before he had even heard it. He doubted that, even with his housekeeper's help, Jim Glenn had written anything people would read.

This meant that Lerner would have to rewrite it from scratch and embellish it with whatever other information he could find out about the first months of Cheyenne's history, when Glenn had been a participant in the making of that history. It would have been easier to have taken notes from an interview and written it himself. Still, he was not one to overlook a nugget in the pile of country rock, and there just might be a nugget or two in this pile.

"I won't take it out," Lerner said mildly, "but what was your reason for writing your life story?"

"My own satisfaction in trying to be honest," Glenn said, "although I have another lofty reason which I gave myself as I wrote it. I've made some God-awful mistakes that I've never forgiven myself for. I want other people to read about them so they won't make them. Of course most men and women are too stubborn or too stupid to learn anything even from their own mistakes, but that's their problem, not mine."

He took his cigar out of his mouth and looked at it thoughtfully. "You see, Lerner, we humans are so selfish and narrow-minded it's beyond all reason. My father understood this and accepted it and lived by his own lights. I didn't understand it until I had to sit here in this miserable chair and look out there at Ferguson Street hour after hour and day after day and month after month and watch people go by, or have them come to my door and ask for money for every damn thing you can imagine. When I finally got it figured out, I knew I had to tell other people . . . I guess I'm a kind of crusader, maybe as bad as the loud-mouthed preachers who keep shouting that we're going to hell if we don't get baptized all right and proper. Most people, including me, don't listen to them, and I guess they won't listen to me, but like I said, it's their problem if they don't listen. I've done all I can."

"I'm a little thick-headed today," Lerner said, "but I still don't savvy what it was you figured out."

"Why hell," Glenn said as if it were plain for everybody to see, "it's what the Bible says about reaping what you sow, only I say it a little different. A man ought to know that if he interferes with other people's lives or their happiness or their rights, and for his own pleasure, it's going to come right back on him. Even if he makes an honest mistake it'll come back . . . After all these years I'm not sure I made a mistake."

He stopped and wiped his face with a handkerchief. He sighed. "You know, I give out so damned quick any more it's pathetic."

He reached down beside his chair, picked up a bell and rang it loudly. A moment later a middle-aged woman in a starched black dress came out of the house and stood looking disapprovingly at Lerner.

"This is the reporter I sent for, Ella," Glenn said. "Fetch my manuscript. I'm going to give it to Mr. Lerner."

"You're getting tired, Mr. Glenn," she said. "I'd better wheel you inside —"

"Go on and do what I said," Glenn ordered, raising his voice. "I know I'm tired, but I've got to do this while I can."

She turned, her dress rustling in protest, and disappeared into the house. "You know, Lerner," Glenn said, "at one time I had a lot of money. I built this house trying to keep up with the Careys and the Kellys and the rest of them. I gave money to some good causes, and now it's been pared down. Just this house and a few shares of stock left and several thousand dollars in cash and some town property. Here's Ron Ballard and Ella Evans — who have been taking care of me for years — expecting to inherit a fortune, which they've earned, but I don't have it to give them. Now isn't that a hell of a note?"

Lerner sensed a tough kind of honesty about this man. Suddenly he wanted to read what he had written. He didn't care how much rewriting he had to do. Tough, basic honesty was a rare commodity. Most of the men he had interviewed held themselves up as paragons of virtue and courage. Before this moment Lerner had not been sure he would take the manuscript when the woman brought it to him. Now he knew he would.

A moment later she came sailing out of the house, handed a cardboard box to Glenn and sniffed as she stared at Lerner. "You'd best leave now, mister," she said. "Mr. Glenn is tired."

"My God, Ella," Glenn shouted, sudden anger putting a depth to his voice that it had lacked before, "I'll tell him when to leave. You go on about your business and leave me to mine."

She made another noise, more of a snort than a sniff this time. Turning with another great rustling of her skirt, she stomped back into the house. Glenn opened the box and took out a sheet of paper. He handed it to Lerner, saying, "My life during the first months in Cheyenne was bound up with several people. It's hard to tell where my responsibility for my mistakes ended and theirs began. We all made them and somehow our lives got tied up in a kind of crazy pattern. The trouble was things got out of hand before I realized it. When I was writing this I kept trying to think what would have happened if I had done something different or made a different decision at any of the critical points in my life. Or if one of them had."

Lerner looked at the paper. There were three names: Cherry Owens Lind, who lived five miles from Cheyenne up Crow Creek; Nancy Rush, who lived in a white frame house on the corner of 16th and Russell; and Frank Rush, who was in the Territorial prison in Laramie.

"Who are these people?" Lerner asked. "I mean, why did you give these names —"

Glenn raised a hand. "I'm going to tell you," he said as if irritated by the question. "I just hadn't got to it. These three people are still alive. I haven't seen Cherry for a long time. Twenty years or more. Nancy comes by to visit me quite often. I haven't seen Frank since the trial. I'm not even sure he's still in prison, but I thought the warden or someone there could tell you where he is."

Glenn settled back, his eyes closed. He went on wearily. "I want you to talk to them after you've read what I've written. Maybe they won't talk to you, especially if they know what they say might be published, but go see them anyhow and in the order I have their names listed. You have to make a judgment concerning the events I've written about after you hear what they've got to say."

"I don't see why it's up to me to make a judgment," Lerner said.

"Well, I'll tell you why," Glenn said. "I may have been lying faster'n a horse can trot. You're going to have to decide. Otherwise you'll just be taking my word. Besides, they were familiar with most of the things that happened to me, but they saw those events through different eyes. Actually, they helped create most of the events I'm talking about. You'll need their viewpoints to round out my story. Now I'll tell you it's time for you to go. I'm so damned tired I can't think straight."

"All right," Lerner said, "I'll talk to them. I'll report back to you after I see them."

"If I'm still alive," Glenn said.

Lerner rose and walked to the steps, then turned, realizing that Jim Glenn might not be alive when he finished interviewing the three people. "You said something in your letter to Alex Dolan about the sun on the wall. He didn't know what you meant and I told him I'd find out."

"You'll know when you've read my story," Glenn said. "I mention it because it was one of my father's favorite sayings."

"Good day, sir," Lerner said. He walked rapidly along the path to the gate and let himself into the street.

As he returned to the hotel, he thought again that he had never before been in this situation, his story already written by the man he was to interview and three more people to see. He wondered if these three had written their stories, and if they would say anything basically different from what Glenn had written.

He would have to tell them he was going to write down what they said. Perhaps it would appear in the *Rocky Mountain News* and later in a book, so the chances were that they would say they had no intention of having their private lives dragged out before the eyes of thousands of readers. But he had promised Glenn he would see them, and he would. Then he wondered if Jim

Glenn had a premonition of death. He'd heard of people who had. The thought occurred to him that perhaps in some way Glenn had kept himself alive until he had been able to turn his manuscript over to another man who was capable of doing something with it.

He went to his room in the Inter Ocean Hotel, opened a window, then filled and lighted his pipe, and settled down to read. The woman's handwriting was excellent. He had no trouble reading it, and once started he did not stop to go down to supper until he had finished.

CHAPTER III

I, James Glenn, could begin by saying, as Charles Dickens had one of his characters say, that I was born. I certainly was, in the bedroom of a small farmhouse in Missouri not far from St. Louis. When I was older, my father told me it was a hard birth, with my mother's labor pains lasting for hours. He thought she was going to die. After seeing her suffer so long, he resolved that he would never make her go through it again, and as far as I know, he never had sexual relations with her after that.

He didn't talk to me about sex, but I suspect that he lacked the drive most men have. It was not, of course, the kind of thing a father would discuss with his son, but I am quite sure he did not have any women after my mother died. I failed to inherit his ascetic temperament. After I grew up, I did my share of drinking and fighting and whoring, and I am afraid I was the source of a

30

good deal of concern to my father.

I do not remember very much about my mother. She died when I was six years old, so she had some influence on my life. I have retained a mental picture of her. However, the picture may not be very accurate. Possibly most of it came from what my father told me about her. He worshipped her, he idealized her, and of course when he talked to me about her, he always made her out to be a sort of earthly angel.

I do know that my mother was not very strong. She made me take naps in the afternoons and she always lay down with me. She was very blond, with blue eyes and a pale skin that never tanned, although she had a garden and spent a good deal of time out of doors in the sunshine. I've always thought of her as being virginal and virtuous and very, very beautiful in an ethereal sort of way. She was indeed an earthly angel.

One of my most poignant memories as a child was standing beside her grave and listening to the preacher tell what a splendid woman she had been, and then spend the next ten minutes begging God to save her soul. It was a clear April day, with a brisk wind, and I remember thinking that the wind would carry her soul right up into Heaven.

Right or wrong about her, she was a very good woman, and my attitude in this regard has influenced my opinion of the "good women" I have known.

My father raised me. He died in the spring of 1867, eight years after we reached Colorado. I left his house soon after we moved to Colorado, and made my own way from that time on, but he did more to shape my life than anyone else, particularly between the ages of six and sixteen.

I know he loved me very much, partly because I was all he had of my mother. Sometimes he would talk to me for half an hour at a time on all kinds of subjects including religion and politics and people in general. Philosophy, too, and most of all, I think, the moral code or system of ethics that each of us take for ourselves.

I didn't have to say a word to prime him. All I had to do was sit quietly and listen. At the time most of what he said was wasted on me, but it wasn't wasted in the long run because in later years much of it came back to me.

It seemed to me then that he was a strange man. I guess he was. In many ways I didn't know him at all. That may sound crazy, but the truth is I never knew the inner man. I have a conviction that he did not know himself. I think he always lived for other people, first my mother, and then me. I also think he lived for causes, particularly the Free Soil movement.

My father hated slavery with a passion I never knew him to feel about anything else. He could not, of course, continue to live in Missouri, which was a slave state, so after my mother's death he sold the small farm he owned and moved west into Kansas. We lived there for ten years until we moved to Colorado.

My father was a hard worker. I remember how he told me repeatedly that when the sun rose high enough to shine on the east wall of the house, it was time to be up and doing. In winter he would not let me stay in bed that long because the sun was lazy during the cold months, he would say, and didn't rise until it was late.

During the spring and summer months, when the field work had to be done, he would say to me while I was still in bed, "Get up, Jimmy. The sun's on the wall." He was seldom harsh with me, but this was the one thing that made him lose his temper. I soon learned, after a few painful sessions in which his razor strap and my backside made contact, that I would feel better if I got up when he called me the first time.

Along with being a hard worker, he was also a gambler. The combination seems to me an odd one. Not that he ever had much to gamble with when I was a boy. He would try, though, even if the bets were for small amounts. He would bet on which bird would fly first if two were sitting on a fence. He would bet on the date the first killing frost would come or when the first snow would fall or whether our cow's calf would be a bull or a heifer.

He was also a very religious man, apparently never considering the possibility that gambling might be contrary to religion. Obviously it was not contrary to his. I will admit that he had a peculiar religion, and although it seems to me that all religions are peculiar, his was more peculiar than most. He had absolutely no use for the itinerant preachers who floated through the country in those days, particularly those who preached hellfire and brimstone sermons, and nearly all of them preached that type of scary sermon.

I have never understood why the preachers put out that kind of teaching. My father often said the same thing. I cannot accept the explanation that they believed it. If they had thought about it at all, they would have seen that it didn't add up. Maybe they never thought about it, but simply accepted it because it was what they had been taught. Or perhaps they sensed that it was what the people wanted to hear and they were not anxious to disappoint their listeners, so they preached "the word" and "good, gospel sermons."

Anyhow, my father always claimed that preachers were the laziest men alive and were the worst kind of parasites, coming around and wanting you to put them up for the night and give them a big evening meal and let them have the pick of everything on the table including the breast of the chicken. They did not, of course, intend to pay for anything.

My father always gave them short shrift as soon as he found out they were preachers. He'd just point down the road and say, "Git. You won't have any trouble finding a sucker who'll put you up." He'd shake his head as the preacher mounted and rode away. He'd say, "I just don't savvy how they can do it, move in on you and take the best of everything and lie about God while they're doing it."

My father always got furious about the way the preachers and the churches treated Negroes, even using the Bible to prove that black people were inferior and created by

God to serve white people, and to go from there and say that slavery was God's way of taking care of the blacks.

"You can twist anything to make it prove what you want it to prove, and that includes the Bible," he would say. "The white people act superior even in church, not letting the Negroes worship with them. You'd think that having to sit beside a black man is going to send you right down to hell."

I've thought about it a good deal, but I have never decided how much my father influenced me and shaped me into the man I became. Of course it's not the kind of thing that can be measured. I am sure my father did nothing to diminish my appetite for lusty living. He never lectured me about it, something for which I am thankful.

He was a philosopher of sorts, and since I have a tendency to run in that direction, I suppose he gave my thinking some direction. I have read a great deal, although books have always been hard to come by. I think my father's influence was the greatest in this area, perhaps in setting up my sense of values and establishing some of my basic virtues, such as my desire to work and my belief in being honest in all things. Also in the more abstract beliefs in God and man, and in man's relationship with man.

As I said, my father's greatest weakness was gambling, and although I have done some gambling, I never particularly enjoyed it. I mean, I could take it or leave it, but my father couldn't. On the other hand, women have always been my weakness. I could never turn one down until I became an invalid, and then it was only because I had no choice.

As far as I could tell, women meant nothing to my father after my mother's death. All of this proves nothing, I guess, except that what is one man's meat is another man's poison, even if the men are father and son.

CHAPTER IV

By the time I was sixteen, when we left Kansas, I was a big, strong boy who could keep up with my father in any kind of physical work, but he refused to involve me in his other activities. For instance, he was mixed up in the border fighting between the Free Soil men and the Border Ruffians who kept making trouble by coming across the line and burning houses and barns and sometimes murdering the anti-slavery Kansans. I mean, I think he was involved in the fighting, but he never talked about it, so it was something I could only guess at.

I had never considered my father a fighting man, but in looking back on our last years in Kansas, I have a feeling he did his share of fighting and he probably belonged to one of the secret Free Soil societies that flourished in Kansas during those bloody years.

He would be gone for two or three days at

a time, leaving me to take care of the chores. He always warned me when he left to keep my eyes open for strangers and my gun handy, and to head for the house if anybody showed up that I didn't know.

The house was built of logs and was a sort of fort with heavy doors and strong bars and thick shutters for the windows. Underneath was a cellar. A tunnel led from it to the cut bank of a nearby creek. If we were ever pinned down and the Border Ruffians succeeded in burning the house, we could get away through the tunnel and probably escape by hiding in the weeds and brush along the stream.

Before my father left on one of these trips and after he came home he always gave me a sort of lame reason for being gone. I never questioned him, because I thought he'd tell me if he wanted me to know. Probably it was better that I didn't know, because I couldn't tell anything if I didn't know it.

We heard a great deal of John Brown in those days. I don't know how much my father had to do with him, but it may have been a good deal. I only saw him once, when he rode past our farm and my father stood in the road talking to him.

I was close to Brown for only a few seconds. As soon as I walked up, my father sent me away to do some chore that didn't need to be done right then, and the one sharp memory I have of him was his fierce eyes. They were the eyes of a zealot, a fanatic.

Somehow I found it hard to put my father in the company of a man like that. He was too gentle, too mild, and yet there were times when he got worked up about slavery and the brutal crimes that some of the slave owners committed. During those times, which did not come very often, I saw in my father's eyes the same wild expression I saw in John Brown's eyes.

I suppose that all men of John Brown's caliber are finally crucified in one way or another. They are John the Baptist men who make way for the Lord, and without them I suspect that man would never progress in a humanitarian way.

I'm sure my father was more of a zealot than I suspected at the time. He may even have been a conductor on the Underground Railroad, but I never knew for a fact that he actually brought slaves to our farm. However, we did have a cave in the side of a hill on the upper end of our place. My father ordered me to stay away from it, saying there were outlaws in the country who sometimes sought refuge there and it was dangerous.

Once I was caught in a violent storm and couldn't get back to the house before it hit, so I sought shelter in the cave. I found plenty of evidence that someone had been there recently. I never said anything to my father about what I had found, but I thought then and I still think that slaves, not outlaws, used the cave.

At any rate, he was never caught. If he took part in the fighting he was never wounded. He was very restless the last year we lived there and kept talking about leaving. I suppose he worried about getting caught or being shot. Anyhow, when the news of the discovery of gold in the Pike's Peak area reached us, he decided to move out there and get rich. It sounded like good adventure to me, so I was all for it.

He sold the farm, bought a herd of horses, and prepared to set out for the gold fields. Before I knew it, we were headed west over the Smoky Hill Trail. I guess there isn't anything that's more of a gamble than buying and selling horses, and I never knew of any kind of man who could look you right in the eyes and lie faster than a horse trader.

My father, being honest, was at a disadvantage, but he had a way of being silent on certain matters that he didn't want the other man to know. Perhaps that was a form of dishonesty, but my father could accept it and keep his moral code intact.

He hired two men and we took the horses through to Denver without much trouble or loss, although the last hundred miles of the Smoky Hill Trail were tough ones, and many a man lost his life in that stretch. We weren't slowed down by women and children, and we had no wagons, so we moved fast. We didn't have any run-ins with either Indians or horse thieves — just lucky, I guess — and ended up in the Elephant Corral in Denver with one of the best horse herds that ever made it up the Smoky Hill.

Everything in Denver was high, but my father expected that. He sold most of the horses at a good profit, keeping one saddle horse, a sorrel, which he gave me, and one team of work animals. He bought a wagon and looked around for a place to settle.

He had no use for Denver, which was tough and wild, and he didn't want to go to one of the mining camps. Eventually he decided on Golden, which was right at the foot of the Rockies where Clear Creek comes out of its canyon. He built a small house and had a big garden, and made a living freighting with his team and wagon between Golden and the mining camps.

I was seventeen the following spring. My feet were too itchy to stay home, so I told my father I was leaving. He took it pretty well, better than I had thought he would. Knowing me as well as he did, I suppose he expected me to do exactly what I did. I'm sure the signs were there to be read, and he was a sensitive man. He handed me one hundred dollars and asked me to write once in a while so he'd know where I was.

I had to do it, and I have never been sorry that I left home, but I didn't find the world as much of an oyster for me to open as I had expected. I went to Black Hawk and worked in a mine, but I couldn't stand being in a dark tunnel day after day. I had to be out in the sunlight and feel the wind on my face.

I quit my mining job and went to work in a store in Central City, but I couldn't stand counter jumping either. Eventually I discovered that I could sell all the firewood in Black Hawk and Central City that I could cut, so I chopped and hauled wood most of the time I was in Colorado.

My first big problem was a place to live. I solved it by building a small cabin in the canyon north of Black Hawk. Of course I didn't get rich cutting and hauling wood, but I was outside and I made a living. I had time for myself, too, if I wanted to go fishing.

The truth was I couldn't stand the regularity of a job working for somebody else and having him boss me around all the time. During the bad winter weather, when there was too much snow on the ground to cut wood, I managed to swallow my pride and work for a carpenter in Black Hawk. Although I rebelled as I always had when I was working for daily wages, I disciplined myself and kept my job. I was glad later on that I had the training.

After the Civil War broke out we heard all kinds of wild stories about an army of Texans that would be invading Colorado, moving north from New Mexico. They wanted the Colorado mines, and unless they were stopped they'd march right on north into Montana and grab those mines. By that time, of course, they would have cut California off from the rest of the Union and they'd have had the mines there, too. The South didn't have the wealth that the North had, and the gold they'd have from the western mines might have saved them.

Anyhow, the last thing I wanted was for a bunch of wild-eyed Texans coming into Colorado and telling me what to do. I knew enough of what the Border Ruffians from

Missouri had done in Kansas. Along with a number of men from Black Hawk and Central City, I joined the First Colorado Volunteers in the fall of 1861 and started learning how to be a soldier in Camp Weld, which was two miles south of Denver.

I guess we were a pretty wild bunch. None of us took to soldiering very well. If I rebelled against the regularity of an ordinary job, I would naturally be more than rebellious when I had to suffer army discipline and believe me I suffered.

Everyone in Denver, I think, was made happy by the orders we received on February 13, 1862, to march south. We moved out of Denver on February 22, the day after a Union army in New Mexico had been beaten in the battle of Valverde.

The march south was no picnic. Until we reached the Santa Fe Trail the road was more of a path than a real road. The weather, as my father often said, was cold enough to freeze the balls off a brass monkey.

When we reached Pueblo, we heard for the first time about the defeat at Valverde and that the Rebel army was marching up the Rio Grande. After we got that news, we knew we had to move because it was going to be up to us to stop the Texans. Most of the regulars that had been in the West had been called East. Even with several inches of snow on the ground we made forty miles a day.

As we were climbing Raton Pass, we had word from Fort Union that the Rebels had occupied Albuquerque and Santa Fe, and would soon be attacking Fort Union itself. We made some kind of record after that, I guess. Carrying nothing but our arms and blankets, we marched through the darkness to the Cimarron River in New Mexico.

We had to stop when we reached the Cimarron because we were simply worn out. Some of the horses pulling the baggage wagons actually fell dead in their harness. We had covered ninety-two miles in the past thirty-six hours, so it was understandable that we were dead tired.

The weather was still bitterly cold. After we rested, we went on to Fort Union, reaching it March 10. We had covered more than four hundred miles in thirteen days. We remained at the fort for twelve days, resting and receiving regulation uniforms. Arms and ammunition, too. The officers decided it was a good time to start drilling us again, but we'd come to fight, not to drill, and we didn't like it any better than we had at Camp Weld.

We had our wish about fighting two weeks later. We left the fort, marching south, and ran head on into the Rebel column in Glorieta Pass. I guess the Texans figured it would be easy enough to take Fort Union, and it probably would have been if the First Colorado Volunteers hadn't been there to stop them. I don't think they even knew we were in New Mexico, so I guess they were somewhat surprised when they met up with us.

We whipped them in two battles, one called "Apache Canyon," on March 26, the other "Glorieta," on March 28. I've met Texans after the war who claimed we didn't whip them at all, but I guess that's like a Texan.

The truth is these battles were very important, sometimes being referred to as the "Gettysburg of the West." The Texans turned around and went home, their commander, General Sibley, arriving at Fort Bliss near El Paso during the first week in May. How anyone, even a braggy Texan, could call that a victory for them is beyond me, but then, I'm not a Texan.

The regiment continued in service in Colorado and neighboring territories through the rest of the war, but I took a bullet in my left leg in the last fight. Although it wasn't a particularly serious wound, it was painful and it was enough to get me sent back to Denver and out of the regiment, which was fine with me. I'd have gone crazy sitting out the rest of the war with no fighting to do.

I had left my saddle horse with my father in Golden. I stayed with him until the soreness was gone from my thigh and I was able to work. He didn't have much to say about what he'd been doing, but he was never one to talk about his personal exploits.

Before the firing on Fort Sumter and in the early months of the war there had been a good deal of Confederate sentiment and intrigue in Colorado, and I suspect my father was involved in some of the activity against the secessionists just as he had been in Kansas. In any case, the trouble had been pretty well settled around Denver by the time I got back from New Mexico.

My father, of course, was glad to see me come home mostly in one piece, and he was sorry to see me leave to return to Black Hawk. He was lonely, and although he never said so, I'm sure he wanted me to stay with him, but now that I felt all right, my feet were itchy again and I had to go.

He continued with his freighting business, usually showing up in Black Hawk at least once a month. He always stayed overnight with me, so we were never out of touch very long.

CHAPTER V

When I'd left Black Hawk to volunteer, I had nailed the door to my cabin shut and had put shutters on the windows. I knew something was wrong, the evening I came back, as soon as I was in sight of the cabin. The door was open, the shutters were off the windows, and smoke was pouring out of the chimney.

I'd heard plenty of stories about men jumping mining claims, but jumping a cabin was a new wrinkle to me. At first I was puzzled and surprised, and then shocked, and finally I was mad. The closer I got, the madder I got. It was a hell of a note, I told myself, when a man goes off to war to fight for everybody who stays home all safe and snug, and then finds that somebody has grabbed his home while he was gone.

I stepped out of my saddle and went into the cabin without knocking or hollering howdy. Two miners were sitting at the table eating supper. They were filthy, and the inside of the cabin was a dirty mess; it smelled worse than any pigpen I had ever seen or smelled.

One of the men yelled, "You never learned no manners, did you, just walking in —"

"It's my cabin," I said. "Git out."

"Oh no, we ain't doing no such thing," the second one said. "We found the place empty, so we moved in."

"Possession is nine-tenths of the law." The first one grinned as smug as a cat licking up spilled cream. "You've only got one-tenth, mister."

By that time I was in a killing rage. It's a miracle I didn't pull my gun and shoot both of them where they sat. Instead, I stomped up to the table and banged their heads together. I did it three or four times until I got a good solid crack that took the fight out of them, and then I threw them out. That gave me nine-tenths of the law and left them with one-tenth.

I grabbed up some dishes and threw them at the men. There was a big bowl filled with hot beans. I guess they'd just taken it off the stove. Anyhow, I hit one man in the face with them, the beans running from his forehead clean down to his chin. He took off down the road howling like a turpentined dog. The other one almost ran over him before they got out of sight.

I yelled at them, "Git out of camp and stay out."

It was a comical sight, I guess, but I was too mad to see anything funny in it. They were running so fast and making so much noise I don't think they heard me, but I never saw them in Black Hawk again, so it seems they took my advice whether they heard me or not.

I didn't feel like starting to clean up that night, so I cooked my supper outside and slept outside. I started trying to make the cabin livable again in the morning. I never had been much on cleaning house, but I cleaned that cabin. It took me three days of throwing stuff out and scrubbing with lye, and I still didn't get rid of that sickening, insidious stink. It lingered for days.

I fetched my team and wagon from the man I'd left them with, but it took me a while to work up customers for my wood. When the snow got too deep late in the fall for me to continue cutting wood, I went to work again for the carpenter I'd worked for before I'd volunteered.

That was the way my life went until the first of October, 1866. All the time I kept thinking I'd save enough money to start some kind of business of my own. I had saved a few hundred dollars, but by that time I realized I was never going to make it if I didn't hit something big. Otherwise I'd be like thousands of other men I'd seen come and go in the mines and spend their life working for wages. I didn't intend to do any such thing, but the trouble was I couldn't see anything big coming my way in Black Hawk or Central City.

There was always the opportunity to invest in a poker game, but my savings had come too hard for that. I had plenty of chance to buy mines, but that, too, was more of a gamble than I wanted to take. Prospecting wasn't for me, either. I couldn't tell country rock from rich ore and I didn't have any real desire to learn the difference.

I'd decided it was my last year cutting wood. I didn't know where I was going, but I knew I was going. I talked to my father about my future. He didn't have any good advice to give me, although he offered to take me into his freighting business, which had been more profitable than my wood-cutting. I was too restless for that, so I thanked him and said no.

He told me he had over one thousand dollars saved and I could borrow it if I found something I wanted. Well, I hadn't found anything, and the more I thought about it, the more I was convinced that it didn't make much difference whether I stayed in Black Hawk or went to Denver. I needed capital and that was the truth.

I'd worked in a store long enough to know I didn't want that. I'd had all the farming I could stomach back in Kansas. I even thought about buying and selling horses, but I didn't know horses well enough or the tricks of horse traders, so I realized that the first good trader I ran into would cheat me out of every cent I had.

I would have liked to own a stage line. Or some kind of contracting business — house-building, for instance. But even if I borrowed from my father, I wouldn't have more than fifteen hundred dollars, and that wasn't enough to set me up in any kind of business.

On the first day of October I fell into a job I hadn't expected. I came back to my cabin after delivering a load of wood in Central City and found two young women waiting for me. They'd driven a buggy up from Black Hawk and were just about ready to leave when I got there.

They introduced themselves as Rosy and Flossie Martin. They were identical twins, good-looking, blond, blue-eyed, and on the plump side. They were dressed fine and fancy in black silk dresses that rustled in quiet luxury every time they moved, bonnets with long drooping plumes, and red shawls that gave them a dignified, respectable appearance and made them look older than they were.

I studied one and then the other, and decided I was seeing double. They looked that much alike. They wore pins on the front of their dresses, one with the letter *R*, the other with the letter *F*. Later on, when I knew them intimately, I discovered that Rosy had a big brown mole on her left buttock. When I was in bed with one of them, that mole was the only way I had of telling which one I had. When they were dressed, I couldn't tell them apart unless they wore those pins.

I guessed their profession, but I wasn't real sure until they told me. They were honest and saw no point in not informing me right away. Rosy said, "We're whores. There are plenty of other names folks call us, especially the women, but when you get right down to cases, that's what we are."

"Do you have any scruples about working for us?" Flossie asked.

"Not a bit," I said, but I'll admit I was

taken back a little by their frank announcement.

"We want a house," Rosy said. "We think men like to be reminded of home even if we're not their wives."

"That's right," Flossie said. "We've got an organ. I play real pretty and Rosy sings real good, so every evening before we transact any business, we'll entertain 'em. That's why we're not gonna set up our place alongside all the other ones. We don't want to get a bad name."

"Hell no," Rosy said. "We're going to have us a dignified business and we ain't gonna stand for nobody being rowdy. If they are, we'll throw 'em out."

I kept looking from one to the other just as I had been. It was the damnedest feeling, kind of like looking at a woman's face and then turning and seeing it in a mirror. I still didn't know what they wanted, so I said, "It sounds good, but what's all this got to do with me?"

They seemed surprised. Rosy said, "We told you. We want you to build us a house. We've bought some land in the canyon below here. We want the house good-sized: two bedrooms, a front room, and a kitchen. A good, big front room that'll have room for the organ and several men. They'll have to sit in it and wait their turn."

"And a privy, of course," Flossie said. "Behind the house."

"A woodshed, too," Rosy added.

"And maybe a small barn," Flossie said, nodding as if dreaming about the whole business. "We're gonna have us a nice horse and buggy. We talked to a man in Black Hawk and he said you'd been working at being a carpenter for several winters. We've got money, and you can take some of your pay in trade."

I wasn't so anxious to do that, though later on I did. Anyhow, the money sounded fine. I said, "I've always worked for somebody else, but I can do it."

"Good," Rosy said. "Start tomorrow."

"In the morning bright and early," Flossie added. "We want the house well enough along to give us shelter before the cold weather sets in."

"Better build the privy first," Rosy said.

"That's right," Flossie agreed. "We're going to live in a tent and watch you build the house."

They were the damnedest pair I ever ran into, but I told myself they just might do all right. Actually I didn't care whether they did or not as long as they had the money to pay me. I hired a man I'd once worked with and we staked out the positions for the buildings and hauled lumber and got started.

We had good luck with the weather and got the house framed up and the doors and windows in before the first bad storm hit us late in November, but it took us a good part of the winter to do the finishing work. By the time we had the wallpaper on and the painting done, we were ready for spring.

We got paid, all right, and I landed another house-building job in Black Hawk, so I kept my man and went right on working. Almost every evening as I went back to my cabin, I stopped at the Martin house and had a cup of coffee with Rosy and Flossie. They had the organ sure enough, and Flossie could play pretty well and Rosy could sing, but they were better cooks than they were musicians, and once in a while they asked me to stay for supper.

Their business was fine right from the start. They gave the men a touch of what they had left back home before they came to Colorado to get rich in the mines, which mighty few of them did. The girls sang some of the old sentimental songs. When I'd spend an evening with them I was surprised how many of those tough old miners would break down and cry like children when Rosy sang "Just Before the Battle, Mother" and "Tenting Tonight."

Most of the men were Civil War veterans and they'd sung these songs themselves. Then Rosy would sing "Juanita," and when she got to "Weary looks, yet tender, Speak their fond farewell," there would be few dry eyes in the room.

The craziest side of the girls came out one Sunday afternoon when we were sitting in the kitchen drinking coffee and eating one of Rosy's chocolate cakes. Rosy was the one who liked to cook and Flossie liked to sew, and both of them wanted to get married.

"Why don't you marry one of us?" Rosy asked. "We'd make you a good wife."

"Sure we would," Flossie added. "We've had lots of practice with men."

I wanted to laugh, but I didn't dare risk it. They'd have run me out of the place if I had. It was plain they were deadly serious. I almost choked on my coffee trying to keep from snorting. Finally I asked, "Who do you think would marry a whore?"

That made them mad. Rosy said hotly, "We ought to chase you up the road to your place."

"If I knew where the broom was, I would," Flossie said, "and I'd hit you over the head every jump you made."

"Where do you think men on the frontier got their wives?" Rosy demanded.

"I'll tell you," Flossie said. "They got them out of whorehouses, that's where. And they made good wives and mothers."

"If you really want to get married," I said, "why don't you get out of your profession? You could find work in Black Hawk or Central City."

"Work?" Rosy demanded. "We don't want to work."

"Hell no," Flossie added. "What we're doing is better than working."

I wasn't so sure about that when I stopped in one evening in May. Rosy looked as if she'd been through a meat grinder. One eye was swollen shut, her nose was twice the size it usually was, and on one side of her face she had the biggest, most painful-looking black-and-blue bruise I ever saw on a human being in my life.

I asked what had happened and Flossie said, "She don't feel like talking much, so I'll tell you. That damned, mean Bully Bailey done it last night. They went into her bedroom and pretty soon I heard her scream. I ran into her room. A couple of men who were waiting in the front room were right behind me. All we saw was Bailey's hind end going through the window."

Rosy's lips were all puffed up, and she had trouble talking, but she managed to say, "I always was afraid of him."

"We don't usually do business with that kind of man," Flossie said, "but we didn't know he was that bad. He just fooled us."

"Now we've got to close down for a while," Rosy said with regret. "I can't let anybody see me this way."

I started looking for Bailey. I knew the bastard and I was surprised when Flossie said that Bailey had fooled them. There wasn't any doubt about the kind of man he was. He was big, taller than me and twenty-thirty pounds heavier. He was a wicked bar-room fighter who would gouge a man's eyes out if he could. I'd seen him whip smaller men than he was, but I had never seen him tangle with a real good small man or one that was bigger than he was.

His real name was Roscoe Bailey, but folks always called him Bully because that's exactly what he was. He didn't like it one little bit, but once the name got hung on him, he couldn't stop people from calling him that.

I found him just after dark in the Western Star. He was bellied up against the bar, wedged in between a couple of his cronies. I didn't say anything to him. I just went up to him and grabbed him by a shoulder with my left hand and yanked him around to face me, then I let him have it right square on his nose.

Well sir, you should have seen the blood fly all around him in a bright red shower. It was just as if you'd squeezed an overripe plum in your hand. He let out a squall of pain. Anger, too, I guess. He shook his head and came at me like a bull, his big fists flying.

I ducked a wild punch and hit him on the chin. It stopped him, but he stayed on his feet, weaving a little and kind of pawing at me. I kicked him in the crotch and I think I must have knocked his balls about six inches higher than they were. He bent over and froze there. I guess he hurt so much he was paralyzed.

"Get out of camp," I said. "If I see you around here again, you'd better go for your gun because I'll kill you. I'll cut your head off and give it to Rosy Martin to hang on her wall."

He didn't move even then, but the men he'd been drinking with came to him and grabbed his arms. They practically carried him out through the batwings. I started toward the door to see if they had left or were fixing to drygulch me and then I saw my father standing in the front of the crowd. I didn't even know he was in Black Hawk.

He'd never seen me like that before. He'd probably never seen me fight anybody. His mouth had sprung open and he was staring at me as if he didn't know who I was. Maybe he didn't; maybe for a few seconds I had not been the son he had raised.

"Let's go home," I said. "I haven't had any supper yet. Have you?"

He shook his head. He followed me out of the Western Star and walked up the canyon past the Martin house and on to my cabin. He didn't say a word all the way there.

Chapter VI

I built a fire and put the coffee pot on. I warmed up some left-over beans and fried bacon, and made biscuits. I set the table and put out a jar of honey, and all the time I was doing this my father sat on a chair at the table and looked at me. I had a funny idea that he wasn't seeing me, and then it struck me that it wasn't the fight that was bothering him. I didn't have any idea what it was, though.

As soon as I had everything on the table, I said, "It's ready. I'll bet your tapeworm is hollering at you."

He didn't say a word until we started to eat. Then he sat staring at his food for a moment before he said, "You handled that big fellow good. You went after him like a mad grizzly."

"I was mad enough," I said, and told him what had happened.

"If that woman is a whore, she's got to

expect some of that," he said. "Not that I condone it. It's just that now and then you find a man who's that way."

"Not if I can help it," I said. "Both women are popular in camp. I'll kill Bailey if he shows up in Black Hawk again and he knows it. He likewise knows that no jury would convict me of murder."

He shrugged and started to eat, but his heart wasn't in it. After a while he asked, "Got any ideas yet about what you want to do or where you want to go?"

I shook my head. "No."

"I've been thinking about the railroad that's being built across Nebraska and ought to be in Wyoming pretty soon. Maybe it is now. I don't know. Anyhow, there's bound to be some good-sized towns spring up along the railroad where there's nothing but prairie now. If you'd take my money and put it with yours, you could buy some property cheap. It's bound to go up."

I hadn't thought of that. It made sense. The railroad would bring people West who would farm or raise cattle, and it would give them the means of shipping their produce back East where the big markets were. More than that, a lot of other people would come with the ranchers and farmers: storekeepers, lawyers, doctors, school teachers, newspaper men, and a lot of others. Why hell, the belt of country along the railroad would be settled and booming in just a few years.

The more I thought about it, the better it looked to me. I'd never been real excited about the mining country. It was a take-out kind of industry that didn't put anything back. Sooner or later the gold or silver or whatever metal was being mined would be gone and the camp would be deserted. Farming and ranching were different — the land would always be there and they wouldn't leave ghost towns all over the country the way mining would.

"You've got a good idea," I said. "I'll think about it some more and maybe head up into that country. I'm ready to quit here as soon as I finish building the house I'm working on. It's about done. You'd better go with me."

"No," he said with more emotion than the suggestion called for. "I've got a feeling that my race is about run. I won't live through the summer, so I might as well stay right here."

I don't know when I had heard anything that shocked me as much as that. I put my fork down and swallowed. All of a sudden I had a crazy kind of hollow feeling in my belly. My father was my only close living relative. I guess there were some cousins back in Illinois, but I didn't know them and I didn't want to.

"Now look," I said. "You're not fifty years old. Most men are in the prime of life at your age. I've never known you to be sick. What are you talking this way for?"

He didn't look at me. He went on eating, taking one slow bite after another. Finally he said, "Well, Jimmy, I'm not superstitious. At least I don't think I am, and I never put any faith in folks who claimed to have second sight, but lately, say the last month or so, I've had some notions about dying. Came on me pretty fast. Dreams, mostly, but they're so real I can't get them out of my mind."

"Dreaming about dying doesn't mean you're going to die," I said. "I don't like to hear you talk that way."

I felt like laughing or crying or just getting up and walking out of the cabin. I don't think anything that had happened to me since I was a child had bothered me like this. I took a drink of coffee and discovered that my hands were shaking. It was so bad I actually spilled some of it, and my cup wasn't full, either.

Even though it all sounded crazy to me and wasn't like my father, who had always been a sane and stable man, I couldn't entirely discount what he had said. I remembered there had been men in the First Colorado Volunteers who had had premonitions that they were going to be killed. They had, too — every one of them.

My father pushed his plate back, his food only half eaten. "It really isn't important, Jimmy. Life is a transient thing as far as this earth-plane is concerned. I've had a good life. Eight happy years with your mother and the good years while you were growing up in Kansas. I haven't seen much of you after we moved here, but I've known what you were doing and where you were. I've been proud of you, too. I know you're the kind of man who'll get along and be able to take care of himself."

He had picked up his fork and was starting to poke at a piece of bacon. Then he put the fork down and raised his head and looked squarely at me. He said, "Jimmy, the sun's on the wall for you."

I knew what he meant, all right. He'd said something like that too many times when I'd been a boy for me to mistake his meaning. He was absolutely correct. I'd spent enough time here in Black Hawk cutting wood and building houses, and now it was time to get on with my life somewhere else, a place where I could make it count.

"Yes," I said. "I'll be on my way as soon as I finish my obligations around here."

"I was thinking about Julesburg," he said. "Right now they say it's hell on wheels, and I guess it is, but they'll settle down after the end of track is pushed on West. It might turn out to be quite a city."

"It might," I said, but I wasn't at all sure. It seemed to be too far away from any place of importance to become a city.

"I finally had a run of luck," he went on. "That's what I'm working up to tell you. I've been a great one to piddle around with little bets. You know that, of course. I've won some and I've lost some, and all the time I kept working and saving when I could. My gambling never amounted to much and I've always come out about even, but a few days ago I decided to try for the big one, so I went into Denver and got into a big poker game."

I had trouble believing what I was hearing. This wasn't like him, either. The little bets like wagering fifty cents on which bird was going to fly off the fence first was his size, not the big poker game. I knew he had played some, but I also knew he wasn't particularly good at it.

I'd watched some games here in Black

Hawk and Central City and I'd seen some big winners, professional gamblers who knew when to press their luck and when to pull back. It seemed to me it was a matter of intuition and the big ones knew when to trust it.

I've talked to some of these gamblers. The interesting part of it is that none of them can pin it down and tell exactly what the feeling is or why and how intuition works the way it does. The trick is to know when to trust it, and even if they can't describe the feeling, they can and do recognize it.

The more I thought about it, the more certain I felt that my father did not understand this or had not done enough big-time gambling to recognize the feeling if it did come to him. I didn't know what a run of luck meant to him, or even what he called big-time gambling. It might be winning or losing fifty dollars. Anyhow, I puffed hard on my pipe and waited.

For some reason he was having trouble telling me about it, maybe because he sensed I found it hard to believe. I'm sure he realized that what he had done was not his customary behavior. Maybe he had even surprised himself, and then I remembered what he had said a little before about living through the summer.

Right then I realized why he had done it. The way he saw it, he wasn't going to live long enough to put together any sizeable amount of money. His savings, like mine, had dribbled in too slowly, so he had decided on the big play — but I still didn't know how big was big.

He'd sat back in his chair all this time without saying anything. He'd been staring into space and probably not seeing anything. Now he raised a hand to his chin and began feeling the deep cleft that was there, a sign that he had something important to say. I'd seen that gesture too often to be mistaken, so I knocked my pipe out and filled it again and waited for him to go on.

"Well," he said finally, "I took all but about fifty dollars of my savings and went to Denver. I had twelve hundred dollars, and with that kind of money I could pick my game. The funny part of it is that I still don't know exactly why I did it or why I drifted into the saloon I did, but when I walked up to a table, I knew it was the one where I wanted to play.

"At first my luck was just average, and then I began getting the big hands. By sunup I was two thousand dollars ahead. I cashed in and came home and put all of it under the hearthstone. You'll find it there when the time comes. You'll have enough to make the big gamble, and that's what you've got to do."

"I don't know what to say," I said, and I didn't.

There was a strange, unreal feeling about the whole business, my father thinking he was going to die soon and going on this gambling spree and then coming here and telling me about it. I got up and went around the table and laid a hand on his shoulder.

"We haven't been together as much as we'd both like," I said, "but I can't face this dying business. It's been good to know that I had a place to go when I got out of the army or any other time when I needed it."

He put a hand up on mine and patted it, but he didn't look at me. I guess both of us were about ready to start crying. It was a new feeling for me. Neither of us was what I'd call sentimental. We'd never talked like this to each other before in our lives. It was a moment before we could speak, and his voice trembled when he did.

"You know, Jimmy," he said, "we make too much of death. Actually, there is no death. We keep right on living. I want you to think of it that way because I know it's true. I never understood that until lately, but I do now."

I pulled my hand away and stepped back. He rose and said, "Let's clean up the dishes and go to bed."

We did, but for some reason I couldn't sleep. I had always felt that my father was a strange man, but this was too strange. Something had happened to him and I didn't suppose I'd ever know for sure what it was. I felt positive it had been more than a dream, but he would have told me if he'd wanted me to know.

I guess it was the way it had been in Kansas when he'd been involved with the Free Soldiers and the Underground Railroad. He didn't want me to get into trouble over his doings, so he didn't tell me about them. Maybe he just found it hard to talk about himself. I knew that what he had said tonight had not come easily.

There are so many things a man experiences but cannot describe in words. It's like the professional gambler who often knows when to push his luck and when to back away but, like I said, he can't tell how he knows. I think it was that way with my father regarding the experience he'd had. All I knew as I lay awake staring into the darkness was that it had been a very profound one.

We had breakfast in the morning and shook hands. Neither of us said anything more about what had happened or had been said the previous evening. I guess we were drained dry.

Three days later a neighbor of my father's rode all the way from Golden to Black Hawk to tell me that he had died of a heart attack. They'd found him sitting in a chair in the kitchen, slumped over the table.

CHAPTER VII

My father's neighbors had been very fond of him. They had taken care of the funeral arrangements before I got to Golden. I slept in his house the first night I was there, although one neighbor, a lanky Missourian named Carew, came over at dusk and asked me to stay with him and his family. I thanked him and said that I'd rather be by myself, and he seemed to understand.

I didn't look for the money that night. It would wait. Too, I was afraid more of the neighbors would drop in to offer their sympathy. Several of them did. They all spoke highly of my father and said what a good neighbor he had been. I did not have the feeling they were saying this just because he was dead. You get a feeling about things like that, and I was convinced they were sincere.

The funeral was the next afternoon. The preacher came by in the morning. I didn't like him at first, but then I just didn't like preachers. I had decided that if he used the funeral service as a means of converting those of us who were sinners, I'd get up in the middle of the service and walk out. I told the preacher how I felt in plain, direct language that he couldn't misunderstand.

He stared at me, shocked, I guess. He said, "Mr. Glenn, I believe you would walk out."

"You bet I would," I said. "I was only six when my mother died, but I remember what the preacher said. He ranted and raved and threw his arms around. It was all about hell. If there was ever an angel who walked this good green earth, it was my mother. Hell had no place in her funeral service."

The preacher was thoughtful for a moment, then he asked, "Have you been saved, Mr. Glenn?"

"Of course I have," I answered. "So has my father. He didn't go to church, but he read the Bible. It's yonder on the table. Take a look at it and you'll see he mighty near wore it out reading it. I was taught by him. I don't go to church, either, but we know a little bit about the nature of God. That's why we know we're saved."

"You sound as if your father was still alive."

"He is, isn't he?"

I don't suppose anybody ever argued with the preacher or contradicted him. I guess some preachers would have jumped down my throat and worked me over verbally, but he didn't. He didn't answer my question, either. He kept looking at me in that thoughtful way he had. Then he asked, "If you know something about the nature of God, you must know what His dominant characteristic is."

"I do," I said. "It's love, and if God is love as the Bible says, He sure wouldn't prepare an eternal hell and cast people into it because they didn't do just what He thought they should. Like getting baptized, for instance, and doing it by a certain procedure."

"Immersion, for instance?" he suggested.

I nodded. "That's right."

"You don't think it makes any difference to God what you do?"

"Of course it does," I said, "but we're not going to be condemned for eternity on account of what we do in one lifetime. There's too much difference in the way we're born. I was lucky with an angel mother and a loving father, but how about some savage Indian who never heard of God? Or a Negro who was born and raised in slavery? Or some sick, ignorant kid born in a family of drunks? I could go on, but you get the point. If God is anything, he's a just God."

"I do indeed get the point, Mr. Glenn." The preacher rose and, walking to the table, picked up my father's Bible. He added quite casually, "You are very much a chip off the old block. You were not home very much, so you don't know that your father and I were very good friends. As a matter of fact, I think I am the only preacher he was ever really friendly with. I often dropped in for an evening and we'd sit up until midnight talking about some of these very things. I must admit he made a good case for his point of view."

He put the Bible back on the table and smiled slightly. "I will miss him a great deal, mostly because I find so few men who force me to stretch my understanding. It's very easy to fall into a rut and preach a safe and sound doctrine. He taught me that I had a greater obligation than that, and I have tried to meet it. I tried to persuade him to come to church because I felt he needed the fellowship, but he never came, so perhaps he didn't."

He walked to the door, then turned back, his face grave. "There is one thing I must tell you because I believe I knew him better than anyone else in Golden. He was very proud of you and he loved you very much. He knew you would never get any more schooling. It wasn't necessary for you, he said, because you would educate yourself. He thought that book learning often made men impractical, and as a result they live in the clouds. You are a practical man, he said, very independent, and you'll make your own way. No matter what happens to you, you will always be able to take care of yourself."

His smile returned then, and he added, "There will be no mention of hell today."

The neighbor, Carew, stopped for me after dinner and took me in his carriage along with his wife and children to the church. The service was not a long one. There were the usual songs and prayers and scriptures, but the preacher's short talk was what I was to remember.

He kept his word. There was no mention of hell, though he did talk about Heaven — not the usual golden streets and harps and angels, but a place of peace and love. He never said my father was there, but I did not for a moment doubt his conviction that it was true. He also said that death was not the end of anything, but a continuation of life.

He talked briefly of his personal loss and the community's loss as well. I could find no fault with anything he said. I knew that if my father was there to hear — and I had a strange feeling he was — he, too, would have approved of all the preacher said.

Afterwards I rode beside Carew to the graveyard. I heard the last prayer, the last song, and I saw the coffin lowered into the grave; then some men stepped up with shovels in their hands and started filling it. The first rock that hit the coffin made a strange, echoing sound. A sob shook my whole body when I heard it. I turned quickly and walked to Carew's carriage and stood there. I had been able to detach myself from the fact of death, but that empty sound was too much for me.

It struck me that the daily business of living was lonely and too often as empty of meaning as that hollow sound of the rock hitting the coffin. For the first time a keen sense of regret stabbed me like a thrust of lightning. I could have spent more time with my father. He always visited me and slept in my cabin and ate his meals with me when he came to Black Hawk. I could have ridden to Golden and spent some time with him, but I had not been here for more than a year.

The preacher shook hands with me and said he hoped we would meet again. Carew returned to the carriage with his family. He waited until the rest of the neighbors had filed past and shaken hands with me, then we got into the carriage and he drove back to my father's house.

On the way I asked, "Did he have any heart attacks before this last one?"

Carew gave me a sharp look, perhaps thinking it was something I should have known. I didn't try to defend myself, though. If my father had wanted me to know, he would have told me. Besides, it was none of Carew's business.

"Yes, he'd had several over the last two years," Carew said. "Most of them were minor. At least, they didn't lay him up very long, but he had a bad one last fall. We all thought he wasn't going to make it."

"Why didn't you send for me?"

"He said not to," Carew answered. "I don't know why."

So that was why he had told me what he had about not living through the summer. I said, "Then he knew he didn't have much time."

Carew nodded somberly. "Yes, he knew. I tried to get him to stop working. He had some money. He could have lived quietly here and spent a little time working in his garden every day. He'd have made out all right, but he said no, that wouldn't do for him. He'd wear out, but he sure didn't aim to rust out. He told me that more than once. I said he could go and live with you, but he said he guessed neither one of you would like that."

I didn't say anything. He was right. We both liked the way we had been living. I honestly believe he would have preferred death to living with me and being dependent on me. It was something the preacher would have understood, but Carew did not. He looked at me accusingly, as if I were to blame for my father's death. By his lights I was, but not by mine.

He pulled up at the front door of my father's house and I got out and thanked him. He drove away, not saying anything. He had done his duty; he didn't want to see any more of me. Most folks felt the way he did, I guess. And then I had a weird sensation. I thought my father was standing beside me telling me not to worry about what Carew and the rest of the neighbors thought. I wasn't. I mentally thanked him for raising me the way he had.

I guess I had not fully realized before how much alike we had been: non-conformists, loners, independent thinkers, and, most of all, men who did not want to depend on anyone else. I went into the house, feeling good. I did not have the slightest sense of guilt, even though Carew and the other neighbors considered me guilty of gross neglect.

I built a fire and cooked my supper. As soon as it was dark, I barred both the front and back doors and hung blankets over the windows. I didn't know how many people in Golden were aware that my father had been lucky in Denver, but there were bound to be some thieves in Golden. I didn't want any of them watching me through a window.

As soon as I had the room ready, I lifted the hearthstone. Under it was a hole containing a number of canvas sacks. I moved them to the table and emptied them, and then I was looking at the biggest pile of gold and silver and greenbacks I had ever seen in my life. I counted it, and then I simply sat and stared at it, thinking of all the things I could do with that much money.

There was more than thirty-five hundred dollars. My father had been right. I could buy a good many lots in any of the railroad towns. If I picked the right one, I would be rich. If I picked the wrong one, I'd be broke. So I was going to gamble, but my bet wouldn't be a piddling fifty cents on which bird was going to fly off the fence first. It would be for all or nothing.

I put the money back under the hearthstone and lowered it into place. I didn't touch it again until I had sold my father's house, team, wagon, and personal things, retaining only his watch and a few small items that were keepsakes more than anything else. The last night I slept in the house I took the money out from under the hearthstone. I placed the gold in a money belt I had bought that day; the rest went into my saddlebags.

I wound up my affairs in Black Hawk as fast as I could, but it was well into July before I was done. By this time I had more than five thousand dollars — closer to six, I guess. I stopped at the Martin girls' house and told them good-by. They kissed me and cried a little and said they'd miss me. Not just as a customer, either, and didn't I want to marry them before I left and take them with me.

"You think I'm a Mormon?" I asked. "What would I do with two wives? I doubt that I could handle one."

"Marry just one of us and the other one will go along as a friend of the groom," Rosy said.

"Yes, that'd be the way to do it." Flossie bobbed her head in agreement. "I would make you a mighty intimate friend. Two women are twice as much fun as one."

"I'll bet they are," I said. "And twice as much trouble, too. I'd sure have problems. If you took your pins off, I wouldn't know which one I'd married until you were undressed."

"Oh, I undress easy," Rosy said.

"So do I," Flossie added.

"Yeah, for the first man who rode by with two dollars in his pocket," I said.

I got out of there then, thinking that if I ever did get married, it would be to a girl of virtue. I rode to Golden and turned north. I had been hearing recently about a new town named Cheyenne in the southeastern corner of Wyoming that was going to be a division point on the Union Pacific. It just might be the place I was looking for.

As I rode, my thoughts drifted back to Rosy and Flossie. They were indeed a strange pair. I had a notion they might turn up in Cheyenne. Business had been slow in Black Hawk all winter, but it was bound to boom in an end-of-track town.

The Martin girls were business women if they were anything. They'd retire someday as rich women, I thought. They'd move to some town where they weren't known, pass themselves off as rich widows, and end up respectably married.

All of a sudden it struck me funny and I began to laugh. Suppose only one of them got married and the single one lived with the married one. If Rosy got rid of that mole, the husband would never know which one he was sleeping with.

CHAPTER VIII

The first night I camped on the bank of the Poudre just below Fort Collins. I rode directly north the next day, but I didn't find Cheyenne, I didn't know how many miles I had ridden, and I didn't knew where the territorial line was.

I began to wonder if I'd gone right past Cheyenne. It couldn't be much of a town yet, so I began to worry. It might have been on the other side of some ridge I'd passed. Maybe I was getting farther away from it all the time. I'd be in Fort Laramie the next thing I knew. That really wouldn't happen, of course; the fort was about one hundred miles north of Cheyenne. I was thinking crazy because I was irritated by my failure to find the town.

Late in the afternoon I saw a ranch to my right and I reined toward it, thinking I might be smart to stay the night there. At least I'd find out where Cheyenne was.

When I reached the buildings, I decided it wasn't much of an outfit.

The house was a shack — no more. The log barn was better, not large, but well built and tight, and would give horses ample protection in bad weather. The pole corral was equally well built and tight. It struck me that whoever owned the spread had put out much more effort for his animals' comfort than his own. I was dead sure of one thing: there were no women here.

I reined up in front of the shack and sat my saddle for a moment, just looking around. I couldn't see any cattle, but there were six horses in the corral: one bay, two sorrels, and three blacks. They were fine-looking, leggy animals that could cover a lot of miles in a day. My sorrel was the same horse my father had given me when we arrived in Denver. I hated to sell or trade him, but he was getting old and I was going to have to buy another mount.

A small, meandering stream flowed past the barn and shack. A short distance downstream the owner had built a dam. A good-sized pond was above it, holding more than enough water to irrigate about forty acres of meadow. He would get a good crop of hay, and I judged the grass was about ready to cut. I guessed that the stream would dry up later in the summer if the weather stayed dry, but the pond was big enough to furnish drinking and stock water all year.

I sat there a good five minutes, but nobody showed up. I decided no one was home, but I hollered "Hello" on the off chance that someone was around and hadn't seen me. Sure enough, the door banged open and a man came out of the shack rubbing his eyes.

"I was sleeping and didn't know anybody was here," he said. "Get down and rest your saddle."

I had no way of knowing what I was getting into or whether anyone else was on the place. If I'd had my druthers, I'd have stayed the night in Cheyenne, but I was tired and my horse was worse off than I was. Still, I hadn't made up my mind when I asked, "Where's Cheyenne? I figured I'd be there before now."

He jerked a thumb toward the north. "It's another five, six miles. Your horse looks plumb tuckered. Better spend the night here. I like company and I don't mind telling you it gets damned lonesome. I've been here two years and if you ask me why I settled in this God-forsaken hole, I won't tell you because I don't know."

He was as tall as I was, a good six feet, his face as brown as the leather of my saddle, with more lines in it than I could count. It was what I'd call a weathered face. It reminded me of some ancient cliff that had been eroded by wind and weather for centuries. He was about my age, maybe a little older, with faded blue eyes and corn-colored hair that hadn't been combed lately and stuck out in all directions.

I stepped down and held out my hand. "I'm Jim Glenn," I said. "I was hoping to get to Cheyenne tonight."

"Ed Burke here," he said, shaking hands. "This prosperous-looking spread is the EB. You wouldn't know it, but I'm a rich cowman." He winked as he threw out an arm in a grandiose gesture. "The range as far as you can see belongs to me. Nobody else is fool enough to claim it. That's why it's mine. All I need is some cows. I've got a herd that's grazing on the other side of yonder ridge." He grinned wryly. "All ten of 'em."

I seldom responded favorably to a man the moment I met him, but I liked this Ed Burke right off. I prided myself on being able to judge men, and although I wasn't always right, I had a pretty good average. I'd learned by hard, bitter lessons.

Black Hawk and Central City always had a lot of floaters. When I'd started to cut and haul wood, I had been taken in by some of them who promised to pay, but after they got the wood they'd manage to put me off by one excuse or another. Before I knew it, they'd left town still owing me. Of course they'd burned up a load of free wood.

As I grew older, I got meaner. The last year I lived in Black Hawk I didn't lose a nickel. One reason was that I had a reputation for being mean and nobody figured it was smart to cheat me. Another reason was that I'd learned to pick my customers.

I never really knew how I judged a man or what kind of measuring stick I used. I guess it was mostly just a feeling. Now it struck me that Ed Burke was all right. I had a crazy idea that I'd like to stay here and throw in with him. I had enough capital to buy a fair-sized herd, and if Cheyenne was destined to grow into a city, it would furnish a market close at hand. Even if it didn't, the railroad would be here and shipping cattle to Omaha or Chicago or St. Louis would be no problem.

Once the idea hit me, I could see a lot of possibilities. For one thing, there was less gamble in a cattle ranch than there was in buying town lots when it's anybody's guess what the town is going to do. I wasn't fool enough to say anything about it, though. I'd look Cheyenne over first and get a little better acquainted with Burke before I made him a proposition.

"I ought to keep riding," I said, still not sure what I wanted to do. I guess my trouble was that I'd made up my mind I wanted to get to Cheyenne before dark and it was hard to unmake it. "If Cheyenne is only five, six miles, I could —"

"If you're thinking you're gonna find a city," Burke interrupted, "you are mistook. You'll find a few people and some tents and shacks, and a lot of street markers and stakes showing where the streets are. But city?" He shook his head. "Hell no. You probably won't find no bed and no place to stable your horse. I'll go throw another antelope steak into the pan. You take care of your horse."

I decided to stay. Cheyenne would be there in the morning. I still wasn't sure why I had taken a liking to Ed Burke. Saying I had a feeling about a man wasn't any answer. Why did I get a feeling? I thought about it as I watered my horse. I offsaddled and rubbed him down and turned him into the corral, and all the time I kept asking myself that question.

I finally decided I liked him because I had a natural sympathy for him. He'd settled here with a tall stack of hopes and he hadn't cashed in on them. He didn't even have a good working ten-cow spread. Chances were he hadn't had enough money to stock his range when he started and he didn't see any better chance yet.

I stood looking at his horses and a question popped into my mind. He didn't need six horses as good as these to operate the kind of outfit he had. Those animals could be driven to Denver and sold for a sizeable chunk of jingle. Why didn't he do that and take the money and buy some cows and a good bull?

Not that it was any of my business, but it seemed to me he wasn't really smart — more of an idealist than a practical man. I knew the world was full of men like him who struggled all their lives to get their heads above water and worked their tails off while they were doing it, and never quite made it.

When I went into the shack, it was hotter than the hinges of hell's front door. He had a good fire going, coffee boiling, and a pan of antelope steaks sizzling. The smell was enough to start my mouth watering and my stomach to rolling around. It had been a long time since I'd eaten dinner. It hadn't been much of a meal anyhow, just crackers and cheese and a can of peaches.

Burke motioned to a chair at the table. "Sit down," he said. "This ain't gonna be no banquet, but there's plenty of what there is." He stopped in front of the stove and stared unabashedly at me for a good minute, then he said, "I don't usually ask a man his business, but I'm going to ask you because I might be some help. Why are you headed for Cheyenne?"

"To buy lots," I said. "I'm not sure Cheyenne is the place, but somewhere along the railroad there's going to be a big town. I aim to get rich off the lots I'm going to buy."

I expected him to give me the horselaugh. It sounded pretty stupid to my own ears when I told it plain out that way, trying to get rich so easy. I was a practical man and it was plain he wasn't, and I could have told him how to run his ranch, but he'd been in the country for two years and he'd been in Cheyenne, and therefore he might be in a good position to say I was stupid or smart to invest money in town lots.

He didn't give me any horselaugh. He turned back to the stove and flipped the steaks over, then he said seriously, "You just might do it. It's my guess that Cheyenne is going to be *the* town. I wish to hell I had a little money to buy some of them lots. Right now the U. P. is selling 'em for $150 apiece. Of course that's gravy for the company because the lots didn't cost them nothing except to survey 'em. They can't afford to price 'em too high or nobody will buy 'em, but I'll bet you right now that within two, three months, when the track gets to Cheyenne, them same lots will sell for five hundred dollars."

That wouldn't be a bad deal for me, I thought. Hold the lots a few months and make better than three-to-one profit. I asked, "You don't think Julesburg will be the big town?"

He gave me the horselaugh then. "Hell no," he said. "There ain't no reason why it should be, set off by itself the way it is in the northeast corner of the state like it is."

He waggled a forefinger at me. "It's different with Cheyenne. They ain't gonna leave a town as big as Denver high and dry, especially when there's a whole territory depending on it with a lot of stuff to ship, so there's bound to be a junction with a spur they'll run south to Denver. It's on a direct line between Fort Laramie and Denver, too. No sir, you can't miss investing in Cheyenne property."

"It sounds good," I said, thinking he had

been studying the situation longer than I had.

"And another thing," he went on. "Cheyenne's been named as a division point. That means jobs and jobs mean men and men mean families and families mean a market."

He shoved the steaks around on the bottom of the frying pan. "Julesburg? Let me tell you about that place. I was there a while back, and I was glad to get out alive. When they call it hell on wheels, they ain't mistook. I've seen some mean, tough burgs in my time, but that one takes the cake. There's more whores and pimps and gamblers and just plain sneak thieves over there than I ever seen before. You get into bed with a whore and she hands you a drink, and that's all you remember till you wake up in an alley with your pockets picked clean. Stay away from Julesburg, Mr. Glenn. It ain't safe for man or beast."

"Chances are Cheyenne will be the same when it's the end of track," I said.

"Mebbe." He shrugged. "Mebbe not. There ain't nobody in Julesburg that's interested in getting law and order. It all depends on the kind of leadership they get in Cheyenne. Now you look like a purty tough hand. You willing to take the lead in handling gangs of thieves and murderers?

Get a vigilante committee to working if the law can't handle it? There's nothing like a few hangings to clear out the riff-raff."

The idea had not occurred to me before, but I guessed right then I'd be up against that decision sooner or later. If I bought lots in Cheyenne, I'd have a stake in establishing law and order. If the law couldn't keep it, a vigilante committee was the only answer.

I had never belonged to one. It hadn't been necessary in Black Hawk, though there had been plenty of talk about forming one several times. Denver had had a very active one. I guess it had been necessary there, but I had never been in favor of forming one in Black Hawk. When a vigilante committee is controlled by the wrong men, you simply exchange one form of lawlessness for another.

"I guess I'd be willing," I said after thinking about it for a minute. "If I'm a property owner in Cheyenne, I'd have to help establish law and order. If we didn't have it, I couldn't sell my property."

He nodded. "That's right. Well, I guess we can eat." He set the table, brought out a pot of cold beans, lifted a pan of biscuits from the oven, poured the coffee, and then forked the steaks into our plates. He was a better than average cook and I was more than average hungry, so the supper tasted like the banquet he'd said it wasn't.

When we finished eating, we went outside into the cool of the evening and filled our pipes and smoked. It was a real easy relationship, with me telling about living in a mining camp and Ed telling about working on a ranch near Trinidad and drifting north and finally deciding to start his own outfit here near the territorial line.

After a while we both yawned and he said he guessed we'd better roll in. I could sleep in the barn because he had only one bunk in the house. There wasn't much hay in the mow, but I raked enough together to sleep on. Then I lay there thinking about my idea.

A good ranch could be made out of the EB. Come to think of it, I wouldn't mind being a rancher. I'd be about as free that way as any way. I guess what I feared the most was being pinned down to a job. I was wondering what Ed would say about having a partner when I dropped off to sleep.

CHAPTER IX

I woke up sometime before dawn. I had no idea what time it was, but it was black dark. For a little while I didn't know why I had awakened; then I heard voices. I sat up and listened, and decided the men were at the corral gate. One voice was Ed Burke's. I had no idea who the other man was.

They were arguing about something, or actually quarreling, from the tone of their voices, but I couldn't make out any of the words. Presently they arrived at some sort of agreement. At least, they stopped talking. A moment later I heard the sound of a horse galloping away from the barn, headed west; then the thudding of hoofs faded and died.

I lay back on the hay, wondering about it. It was a fair guess that someone had ridden in during the night, got Ed out of bed, and swapped horses with him. When it was daylight, I left the barn and had a look at the horses in the corral. One of the blacks was gone and a strange buckskin was there. He'd been ridden hard, and judging from the way he stood with his head down, I had a hunch he might not be any good again.

Smoke was lifting from the chimney of the shack. The door was open, so I stepped through it and saw that Ed was standing at the stove frying bacon. He saw me and nodded, saying, "Howdy. You sleep all right?"

"Yeah, fine," I answered, "except that during the night I heard a couple of men talking. One of them sounded like you."

"Yeah, it was me," he said in an offhand way. "It's happened before. The U. P. has some surveying crews in the Black Hills trying to locate the best route over them mountains. It's a purty good grade west of here, you know. The story is that General Dodge discovered the pass by accident one time when the Indians jumped him and his party, but of course the route the railroad will take has to be exactly the right grade, and be staked out now so that the graders won't have no trouble following it. They'll be laying rails over that summit before snow flies."

"What's that got to do with your night visitor?" I asked.

"Hell, didn't I tell you?" He wiped a hand across his face. "Sometimes I think I'm getting old before my time. You know, my pa was that way before he died. Of course he was over sixty, and I'm only twenty-seven, but I'm getting about as forgetful as he was. I recollect one time when the sheriff stopped to get him for helping and abetting an outlaw when he was trying to cross the line into Mexico —"

"What's this got to do with your night visitor?" I asked again, knowing by this time that he was trying to avoid giving me an answer.

"Nothing," he said. "I was just aiming to tell you about my pa. Say, the coffee's done. Why don't you get your cup yonder and pour yourself a cup."

I did, and decided to quit asking questions. Maybe he had his reason for not wanting to answer me. It wasn't any of my business, but it did look queer, and I couldn't help wondering about it. I guess he thought about it a minute and decided it would be better if he told me.

"That feller who was here last night was a messenger for the railroad," he said. "You see, General Dodge or some of the other mucky-mucks who are east of here at the end of track, wherever that is, or maybe clean back in Julesburg, want the surveyors to do something or not do something they've been doing so they send a man in a hurry to tell 'em. I don't know what kind of message this bird had, but he was in an almighty fidget to get there."

"From the looks of that buckskin in the corral," I said, "he must have ridden hell out of him."

"Yeah, I reckon he did," Ed admitted, "and I ain't sure that I came out real good on the trade, but he gave me some boot, so I won't lose much if the buckskin lays down and dies. We augered some about how much boot I was to get, but I figured the railroad could afford to pay me purty good the way they throw money away on other things."

He poured coffee, then pulled a pan of biscuits he'd been warming up out of the oven and forked the bacon into plates and got out his jar of honey, so we ate pretty well again. We didn't say much as we ate, but I kept thinking about his story of the railroad messenger. Somehow it didn't ring quite right, but then maybe he accepted the story the fellow had told him. It didn't make any difference to Ed why the man was in such a hurry to get to the Black Hills as long as he got the money he wanted.

After we finished eating, I said, "Time I was moseying along."

"No sense you being in a hurry," he said.

"I'll clean up the dishes and ride with you. I ain't been in Cheyenne for several days. Maybe it's growed since I saw it. Anyhow, it'll be plenty lonesome after you leave and I don't think I can stand it. Sometimes I feel like going outside and barking at the moon like a coyote."

"Sure," I said. "I've got no reason to hurry. I guess they won't sell all of their lots before noon."

He snickered. "No sir, they won't, and that's a fact. From all the streets and lots they've measured off, you'd think the U.P. was figuring on Cheyenne being another Chicago."

I went outside and filled and lighted my pipe. I strolled over to the corral and stood studying the buckskin. He didn't look any better than when I'd first seen him. I thought it was probable he'd do just what Ed said — he'd just lie down and die.

I didn't see the two men ride up until they were almost at the door of the shack. They didn't see me at all, and after I'd had a look at them, I decided maybe it was just as well they didn't see me until I wanted them to, so I stayed there at the corral with about half of it between me and them.

They both carried stars, but that didn't prove anything to me. They were two tough-looking gents, and I'd seen plenty of men toting stars who were just one jump removed from being outlaws. Some weren't even that one jump removed, so I figured it would be a good thing to find out what they were up to before they saw me.

They got off their horses and stood looking around. Ed either hadn't seen them or had decided to ignore them. Now one of them called, "Hello! Anybody here?"

Ed came to the door and stepped outside. "Yeah, somebody's here."

That was all he said, but he was wearing his gun now, which he hadn't been doing before, so I made a guess that he'd seen these men and decided he'd better not take any chances.

They looked him over, silent and cold and somehow threatening without saying a word. Ed looked right back at them, his hand close to the butt of his gun. I didn't know then how much he was figuring on me taking chips in the game, but even if I stayed out of it I had a notion he'd smoke both of them down before they could pull a trigger.

One of them, the taller one, said, "I'm Chip Rawls, United States Marshal. This is Harry Jones, a deputy United States Marshal. Who are you?"

"Ed Burke, if it's any of your business," Ed said. "What's on your mind? I don't have all day. I'm getting ready to ride into Cheyenne."

"You've got plenty of time to talk to us," Rawls said. "Did you see a man riding past here during the night by name of Poke Kelly? He was forking a buckskin."

"Not that I know of," Ed said. "Now if you'll get on about your business, I'll —"

"Easy," Rawls said. "Just take it easy. I told you that you've got plenty of time to talk to us. Did anybody ride through here last night?"

Ed stood looking at them for maybe thirty seconds, then I guess he decided it wasn't any good to lie, maybe thinking about the buckskin he had in his corral. Finally he said, "Yeah, a man stopped here during the night and traded me his tired buckskin for a fresh horse; then he rode on west."

"Why didn't you hold him?" Rawls bellowed angrily. "That was Kelly. He robbed a stage south of here and killed the messenger. What do you think we're here for?"

"He didn't tell me his name was Kelly," Ed said sharply, "and he sure didn't tell me the law wanted him for holding up a stage and killing a messenger. You take me for a mind reader or something?"

"I think you're either a damned fool or you're in cahoots with the pack of outlaws who are all over this country," Rawls said testily, "and you sure don't look like no fool. I'm arresting you for conniving with a known outlaw and giving him aid and sustenance in his flight from justice."

"You ain't arresting me for nothing," Ed said. "You can make up your own law and charges all you want to, but you can't make 'em stick around here. Just leave me out of it. If you try arresting me, you'll be buying yourself a hole in the ground."

Then Ed did a fool thing, or that was the way it seemed to me. He made a slow turn and gave the two lawmen his back before he stepped into the shack. Rawls started to go for his gun, but I moved away from the corral and yelled, "Hold it."

Rawls had his gun out of leather and almost leveled. I believe he would have shot Ed in the back, but when he heard me he froze, his gun within inches of being lined on the middle of Ed's spine. The hammer was back, so it must have been all he could do to keep from pulling the trigger.

"Mister," I said, "if you had shot Burke in the back like you were fixing to do, I'd have killed you right where you stand. I don't believe you are a United States Marshal. I never knew one who would shoot a man in the back."

Rawls turned around and eyed me for a while, so furious he was trembling. Finally he asked, "Who the hell are you, another member of this wolf pack?"

"I'm not a member of anything," I said. "My name's Jim Glenn. I lived in Black Hawk until I sold out a few days ago. I'm headed for Cheyenne. I stayed here overnight and Ed Burke was kind enough to give me supper and breakfast. It's a good thing I was here on this particular morning or you'd have murdered him. Packing a badge doesn't give you an excuse to murder a man."

"I wasn't going to shoot him," he said, sort of half-hearted with his lie. "I was fixing to put a slug past his head so he'd turn around and tell me what he knew about Poke Kelly."

He eased his gun back into leather. I was still mad. Either these men were pretending to be U.S. lawmen for some reason of their own, maybe hoping to run Kelly down and relieve him of any loot he had taken off the stage, or they were disgraces as lawmen. Either way, I had a feeling I'd just as soon kill both of them as not. I carried my feeling a little further. I even had the notion that the world would be a better place to live in if they were dead.

I dropped my gun back into leather. I said, "Rawls, you are a ⬛⬛-damned liar."

I figured that would make him go for his gun. If he had, I'd have killed him sure. I guess I was so mad I was a little bit out of my head. I was hoping Jones would draw, too. They were both facing me, and even if they weren't very fast with their guns, one of them would probably have plugged me, except for one thing.

Facing me, they had their backs to the shack, so the situation was reversed to what it had been. They didn't know whether Ed was standing there in the doorway or not. As a matter of fact, he was, his gun in his hand, and he could have smoked both of them down while they were drawing on me.

Rawls stood there steaming for quite a while. His pride was hurt, and pride was a vital part of a man like that. In the end he wanted to live more than he wanted to recover his pride, so he didn't force any-thing.

After a time Rawls said, "Harry, go take a look in the corral."

I moved into the open, away from the cor-ral toward the barn, so there wasn't any chance that the deputy could get behind me. I aimed to watch him and Rawls at the same time. Right then the weather was pretty sticky. It wouldn't have taken much to start the ball.

Jones must have sensed that because he didn't make any effort to get around to the other side of the corral. He walked to the gate, very slowly, had his look, and came back. Ed was still standing in the doorway and Jones couldn't help seeing him.

"The buckskin's out there, all right," Jones said.

Rawls swore. He said, "Let's ride, Harry. We're wasting time with these two buckos." He swung into the saddle, then he leaned forward and said to Ed, "I think you knew who Kelly was and I think you didn't want to stop him. If I ever get any proof that you're working with the outlaws, I'll be back."

"I'll welcome you," Ed said coldly.

He didn't say any more, but I think Rawls got the point that Ed would welcome him with a dose of lead. Anyhow, Rawls and Jones rode west, hoping, I suppose, that they'd pick up Kelly's trail. I walked to the shack, saying, "Ed, you are a complete idiot for turning your back to men like that. I don't know yet whether they were lawmen or not, but that's not the point. Rawls is a killer."

Ed wasn't offended. He just grinned at me as he said, "I knew you were out there."

"You're still an idiot," I said. "You didn't know me well enough to be that sure I'd take a hand in the game. A lot of men would have stayed out of it."

He shook his head. "I'm a good judge of horseflesh and men. It didn't take me long to size you up, Jim. You're a hell of a tough man and I figure we're gonna be friends. You couldn't have stayed out of the ruckus any more than you could fly. Now saddle up. I'll be finished up here in a little while and we'll light out for Cheyenne."

I turned on my heel and went back to the corral and saddled my horse. What could you say to a man who talked to you that way? I still didn't know whether Ed really believed what Poke Kelly had said about being a Union Pacific messenger, or whether he just didn't give a damn and was perfectly willing to swap horses with an outlaw who was running from the law. Either way, I had a hunch Ed was right about us being friends.

CHAPTER X

We rode into Cheyenne before noon and I will have to admit I was disappointed. I had seen some primitive Colorado mining camps, but I had never seen any place as primitive as this. You couldn't dignify it by calling it a town.

I saw a few log houses, others built of cross ties which had been set on end to form the walls and were covered by canvas for roofs, a few with posts set in the ground for corners with nothing but canvas for walls; but most of the settlement consisted of plain, ordinary tents. I had the impression that Cheyenne looked more like a county fair than a town.

I groaned, and Ed looked at me and grinned. "I told you not to expect much of a town," he said.

I nodded agreement. "I know. But I did expect to see more of a town than this."

He threw out a hand in a wide, inclusive

gesture. "You can see it's gonna be a big city. Look at the stakes marking the streets and lots. The signs telling you the names of the streets are all in place so you can't get lost among the tall buildings. I've heard the railroad has surveyed four square miles, so they're sure expecting it to be a city."

I could see that, and if I'd had any doubts about investing my money in Cheyenne lots, I lost them at this point. I was going to take my father's advice and gamble big. Either I'd be rich or I'd be starting over. All of a sudden I felt a thrill bigger than I had ever felt before in my life. I was getting in on the ground floor and the only way I could go was up.

Ed reined to a stop and dismounted in front of a big tent with a sign: HEAD QUARTERS SALOON. "I'll go in here and wet my whistle," he said. "You want a drink?"

I shook my head. "No, I'm going to buy some town lots and get rich."

He laughed. "You'll do it, Jim. You'll do it as sure as hell's hot. Well, I'll see you once in a while. I figure I ain't gonna stay out there on the EB and rot, so I'll come to town and turn my wolf loose."

"Thanks for putting me up and feeding me," I said.

"I enjoyed it." He laughed again. "The part I enjoyed the most was when you threw your gun on that bastard of a United States Marshal. I hate 'em. If I ever run into him in town, I'm likely as not to jump him."

"No sense getting in bad with the law," I said.

"If he is the law," Ed said. "So long."

He nodded and went into the big tent. I rode on down the street, noting that I was on Eddy. I rode quite a ways on it, clear past the last tent, not turning around until I came to 24th. Then I followed it one block to the next street, which was Ferguson, and rode back on it to 16th, where I had started.

It wouldn't be a tent city for long. I must have seen twenty buildings in the process of being built, and I had never heard so many hammers in my life. I wouldn't have any trouble getting a carpenter's job if I wanted it, but I was going to do my own carpenter work and hire some men to boot if I could find them.

I turned east on 16th to Hill and rode along it for eight blocks until I reached 24th again. It struck me that the business section would be in those blocks close to 16th on Eddy and Ferguson, and maybe Hill, and the lots farther out would be in a residential area.

I returned to 16th Street on Ransom, which paralleled Hill. By this time I knew what I wanted if the lots were still available, and I had a pretty fair notion of the way the town would grow, so I hunted until I found the Union Pacific land office. I tied my sorrel in front of the tent and went in, carrying my saddlebags.

"I want to see a plat of the city," I said.

"Certainly." The clerk turned, picked up the plat from a table behind him, and laid it on the counter in front of me. "You are interested in buying some lots?"

"I'm not just interested," I said. "I am going to buy some."

"Good." He rubbed his hands together the way a greedy banker would when he's taking a big deposit. "Very good. You won't go wrong, my friend. Cheyenne is destined to be the biggest city in the area. The railroad company has designated it as a division point, you know."

"How big are the lots?"

"Sixty-six feet by a hundred and thirty-two," he answered. "Very generous lots."

"Where will the tracks run?"

"South of 16th," he said.

"The lots colored black are the ones that are sold?"

"Correct," he said. "We have done very

well for the short time we have been selling town property."

Most of the lots in what I had guessed would be the business section were sold, but I found a few that looked good, mostly on Eddy, and then I began picking up lots farther out that would be in the residential section. I figured I had got here just in time and that in a few days most of the lots that had a quick future would be gone.

When I had made a small pencil mark on my thirtieth lot, I said, "I'll take these."

Well sir, by the time the clerk had added up the number of small pencil marks I'd made, he had the goggle-eyed look of a man who was in a state of shock. He looked me over, very carefully this time, and asked, "You sure you can pay for them?"

That irritated me, but I held onto my temper. I said, "I'll pay for them."

"Cash for all thirty?"

"Right."

"That will be forty-five hundred dollars," he said as if he didn't believe there was that much money in the world.

I opened my saddlebags and began taking out money. By the time I finished, I had exactly $1,217.50 left. I walked out with empty saddlebags, all of my cash in my money belt, but I owned thirty pieces of

Cheyenne property. I wished my father was beside me to look the lots over. I think he would have been proud of me.

I stepped into a tent restaurant on Eddy Street and had my dinner, then I spent the rest of the day looking at my lots. I picked one out on the corner of Eddy and 22nd where I was going to build my house, then I hunted up a lumber yard and asked if plenty of lumber was coming in.

"You bet," the dealer said. "We've got every teamster we can hire hauling lumber from Denver. We've got other stuff — windows and doors and hinges and nails and so on — coming in from Julesburg. Besides that, several small sawmills are starting to operate in the foothills southwest of here. Now what can I do for you?"

I had figured out the size house I wanted — not big, but big enough for me and a guest if I had one. Maybe I could return Ed Burke's hospitality some time. I told the dealer what I had in mind and where I was going to build, and he promised to have the lumber out there in the morning. They were short of windows and hinges, and I might have to wait a few days for them.

"Do you know of any carpenters I can hire?"

He gave me a derisive laugh. "Carpenters," he said. "Mister, have you listened to those hammers? Some of the hammers ain't in the hands of carpenters. They're just hammer-and-saw men who are earning carpenter's wages because there ain't any real carpenters to be had. No sir, I don't know of nobody you can hire."

"I'll build my house myself," I said, "but I want to put up a business building later on and I'd like to get it started as soon as I can. If you hear of any good men who want to work, send them to me."

"I'll do that," he said with a kind of a sneer. "Yes sir, I'll sure do that."

I didn't like him worth a damn. I went back to my horse and I stopped, flat-footed, my breath going out of me. Just as I reached the sorrel, three men left a tent saloon across the street. The big man in the middle was Bully Bailey as sure as I was a foot high. The other two were probably the men who had been with him in Black Hawk, though I couldn't see them well enough to be sure.

It came as no real surprise to see Bailey in Cheyenne. A new wild town was bound to attract riff-raff like Bailey. Still, I was stunned to actually see him. I stood there watching him until he disappeared into another saloon down the street, then I mounted and rode to the Great Western

Corral and left my horse there.

I walked to my lot on Eddy and 22nd where I intended to build, carrying my saddle blanket. The night was going to be a warm one and the blanket was all I'd need. I was determined to sleep on land that I owned the first night I was in Cheyenne. But I couldn't get Bully Bailey out of my mind. I didn't know whether he had seen me or not, but if he hadn't, he soon would in a town as small as this.

The truth was I was scared. I wasn't scared of any man alive that I could fight while I faced him, but I knew I'd never have a chance to face Bailey again. He wouldn't risk it, so he'd wait until he had an opportunity to smoke me down some night when the moon was full and light was strong enough for him to see me. He'd shoot me in the back and I wouldn't even know he was there.

I just didn't know how any man could defend himself against an attack like that.

CHAPTER XI

I worked practically every waking hour on my house during the first month I was in Cheyenne. I had a strange feeling about it. I don't know why I had it or where it came from, but the thought kept nagging me that time was running out for me.

Not that I was afraid to die. I just didn't want to die until I had accomplished something. It seemed to me that it was a great tragedy for a young man to die without making his mark in the world. It might be only a scratch, but he should have done something. So far I hadn't even made a scratch. I told myself I was going to finish the house, at least, then I was going to start living in Cheyenne, to become a part of the town.

I didn't believe in ghosts, I had never had the slightest interest in spiritualism, I had always believed that life took a different form after death and that anyone who had died could not communicate with those of us who still lived in the flesh. My belief hadn't changed, but still I could not rid myself of the notion that my father was prodding me with the familiar words, "The sun's on the wall, Jimmy."

So I worked as hard as I could and had the house finished late in August. Several times Ed Burke stopped by and gave me a hand. He was a fair carpenter and painter, and I was thankful for his help. Too, he was pleasant company and I enjoyed visiting with him.

It struck me that Ed was neglecting his ranch. He hated hard work, and that included putting up hay. I offered to go out and help with his haying, but he wouldn't let me. I had enough to do, he said, and of course I did. He finally got it cut and stacked, but I'm sure he fooled around so long that he lost some he could have saved.

I learned one thing about Ed very soon — ranching was really not his interest. But I will have to admit that I couldn't find out what was, unless it was women. Whisky, too, I guess, and maybe poker, though he never seemed to lose or win much. I think he played just to pass the time. He appeared to be satisfied if he came out even.

Ed Burke was pleasant and good-natured

and easy to have around. He was perfectly happy if he had a place to sleep out of the weather and three meals a day. I was a little impatient with him because he never seemed to have a serious thought in his head. The notion that he had something to accomplish in this life never occurred to him.

Ed was a spectator of life, not a participant. He was amused by almost everything he saw. He laughed about the whores he bedded down with. He'd say, "They're cows, Jim. Just about as sensitive as any old cow you ever saw, lying on their backs and chewing their cuds with a far away look in their eyes as if they're thinking about what they're gonna have for breakfast, and all the time I'm working like hell. They don't want nothing but your money. Lazy — that's all they are. It's easier to make a living on their backs with their legs spread than it is to keep house for a husband."

He made some snide remarks about the men who were trying to set up a temporary government in Cheyenne. They were men who had some talent for leadership and honestly desired law and order in Cheyenne and didn't want it to become another Julesburg. Most of them owned property, and they knew that their property would not increase in value unless we had law and order.

I took as much part in setting up a town government as I could. Not that I had any ambition to be a leader. It was just that I had most of my money invested in Cheyenne property, and I wanted that investment to grow. I was perfectly satisfied to let the older, wealthier men assume leadership, so I didn't say much, but I attended all the meetings and voted when the time came.

The end of steel was moving steadily toward Cheyenne from Julesburg and would reach Cheyenne sometime in the fall. When it did, the riff-raff that made Julesburg a hell on wheels would move in on us. The trick was to be ready for them when the time came.

The first step was a mass meeting of the citizens of Cheyenne on August 7. A committee was appointed to draw up a charter. This was presented the following day. Two days later we held an election in Beckwith's store, the polls being open from three P.M. to ten P.M. There were three hundred and fifty votes cast, and I'm guessing this was mighty close to every man in town who was eligible to vote. H. M. Hook, who owned the Pilgrim House Hotel and the Great Western Stables, was elected mayor.

We finally had a Provisional Government, just about a month after the first permanent settlers had arrived in Cheyenne. It was a little better than no government, but not much, because it didn't have any legal power.

We were a part of Dakota Territory. Maybe that was better than being part of Colorado, which none of us wanted, but the seat of government of Dakota Territory was at Yankton, which was one hell of a long ways from Cheyenne. It was quite a while before the people in Yankton got around to making our government official. I guess they figured we weren't really a part of them.

Anyhow, Ed would be working along beside me and then for no reason at all he'd start a tirade about the men who were on the town council and the mayor and the marshal.

"Just like a bunch of overgrown kids playing a game," he'd say. "Somebody's got to be big and these are the jaspers who want to be it. Passing laws about paying good money for a license to carry on a business. Hiring policemen. Building a jail. My God, Jim, don't they have enough to do just running their own business?"

He was completely unreasonable about the whole thing. At times I thought he was an anarchist at heart who didn't want any kind of government. Actually he just wanted to be free, without any restraint, I guess, though I couldn't see how any of the laws passed at the council hurt him. Finally I told him he'd lose his cattle, and horses too, if there weren't some rules that men had to live by.

He snorted and said he guessed that wouldn't be much loss — just a dozen skinny old cows and a few horses. "Oh, I know we've got to have some rules," he admitted, "but a Vigilance Committee can take care of it. What we've got is a bunch of men wanting to lord it over the rest of us and playing at having a government. It ain't no answer. Sooner or later we'll get an official government and then we'll have our problem licked. We don't have it licked now and there's no use fooling ourselves."

"The men we've elected strike me as being responsible," I said. "I don't know when we'll get that official government you're talking about, and neither do you. What I do know is we've got to have something right now. That Julesburg bunch will be here in another two, three months, and they'll take the town over if we don't have some government."

"Get a vigilance committee together," he

snapped. "I tell you a few hangings will straighten things out in a hurry."

I didn't argue any more about it, but I didn't know why he was so set on a vigilance committee handling the outlaws. A few hangings would straighten things out, all right, but there wasn't any guarantee about who would be on the rope-end of the hangings. It might be me. The truth was I was just as scared of vigilantes as I was of the Julesburg riff-raff.

Outside of this one subject, Ed was a reasonable man and we got along fine. I couldn't figure out why he was so irrational about the Provisional Government. And it wasn't just with me. He had several arguments in the saloons, especially after he'd had a few drinks, and he'd usually wind up in a fight. I got so I didn't even ask him how he received the black eye he was sporting, or the bruised lip. I just assumed he'd been holding forth on the Provisional Government again and had been talking to the wrong man.

The more I thought about it, the less I understood it. Ed was a man who couldn't or wouldn't discuss politics or foreign policy or religion or philosophy. As I said, he didn't seem to have a serious thought in his head except on this one subject. Finally I got so I quit talking about it, figuring that everybody had an irrational streak if you looked for it long enough. This question of the Provisional Government was Ed's.

Before August was over I had speculators looking me up and trying to buy some of my lots. I was offered five hundred dollars for them, and although that had looked like a good price when Ed had mentioned the figure to me the night I'd stayed with him, I didn't think it was so good now. I had a hunch property values were going higher and that I'd do better to sell at the top of the market, if I could guess when that was going to be. I didn't know, of course, but I was dead sure it hadn't topped out yet.

More people were moving to Cheyenne every day. They lived in some of the damnedest places a man could imagine, sometimes nothing more than dugouts or wagon boxes or the poorest kind of frame houses that were no better than shacks.

Somebody said, "The houses of Cheyenne are standing insults to every wind that blows." It was true enough for most houses, but mine was different. I could have sold it for a good profit even before it was finished, but I wouldn't listen to any offer — I was determined to live in it myself. I guess I figured that a man was judged by the house in which he lived, and for a time I was close to being the Number One Citizen of Cheyenne, if a man is judged by his house.

Fort D. A. Russell was established on the northwest outskirts of Cheyenne. It became one of the major forts throughout the long period of the Indian wars on the plains and was retained as a permanent post after the others were given up. Camp Carlin was also set up near Cheyenne, a supply depot for fourteen forts within a radius of four hundred miles. It was always a beehive of activity, with its thousands of horses and more than one hundred freight wagons and pack trains and the five hundred men or better who worked there.

All of this added to Cheyenne's business, helped boost property values, and made a bigger demand for good houses. I could have done well just building houses that fall and winter, but I was bound to put up a business structure. I owned several good business lots, and I could do the work myself. There was a constantly growing demand for such buildings, and now that I owned considerable town property, my credit seemed to be unlimited.

I knew I could rent my building as soon as it was finished. I didn't know exactly how much rent I could get, but I was certain that any reasonably good building would be excellent income property and I was determined to make it big while I could. I was, as my father had once suggested, making the big gamble and I saw no reason to cash in now with luck running my way.

Building materials were pouring into town, so there was a better supply than when I had started working on my house in July. Freight outfits were on the move all the time between Cheyenne and Julesburg to the east and Denver to the south.

One interesting thing happened that I didn't see because I was still working on my house and never left it until it was too dark to work. Then I usually went to the business part of town for my supper and a drink. I always fixed my own breakfast and dinner, but more often than not I went to a restaurant for supper. By the time I quit work every day I was too tired to fool with building a fire and cooking a meal.

I didn't hear about this incident until it was over, but apparently a bunch of Julesburg speculators, judging Cheyenne to have a better future than Julesburg, came to town and squatted on several town lots, refusing to accept the fact that the railroad company owned the lots and had the authority to sell them.

I suppose the Julesburg men had been breathing the lawless air of their hell-on-wheels town so long that they figured they'd find the same air in Cheyenne. Their argument that the site of Cheyenne was public domain and they had a right to squat on it was stupid, but they did their damnedest to make it stick. They refused to move off the lots, so the Union Pacific men sent to Fort D. A. Russell for help.

Before the squatters knew what had happened, troops arrived and drove the settlers south at gunpoint. There wasn't any argument or debate about the matter until the squatters were across Crow Creek. After that there was a palaver, but the settlers were not allowed to return until they recognized the right of the Union Pacific to sell the town lots.

This affair wasn't particularly important except that it pointed up the need for tough law enforcement. The soldiers were stationed at Fort D. A. Russell to help the Union Pacific, especially against the Indians, but it has always been a question in my mind which was worse, savages who fought to protect their homes or white outlaws who were supposed to be civilized. In any case, the soldiers couldn't always be depended on; the garrison was never a large one, and if the men were chasing Indians, there might not be enough soldiers left at the fort to put down a riot.

I kept my eyes peeled for Bully Bailey and his friends, but I didn't see or hear anything more of them. Maybe Bailey had seen me at the same time I saw him and he wasn't ready for a showdown with me yet. That didn't mean it wasn't coming sooner or later, but at least I had a peaceful month.

That is, my life was peaceful until I met Preacher Frank Rush. I suppose that in a town the size of Cheyenne I was bound to meet Frank sooner or later, but sometimes I think there are absolute laws of cause and effect that dictate a man's destiny, laws we don't understand any more than we understand gravity.

Anyhow, my meeting Frank Rush marked the beginning of a number of important events in my life, and my month of peace came to an end.

Chapter XII

I had seen Frank Rush on the street a number of times and I knew he worked for the Cheyenne and Western Freight Company, but that was all I did know about him. He was a big man, a good six-foot three-inches tall and broad across the shoulders, with the biggest hands I ever saw on any human being. I guessed he weighed two hundred and twenty-five pounds, maybe more.

These were obvious facts I had noticed about the man when I would pass him on the street as I was going downtown for supper. I assumed he lived near my house because he was always walking north toward it, passing me going in the opposite direction.

He was a man you couldn't help noticing and I had been curious about him. I hadn't the slightest notion that he was a preacher until one evening in September when I

131

stepped into the Head Quarters Saloon for a drink.

I'd finished my house and had found a couple of carpenters who were willing to work for me. They had just arrived in Cheyenne and hadn't found anything better. I had started my business building and was working on it by myself when they stopped by and asked if I could use a couple of good men. I said I'd find out how good they were and for them to show up at seven o'clock the following morning.

They were pretty good carpenters at that — better than I had expected — so I hired them. After that we moved right along with the building. Before we even had the roof on, three men who were looking for store buildings jumped me about renting it.

The Head Quarters Saloon had moved out of the tent and into a frame building. The owner even hired a brass band that banged away every evening in front of the saloon. It made more noise than music, but it did pull in a crowd.

On this particular evening I had had supper and decided I needed a drink before I went home. I guess I was lonesome. I hadn't seen Ed Burke for several days, and although I worked well with my two carpenters, they were both family men and we didn't spend any time together after we knocked off work. I was never a man to pick up superficial friends the way Ed Burke did, so I think it was the need to be with people more than the hunger for a drink that drove me into the Head Quarters that evening.

The place was jumping. Several soldiers from Fort D. A. Russell and Camp Carlin were there, a bunch of freighters who operated between Cheyenne and Fort Laramie were bellied up against the bar, some others were playing poker, and a dozen or more graders had come in from the railroad camps, so altogether it was a motley crew, as the fellow said.

Several girls who had rooms upstairs were circulating through the crowd trying to drum up business. One of them propositioned me the minute I came through the batwings, but I didn't want any part of her. She was too fat for me. I remembered reading in the newspaper a sardonic article on the entertainment offered the men in Cheyenne. The author mentioned the Teutonic girls that one of the dance-hall operators had imported from St. Louis. He said they danced and stunk by turns, and after looking at these girls I could believe it. I couldn't help thinking of Ed Burke calling them cows.

Anyhow, I'd been working too hard to get horny, so I told the girl no, got my drink at the bar, and found an empty table over next to the wall. I sat down, thinking I hadn't had a woman for a long time and wishing Rosy and Flossie Martin would show up here. I had expected them before this and had even considered writing to them.

There was a lot of racket in the Head Quarters, all the kinds of noise that's natural for a crowded saloon. Several men at the bar were trying to sing, but their music was worse than the brass band out in the street. Some of the racket was just loud talk. Now and then a man would yell in anger and a fight would start, but the bouncers soon got it stopped. Several card games were going on, and once in a while when the big noise died down you'd hear the click of chips or the banging of a glass on a tabletop.

I sat there and nursed my drink and looked and listened, and all the time I was thinking what a waste of time and money it was. On the other hand, a good saloon like the Head Quarters was a kind of club, and I'm sure it served a worthwhile purpose for many of the men who were there.

I didn't see Frank Rush when he came in. The first I was aware of him being in the saloon was when he raised his hands above

134

his head and shouted, "I want to talk to you men this evening."

He got everyone's attention, all right. This was the first time I'd ever seen anything like this happen in a saloon. He had a great, booming voice that could be heard above the din. Men stopped talking and drinking and playing cards and turned to look at a man who had a voice like that and the temerity to go with it.

The silence wouldn't last long, of course, but he took advantage of the few seconds that it did last. Again his great voice boomed out. "I'm Frank Rush. Some of you know where I work at the Cheyenne and Western Freight Depot. I'm doing that temporarily to feed my wife and myself until I can get a church started. What I want to talk to you about tonight is the gospel of Jesus Christ and the great love He has for all of you."

The men were still listening, most of them not knowing what to make of this. One of the poker players who had been sitting at a table next to mine jumped up and started plowing through the crowd toward Rush. I judged he was a professional gambler by the way he was dressed.

"Jesus Christ," the gambler yelled. "Who the hell is he?"

"If you listen you'll find out," Rush said.

"Go back to your table and sit down. I won't take long. You men have been worshipping Satan twenty-four hours a day. You always have an attentive ear for his siren call to sin. Now I'm asking you to listen for ten minutes to the gospel of Jesus Christ."

"Nobody wants to listen to that stuff," the gambler yelled. "Get out of here, you gospel-spieling bastard. I've got a game going and, by God, I don't intend to let you stop it."

He was a big man, but not as big as Rush. He had his share of guts, though, or maybe he was running a bluff, thinking that any man who called himself a preacher wouldn't actually stand and fight. But Frank Rush didn't back up an inch. When the gambler was a step from him, he swung a fist at Rush's face. The preacher didn't duck or turn away. He simply blocked the blow with his big left arm and hit the gambler with his right.

I guess Rush must have caught the man right on the button. From where I sat, it looked as if that punch actually lifted the gambler clear off the floor and launched him into flight. Anyhow, he surely went up and back down. His head hit the bar. He bounced off and sprawled flat out on the floor.

There was a thudding sound when Rush hit him — I'd heard the same sound in dozens of butcher shops when a butcher is softening up a piece of tough meat — and then the hard crack of the gambler's skull hitting the bar. After he lay sprawled on the floor I heard a strange sighing sound come out of the crowd. I guess a lot of breath was being let out all at the same time.

Rush held up his hands again and said, "I apologize for the interruption, gentlemen, but there are times when a minister has to strike and strike hard to get the opportunity to tell the gospel story. Most of you have heard it, probably when you were children. Apparently you have forgotten it or you wouldn't be in a place like this, sinning and sending your immortal souls to hell as fast as you can."

I guess the gambler had a partner at the table. I saw him get to his feet. But he didn't look the part of a gambler. As a matter of fact, he was dressed like one of the freighters. There were four others at the table. This one had a fine, tall pile of chips in front of him, so I figured he was a capper, working hand in glove with the gambler who had tackled Rush. The two of them, playing together, could and probably had been taking the freighters to a cleaning.

As I say, this was guess work, but it was plain he was up to something, although I didn't know what it was for a few seconds. He took two steps away from the table as Rush started to talk. I was on my feet and edging toward him, still not certain what he was going to do. I wondered why nobody else was interfering or was even concerned about his intentions.

Maybe the other men at the table wanted to get on with the game and didn't care what happened to Rush, or maybe they just didn't want to have anything to do with another man's fight. It was Rush's trouble. That was plain enough, and it was equally plain he hadn't noticed the fellow.

Then the man drew his knife, and of course there wasn't any doubt then about what he was going to do. I got to him just as he brought his arm back to throw the knife. He was quite a distance from Rush but I'd seen men who could be as dangerous with a knife at that distance as a gunman would be with a Colt .45. Put a piece of steel like that into a man's belly and he was dead. I figured Frank Rush didn't deserve it.

I caught the man's arm just before he was ready to let go, and I twisted it hard. He yelped and cursed me and tried to struggle, but I didn't give him much chance. I jerked him back and forth a few times and pulled him around as he dropped the knife, then I slugged him in the soft part of the belly.

He bent forward, his mouth springing open as he struggled for breath. I hit him a second time on the chin. He staggered back, sprawled over a chair, upset a table, and landed on the floor with a great clatter, his arms flung out. I had knocked him cold.

Rush stopped talking long enough to see what the commotion was about. For a few seconds there was silence again, and then that long, drawn-out sigh. A freighter over by the bar laughed shakily and yelled, "Look at 'em, lyin' there like a couple o' sleepin' babes."

Most of the men laughed and another one, a soldier this time, called, "Go ahead, preacher. It won't hurt to listen to a sermon. I guess most of us ain't heard one for a long time."

They listened better than I thought they would. I listened, too, and I was disappointed but not surprised by what he said. Although I didn't time him, it seemed to me he spent one minute on the love of Jesus Christ and nine minutes on the misery and horror and suffering of a soul burning in hell. I was reminded of my mother's funeral sermon and all the other sermons I had heard a long time ago.

Rush finished with, "Next Sunday morning I am holding religious service in front of my tent on the corner of Ferguson and Twenty-third Streets. You are all invited. Thank you for your attention."

He came to my table then. I was surprised because I wasn't sure he had seen what had happened. He had, all right, because when he reached my table he held out his hand, saying, "I'm obliged. I'm Frank Rush, as I'm sure you know."

"Jim Glenn," I said as I rose and shook hands with him. "I admire the way you handled yourself."

"I can say the same about you." He looked at me for a moment and then shook his head. "How can one man thank another for saving his life?"

"You don't," I said. "Forget it. I just thought you deserved to be heard."

That seemed to trouble him. He said, still looking straight at me, "You mean the gospel needs to be heard."

"I don't think you preached the gospel," I said. "In fact, I admire you and your courage for coming in here, but I don't give a damn about your theology."

That troubled him, too. He moistened his

lips, and then he said, "You sound like a man who has given a good deal of thought to the subject."

"I have," I said.

"I see." He moistened his lips again. "This is not the time or the place to discuss it, but someday we will. You are erecting a building on Sixteenth Street, aren't you?"

"Yes," I said.

"I'm going to quit my job with the freight company," he said. "I'm an excellent carpenter. Can you use me?"

That floored me. I guess I stared blankly at him, because I couldn't make much sense out of it. I asked, "Why do you want to work for me?"

"Perhaps you will pay more than the freight company," he said. "Perhaps I like carpentry work better than loading and unloading freight wagons."

"There are a dozen men in Cheyenne who would give a good carpenter work," I said. "I don't understand why you've been working for a freight company until now and then decide you want to work for me."

He looked straight at me. He said without flinching or looking away or doing anything that would detract from the appearance of honesty that I'm sure he wanted to give, "Is it something you have to understand? Isn't

141

it enough that I want to work for you? If you find that I'm not an excellent carpenter, fire me tomorrow night. My day's work won't cost you a cent if you don't like what I do."

"Fair enough," I said.

"I'll be a little late because I'll have to go to the freight depot and tell them I'm quitting," he said, "but I'll be with you before noon."

He was, and it didn't take me all day to realize he was as good as he said he was. I'll have to admit he was a better carpenter than I was. I didn't realize for quite a while that this was his way of thanking me for saving his life.

CHAPTER XIII

We made excellent progress with the building the following week. I could thank Frank Rush for that. He was a good man to have on my payroll any way I looked at him. He wasn't the preacher type. That is, he never tried to convert any of us and he didn't have that pious, holier-than-thou attitude of authority I had come to associate with preachers I had known.

One afternoon a carriage drove by that was filled with whores. They ignored us as well as all the other men who were on the street, so obviously they weren't trying to work up any new business. Apparently they were just out for some fresh air.

About an hour later the carriage returned. You never saw more sedate and dignified women in your life than this bunch. One thing was sure: they weren't going to get themselves arrested and kicked out of town for creating a disturbance.

The two carpenters who had been working for me before I hired Frank stared at the women both times they passed and made some lewd remarks. Frank stared, too, but there was nothing licentious in his expression. You can tell a good deal about a man's attitude toward women, good or bad, in how he looks at them and what he says when he looks. I guess I wasn't surprised when I saw an expression of sympathy on his face.

Frank didn't say anything when they drove by the first time, but when they returned, he said in a low voice, "Poor things," and turned back to the board he had been sawing.

After that I had a lot more respect for Frank than I'd had before, but in a different way. I didn't agree with him that they were poor things. I'd had enough experience with whores to believe that most of them were like Rosy and Flossie Martin in at least one way: they preferred their profession to working for a living. Frank was probably as ignorant as hell about women like that, but he didn't condemn them. The way I saw it, he deserved a lot of credit for that.

After we quit working that evening, he said, "Jim, I want you to meet my wife Nancy. She asked me to have you come out

144

for supper tomorrow evening."

I didn't want to go. I knew they lived in a tent and that it would be hard for a woman to cook a meal for company under such primitive conditions. Too, I just wasn't interested in meeting a married woman. Since she was a preacher's wife, I figured she'd be a dull, mousey woman who would be about as interesting as an Indian squaw whose conversational ability was limited to "ugh" and "how."

I couldn't turn him down, though, so I said I'd come. The next night I went home and washed up, changed to a clean shirt and walked to the Rush tent. I'd been past there a number of times and knew where it was, but I hadn't seen Mrs. Rush until that evening. I was amazed when I met her, astonished, even shocked. She was about as far removed from being the dull, mousey woman I had expected as a woman could be.

She gave me a good smile when Frank introduced us. By that I mean an honest, friendly smile. It wasn't the perfunctory smile that some women can put on and off as the situation demands just as they put on and take off a pair of shoes. It wasn't a phony, too-sweet smile, either. I'd seen plenty of times when a woman knew this was the reaction that was expected of her, so she performed to satisfy the expectation. With Nancy Rush it struck me that she smiled because she meant it and the smile came right from her heart.

"Frank has talked about you so much, Mr. Glenn," she said. "I know he's thanked you for saving his life, but I want to add my thanks, too."

She offered her hand and I took it, and found myself as tongue-tied as a bashful boy meeting a pretty girl. I was disgusted with myself, but I managed to mutter something about being glad that I'd been able to do it.

"Supper will be ready in a few minutes," she said, and turned back to the Dutch ovens and the coffee pot she had on the fire.

To cover my embarrassment I got my pipe out and filled it. When I glanced at Frank I thought he seemed amused. He said, "You see why I'm proud of her."

"Yeah, I sure do," I said.

I told myself that if I could find a woman like that I'd marry her tomorrow. I also thought that Frank Rush was a damned fool for making her live in a tent. Fall would be here soon and the nights would be cold, and then winter would be along.

Although I hadn't spent a winter in Cheyenne, I knew it could get almighty cold.

With the kind of wind we often had, it would simply be unbearable in a tent. So far Frank had shown no intention of trying to find a house in which to spend the winter. At least he'd never mentioned it to me.

I lighted my pipe and puffed on it, my eyes on Nancy Rush. It's hard to describe her in words because I had a feeling about her that didn't come from anything that stemmed from my five senses. Oh, there were physical features I could mention. She was a pretty woman with strong physical features, dark brown eyes, and black, black hair. She was quite tall and had an excellent figure, with high, proud breasts and a slim waist and what must have been perfectly proportioned legs — judging from the bit of ankle that showed every so often. She looked a good deal younger than Frank, maybe by as much as ten years. I guessed she was about twenty-five.

Presently she handed me a plate and tin cup. There was humor in her dark eyes as she said, "I'm going to ask you to help yourself, Mr. Glenn, as soon as Frank asks the blessing. You'll find stew in one of the Dutch ovens and biscuits in the other. Coffee, of course, in the coffee pot. Don't be bashful. We're short on variety, but long on quantity."

I took the plate and cup, unable to keep my eyes off her. I saw the redness of her lips against her white teeth, but again, it wasn't her physical appearance that hit me so hard. I kept trying to pinpoint it, and then I had a hint of what it was. I sensed a maturity about her that went beyond her years; I noted the self-possessed curve of her lips, which I had never seen in another woman, but then I had never met another woman like Nancy Rush.

I guess Frank was as hungry as I was. Anyhow, his grace was a short one. Then he lifted the lids from the Dutch ovens and I helped myself. The stew had plenty of meat and several vegetables. I took a biscuit and poured my coffee and picked up my silverware from the pile she had placed on a napkin beside the fire.

The stew was excellent, the biscuits white and flaky, the coffee strong and black the way I liked it. As I ate, I kept glancing at Nancy, still trying to put into thought-words the feeling I'd had about her the moment I'd seen her. Gradually I worked out more than the hints I'd had of her maturity and self-possession.

She was a slim and shining girl who loved life. I thought she should have found it exciting — then I was stopped again because I suddenly had a very strong feeling she didn't. I don't know why this feeling came to me. It may have been my imagination, but I felt she was disappointed, perhaps frustrated.

We ate almost in silence, with only an occasional exchange of conversation. When I glanced at Frank, I had a notion he was quite satisfied with himself and with Nancy and with his life in general. I turned this over in my mind, but I failed to find any good answer as to why he would be satisfied and Nancy wouldn't. Again I realized that this could be my imagination, but I didn't think so. I had learned a long time ago to trust these hunches or feelings that came to me about people.

Nancy was an exciting woman, and it didn't make sense, if I was right, that she was unable to find excitement in her life with Frank. He was a hell of a good man. He should have been a good husband. I saw lines of discontent around her eyes and I became more certain I was right about them as the minutes passed.

When we finished eating, Frank rose from where he had hunkered beside the fire and dropped his plate and cup and silverware into the wreck pan. He said, "I've got a call to make, Jim. You'll have to excuse me, but I hope you'll stay awhile and talk to Nancy. She's alone all day and she doesn't have any friends here, so she gets pretty lonesome."

"Sure, I'll stay," I said. "I've got nothing to go home to."

After he left, I knocked my pipe out against my heel and filled it again. Nancy rose and poured water into a pan that was set on the fire, then glanced at me and smiled. She said, "I suppose you're wondering why Frank left to make a call when he invited you here for supper. Well, it's a man who has come to Christian service every Sunday since we've been in Cheyenne. His name is Ole Svensen. He's very sick. He was so sick last Sunday I didn't think he'd be able to stay here for all the service."

She shrugged her shoulders, her face turning grave. "If it wasn't Ole, it would be someone else. Frank is calling on somebody every evening. He has to call in the evening because he doesn't have time during the day." She laughed and added, "I guess you know that."

"I was wondering about something else," I said. "Why does Frank go off and leave a pretty wife with a man he doesn't know very well?"

"He knows you, or thinks he does," she said, "and he would never think of me doing anything wrong. You see, he always expects people that he loves or likes to do the right thing."

I had learned in the few days I had worked with him that he was a naive man in many ways, and this seemed additional proof of his naiveté. I didn't say that to Nancy, but it was plain that she thought the same of him. She washed the dishes and I sat puffing my pipe and wondering what was safe to talk about.

"You have a fine house," she said. "I've walked past your place several times. I get so tired of nothing to do and just sitting here in a tent under a hot sun all day."

"I'm enjoying my house," I said, and then I asked the question that had been in my mind ever since I'd hired Frank. I just hadn't had the courage to ask it before. "How do Frank's religious services go? Does he have a crowd?"

She glanced at me, grimacing. "Would you say half a dozen people make a crowd? No, he will not get a crowd until he has a church building. He's saving every cent he can to put one up."

"Where?"

"On this lot," she answered. "It's the only

property he owns."

"I thought he'd build a house on this lot," I said. "One to live in."

"Oh no." She smiled briefly. "A house to live in is not important. A church building where he can preach the Word is. He says he can't go on trying to preach in saloons where he interrupts men's sinning. They hate him when he does. He can't get people to come and stand in all kinds of weather, either."

"What will you live in?" I asked.

"The tent. He'll move it to the back of the lot when he starts his church building."

I couldn't believe it. I said, "You can't live in a tent all winter. It gets cold here. Awful cold."

"I know," she said, "but Frank doesn't. He won't know until the cold weather gets here."

I took my pipe out of my mouth and let it cool in my hand. Knowing that Frank Rush was impractical was one thing, but hearing it from his wife this way was something else. The strange part of it was that he was such a good craftsman, being practical in the material way of handling a saw and hammer. But on other matters in which he had to look ahead, he seemed just plain stupid.

"The end of steel will be here before

long," I said, "and Cheyenne will be another hell on wheels. Aside from the cold weather, it wouldn't be safe for a woman to live in a tent. I don't know whether they'll get the rails past Cheyenne and over Sherman Hill by this winter or not, but if they don't, this town will be jumping. You simply won't have a house to live in."

"I've thought of that," she said, "but Frank hasn't."

"Then tell him," I said. I guess I said it rather loud. I was out of patience with both her and Frank. Even a squirrel had enough sense to get ready for winter. "My God, tell him. If he can't look ahead by himself, you've got to do it for him."

She picked up her pan of dishwater and walked to the rear of the tent and threw it out. She came back, put the pan down, and wiped her hands on her apron. She said, "Mr. Glenn —"

"Jim," I interrupted.

She nodded. "Jim, there is one thing about my husband you might as well know right now. He never believes anything I tell him. I don't think he'd believe anything you would tell him. He has to see things for himself, and by that time it's usually too late. For instance, I told him it was dangerous to go into a saloon and preach, but he didn't believe it until that man tried to kill him with a knife — the one you stopped."

I put my pipe into my pocket and rose. She stood motionless, looking at me. I walked around the fire to her, wanting to take her hands, wanting to put my arms around her and tell her that her life could be filled with joy and pleasure and laughter, that it was what she deserved and she was being wasted on Frank Rush.

I didn't do any of those things. I stopped three feet from her and said, "Nancy, you shouldn't be living like this even in good weather. Why couldn't you and Frank move in with me? I have two bedrooms. You could keep house for me in exchange for a decent place to live. I wouldn't charge you any rent."

Most of the time since I had first arrived she had looked at me squarely if she looked at me at all, but now for the first time she lowered her eyes and shook her head. She said, in a tone filled with misery, "You know I couldn't do that and you know why."

"I'd better go home," I said abruptly. "Thank you for the good supper."

"You're welcome," she said. "I hope you'll come again."

I walked away quickly, not trusting myself to stay longer or to say anything else to her.

I did not understand what had happened, but I knew very well that for the first time in my life I had met a woman I wanted. I also felt she wanted me. That was as far as it would go — just the wanting, never the fulfillment.

I saw an empty tin can in front of me. I kicked it halfway down the block, so far that I lost sight of it in the twilight. This was one hell of a note, I told myself. Well, one thing was sure. Frank Rush would never know how I felt about his wife.

CHAPTER XIV

Every day for several weeks I intended to say something to Frank about building a house for him and Nancy. I knew better than to suggest that they move into my house. I did indeed know what Nancy had meant when she'd said she could not do that and I knew why.

There wasn't any hope, either, that I could persuade Frank to build a house instead of a church, so I didn't try. The only plan that might work was for me to build a house on one of my lots and rent it to them. I would have made it rent free, but I suspected he had too much pride for that kind of arrangement.

They say hell is paved with good intentions. I guess it is. Anyhow, I just never got around to saying anything to Frank about a house. I had plenty of chances to talk to him and I wanted to, but I never did. Then, when my building was almost finished, something happened that took my mind off Frank and Nancy Rush.

I was standing in the doorway of the building looking around and wondering what I should do with it when Ed Burke stopped by. He had worked for me several afternoons and knew Frank and my other two carpenters, but it had been a week or so since I'd seen him. I thought he probably had not come to town during that week.

"Howdy, Ed," I said. "Haven't seen you for a while. I guess you've been busy."

He said, "Naw, I've been out of town. I mean, out of the country. I never work enough to be busy. I ain't like some jaspers I know who are working themselves into an early grave."

I was exasperated with him. I'd never had much use for lazy men, and the better I got acquainted with Ed, the more I realized he was just plain lazy. This was true as far as his ranch work was concerned, certainly, although when he worked for me, he put out all the effort I could ask of a man.

"Oh hell," I said. "I don't work hard enough to end up in an early grave. On the other hand, there is an old saying about no work and all play makes Jack a dull boy."

He gave a short laugh. "Then I sure am a dull boy." He motioned to the interior of the building. "What are you fixing to do with this place."

"I haven't made up my mind," I said. "I've had plenty of opportunities to rent it, but I keep putting it off. It's big enough for a general store, only I've been thinking it would be better to run a partition down the middle and make two big rooms. I'd get more rent that way. That's why we put two doors on the street and two on the alley. I could rent half of it for a restaurant and the other half for a saddle shop or something of the sort."

He nodded in an absent-minded way and shifted his weight from one foot to the other. I don't think he heard what I said. He was nervous and I wondered why. Most of the time he acted as if he didn't give a damn about anything except getting his next meal or his next drink, but something was working on him now and I was curious about it.

He took a cigar out of his pocket and stepped back out of the doorway and stood with his back to the wall. He tried to light the cigar, but a sudden gust of wind sent a cloud of dust down the street and put his match out. He swore and moved past me into the building. This time he got his cigar going and flipped his match into the street.

"You know a tough bird named Bully Bailey?" he asked, trying to sound as if the question wasn't important, and failing.

That startled me, because I almost had succeeded in putting Bailey out of my mind. For a while after I'd seen him and his friends in Cheyenne I'd been plenty scared, Bully Bailey being the kind of man he was, but after all this time I'd decided that the three men must have left the country. Now, judging from Ed's expression and his tone of voice, I guessed they were back in town.

"Yeah, I'm sorry to say I know him," I said. "Likewise a couple of buckos who travel with him."

"They're still with him," he said. "They don't amount to much, but Bailey's a bad actor. Take my word for it. I know."

"So do I," I said. "He's a coward, but some of the most dangerous men I ever ran into are cowards."

"Right," he agreed. "Well, it seems that all three came to town about the time you did and then left for Julesburg, but it got too hot for 'em there so they came back to Cheyenne. Bailey's been drinking, and when he gets enough coffin varnish in him, he gets a loose mouth. Now he's been making some tall threats about you, saying he's gonna stop your clock for good."

159

"I'm not surprised," I said. "I'm going to have to kill the bastard. I saw him and his friends here, but when I started looking for them, they had disappeared. I'd better start looking again."

"I'll help you," he said.

"Oh no you don't," I said. "This is my fight and I'll handle it."

He chewed on his cigar awhile, then he said grudgingly, "All right, go ahead and get yourself killed of bravery. That's what you'll do."

"No I won't," I said. "I never saw the day I couldn't handle Bully Bailey and his friends."

"If you get a chance to see 'em," he snapped. "By God, Jim, you are the mule-headedest man I ever seen. I don't know why I waste my time worrying about you."

"Neither do I," I said. "I'll go get my supper. Afterwards I'll start looking for Bailey." Then I thought of something and asked, "How come he's called Bully here in Cheyenne? He always hated the name, but it got fastened onto him in Black Hawk and he couldn't get rid of it."

"It wasn't his idea. Some men besides you had met up with him before he got here and knew what he'd been called, so they pinned the name on him again. Fits him, too. I've met a lot of men I thought were tough birds, and liked them, but this damned Bailey ain't really tough. He's an animal." Ed shook his head. "No, I can't say that. It insults the animals. He's just plain mean."

"He is that," I said, remembering what he'd done to Rosy Martin. "Well, I'll go find some place to eat."

"Say, there's a new restaurant in town," he said. "It's called the Cheyenne Eatery. It's in a tent a block west of here, on Ferguson between 16th and 17th. Have you tried it?"

"No, I haven't," I said.

"It belongs to a young woman who just got to town. I claim she's the best cook in Cheyenne. Trouble is she's trying to run the place by herself, so the service is slow when she's crowded, but a meal is worth waiting for. Her name's Cherry Owens. A right purty filly, too."

"I'll try it," I said.

"You do that," he said. "If you don't get a good meal, I'll pay for it."

"Fair enough," I said.

He started off down the street, walking north. I wondered what he was up to. I stood there several minutes watching him until he disappeared. The saloons weren't in that direction. None of the brothels were,

161

either, so I was curious about where he was going.

Finally I shrugged my shoulders and decided to hell with it. Anything he did was his business and none of mine. I liked him and enjoyed his company, but he didn't have the same goals I did and I often wondered what we saw in each other. Sometimes I wasn't sure what my goals were, but I had some, and more often than not I didn't think Ed had any.

I walked to the corner and turned toward Ferguson Street. I found the Cheyenne Eatery without any trouble. There were just two cowboys sitting at the counter, so the service wasn't as slow as it would have been if the place had been crowded.

Ed was right about the girl on two counts. She was a pretty filly, about twenty, I guessed, small, just about big enough to be called Watch Fob or Trinket or some such name, and she could move. She went on the dead run after she took my order and again when she brought my plate of food. I thought she'd wear herself out in a week at this rate, if she had to go on being both waitress and cook.

She was blond, and her eyes, a bright blue, had a way of taking a person in with one sweeping glance. Her hair was gold-yellow with touches of red in it. She had brushed it back from her forehead and tied it in a bun at the back of her head. It was a little too prim, I thought, and decided she would have been more attractive if she had used a little curl.

As for the food, Ed was dead right on that, too. I had never tasted a better steak in my life, the biscuits were light, the custard pie excellent, and the coffee wonderful. When I had finished eating, I sat there with my second cup of coffee, looking at her. The two cowboys had finished and left, so for the moment I was alone with her.

I guess she sensed I was staring at her. She had moved to the front of the tent and was standing there looking out into the street. Suddenly she turned and came back to where I was sitting. I was a little uneasy, thinking she might chew me out for staring rudely at her.

"Do I pass inspection?" she asked, smiling.

At least she wasn't irritated because I'd been staring at her, but I guess my face got red anyway. It felt hot enough to be red. I managed a wink and a weak grin.

"You certainly do," I said, "but I was sitting here worrying about you. You can't handle both sides of this business. You'll die

163

of exhaustion."

She curtsied. "Thank you for your concern, Mr. . . ."

"Glenn," I told her. "Jim Glenn. We don't have many women like you in Cheyenne, so we treasure the few we do have."

She had been sarcastic, but now I realized she had turned serious. She studied me for a moment, chewing on her lower lip thoughtfully. Finally she said, "Maybe I misjudged you. I half believe you meant what you just said."

"Of course I meant it," I said testily. "And another thing. I don't know where you came from, but you can't run a restaurant in a tent in Cheyenne after cold weather gets here."

"I know that," she admitted. "I come from Denver, so I don't have any illusions about Cheyenne being in the tropics during the winter." She shook her head. "You see, I'm not in any position to be choosey. I couldn't find a building when I got here, not one that I could afford to rent."

She motioned toward the rear. "I have a small tent back there which I use for my living quarters. I can make out fine for another month or so. Buildings are going up all the time. I'll find something by then."

"I have a building we're just finishing," I

said. "I can fix it up for you in a day or two. We'd just have to run a partition down the middle."

Her eyes narrowed and her mouth firmed out and I could feel the anger begin to build and then the outrage that took possession of her. "Mr. Glenn," she said, tight-lipped, "I know how men operate. You might as well get it through your head right now that I can't be bought by the best building in Cheyenne. I'll pay my way as I go, or I won't go. I'm not looking for any easy way."

I sat there looking at her and wondering what I'd said that had made her so mad. I guess it took me about thirty seconds to understand what she was saying. When I did, I got mad. I slid off the stool and tossed a four-bit piece onto the counter, then I walked out of the tent, leaving half a cup of coffee. I was tempted to go back and tell her to go to hell, that I wasn't trying to buy her as she seemed to think. If I wanted to buy a woman, I knew where to go.

I stopped and turned around, and then it struck me that she had been close to crying when she'd said all that about not being bought. She was young and pretty, and of course I had no way of knowing how many men had tried to take advantage of her. It was plain enough that to her all men were alike. Maybe that had been her experience with men.

After thinking about it a moment, I turned around and walked away. I didn't see any sense in begging her. If she thought this about me, she'd just have to think it. I doubt that any defense on my part would change her.

I walked along Ferguson to the nearest saloon, realizing that I should have sympathy for her. I knew a good deal about men, and I'll have to admit that many of them are exactly the kind she took me for.

It was dark when I began looking for Bully Bailey and his friends. I tried every saloon in town, but they didn't seem to be in Cheyenne. I didn't look in any of the brothels, thinking there wasn't any use. They'd be in bed with some of the whores if that was where they were. All I could do was to wait and try again tomorrow night. They were the kind of men who would show up in one of the saloons sooner or later if they were in town.

One thing did bother me. It seemed to me that I kept running into Ed Burke all evening. Or if it wasn't Ed, it was Frank Rush. I wasn't surprised at seeing Ed, because when he was in town he wandered around aimlessly from one saloon to another, but I knew Frank didn't drink and that he had given up trying to preach in the saloons, so I did wonder about that. I didn't ask either one what they were up to. It was their business. Certainly it wasn't any of mine.

By ten o'clock I knew I had to give up. I started north on Ferguson Street, tempted to stop at the Cheyenne Eatery and get a cup of coffee. If Cherry Owens gave me a chance, I'd tell her there was no price tag on my building as she had assumed.

I didn't get there. Not right then anyhow. Two men jumped me and a third one came at me from somewhere behind me. I guess it was that way, though I hadn't known I was being followed.

I didn't have any chance. I caught one of them with a good punch to the jaw that knocked him down. I kicked another one in the belly and drove the wind out of him, but the third one slammed a fist into my throat. I caught a glimpse of his face just as he hit me and saw he was Bully Bailey.

I was on my knees trying to breathe, but it seemed my throat had closed up and I was in the horrible, helpless condition of being unable to suck any air into my lungs. I felt as if my throat had collapsed or that my windpipe had been cut.

From a great distance I heard Bailey's voice: "I'm gonna kill the bastard."

One of them kicked me in the ribs. Pain knifed all through my belly, but I was breathing again. I started to get back on my feet when the roof caved in. I guess one of them slugged me with a gun barrel. Or maybe picked up a club. I didn't see him hit me, so I'll never know what he used. All I know is that the whole world turned black and I wasn't aware of anything until I came to in Cherry Owens' tent.

CHAPTER XV

I was unconscious for a long time, an hour or more from what Ed and Frank told me later. When I came to I was aware first of a whacking headache that I thought was going to split my skull any second, and at almost the same time I was aware that my chest hurt like hell every time I took a breath.

Later, when I was able to focus my eyes, I made out Frank's face. He kept shaking his head and saying something about wishing that Ed would hurry and get back with the doctor. Cherry Owens was kneeling beside me. She had a bucket of water next to the bed, which was just a mattress and a couple of blankets spread on the ground. She would wet a cloth in the water, then squeeze it as dry as she could, and finally lay it across my forehead. After a minute or two she would lift the cloth and repeat the process.

"The bleeding's stopped," she said. "I thought it would. The cut isn't deep, but I'm worried about that knot on his head. I'm positive he has a concussion."

"And some broken ribs to boot," Frank said worriedly. "Where is that doctor?"

"Don't expect the doctor to do any good," Cherry said. "All anybody can do is keep him quiet."

I looked at Cherry and then at Frank. I managed to say, "I'm all right."

I heard Frank's great sigh of relief. "Well, doggone it, Jim," he said. "That's not exactly your normal voice, but I'm sure glad to hear it."

Cherry smiled and sat back, her hands on her knees. "It is indeed good to hear your voice," she said. "We wondered if you were ever going to come around."

I guessed I was in the tent that was her living quarters. I said, "I'm in your bed and it's time you were using it. Get me home, Frank."

"You can't be moved," Cherry said sternly. "I've had a little nursing experience, and one of the first things I learned was that anyone with a concussion has to be kept absolutely still, so don't roll around or move any more than you have to. You are staying here."

"Where will you be?" I asked.

"Right here beside you," she said. "I've got other blankets. I don't mind not sleeping on the mattress. The ground is just about as soft."

"Aren't you afraid to sleep in the same tent with me?" I asked.

She laughed softly. "I've had some experience with men," she said. "That's how I had my stint of nursing, if you could call it that. No, I'm not afraid to sleep here. Your spirit is probably willing, but your flesh will be weak for quite a while."

Frank was grinning from ear to ear, but I didn't see anything funny about what was being said. The girl was a fool; she didn't know men as well as she thought she did. But when I started to raise up on one elbow to tell her a thing or two that she didn't know about men, I could have sworn my head was splitting open, and I fell back on the pillow.

"You see?" Cherry said triumphantly. "You're going to be right there on that mattress for a while."

Ed came into the tent with a short potbellied man who carried a black bag and smelled of whisky. I told myself that every frontier doctor must be a drunkard. Maybe that was the only kind who came west, and their drinking was what had made them leave their home practice. I figured this one would want to operate right away, but he didn't.

He set his black bag on the ground, dropped to his knees and felt of my head. He said, "Hmmmm, he's got a concussion." Then he felt of my ribs, pressing too hard on my left side, and in spite of myself I let out a yip of pain and clenched my teeth. He said, "Hmmmm, he's got some broken ribs, too."

He rose, picked up his black bag, and turned to Ed. "Keep him here for at least twenty-four hours. Feed him lightly. Try to keep him from being active for a week or more. It'll be a month before he gets over this. That will be five dollars."

"You old fraud," Cherry cried. "You didn't tell us a thing we didn't know."

The doctor nodded amiably. "Certainly I'm an old fraud, my dear, but I have no idea how you found out. It wasn't my idea coming, you know. Your friend here used the muzzle of his gun as a gentle persuader to induce me to leave a very interesting poker game. Besides, I never suspected you would know so much about medicine. Now the five dollars please."

Ed handed him a five-dollar gold piece.

He said, "Thank you," and left the tent.

"That kind of doctor makes me so mad," Cherry said.

"We don't have much choice of doctors," Ed said. "I guess I wasted my five dollars, but maybe it will help to keep Mr. Jim Glenn flat on his back where he belongs."

"For twenty-four hours," I said. "No more. Tomorrow evening you're taking me home."

"Well now," Ed said, "if I had a purty nurse like this one, I wouldn't want to leave."

"I've got to," I said, "because if I stay here I might get better, and if I did, the flesh might get as willing as the spirit."

"All right," Cherry said. "You'd better go tomorrow evening. Bring a team and wagon, Mr. Burke. He won't be walking for a few more days."

"The offer of my building had no strings attached to it," I said. "I'd still like to rent it to you."

"Very well, I'll accept your offer," she said. "I'm sorry I said what I did, but the words were out before I realized I should have explored your offer before saying anything. The only excuse I have is that I've lived my life among men since I was fourteen. I know exactly what most men are like. My mistake was not finding out that you are different from most men."

"Oh, he's different from other men," Ed said maliciously. "He's so different you can trust him any time and under any circumstances."

"Shut up, Ed," I said. "That's not true and it's why you're getting me out of here tomorrow evening. Frank, start putting a partition down the middle of our building and fix her half of it the way she wants it."

"With living quarters in the back?" she asked.

"Of course."

"Thank you, Mr. Glenn," she said. "Thank you very much."

I saw she was close to tears. Life had been hard on her, I thought. I wasn't sure she'd had all the experiences with men she claimed she had, but any young woman as attractive as she was who had made her own way in boom towns like Cheyenne and had kept herself decent was to be admired. I did admire Cherry Owens.

I didn't want to embarrass her any more than I had, so I looked at Ed and asked, "What happened? I thought Bully Bailey was going to kill me. He said he was."

"He was trying to when we got there," Ed said.

"Just how did you happen to get there?" I asked.

"I was worried about you," he said. "You're so damned stubborn. The way Bailey had been running off at the mouth I figured he was gonna try tonight, which same he did. He was purty drunk, and when a man like Bailey gets drunk, he gets mean, so I went after Frank as soon as I left you." He nodded at Frank. "You tell him what happened."

"Ed was pretty excited when he got to my tent," Frank said. "He told me you'd be dead before midnight if we didn't keep an eye on you. You might be dead anyway, Bailey being the kind of man he is, and you being stubborn and confident the way you are, so I came downtown with him and we tried to follow you as much as we could without being too evident about it. When you started home, we trailed along, but we were too far back to keep them from jumping you. We got there as soon as we could and gave them a little trouble. They got away, though."

"We gave 'em more'n a little trouble," Ed said, grinning. "You should of seen Frank. He was a one-man gang. He didn't need me. He went after 'em like a bull buffalo, banging heads together and throwing 'em around like rag dolls. At first we thought they had killed you. We packed you over here to Miss Owens' place and she looked you over and said everything the damned doc said."

My head still hurt as much as ever and I wasn't taking any deep breaths. I closed my eyes. I was just too tired to keep them open and I hurt too much to keep on talking. All I could think of was that Ed Burke and Frank Rush had saved my life. Maybe I was too stubborn and self-confident, but I had never depended on other men for help and I didn't figure on starting now.

As soon as I was able, I decided, I'd hunt Bailey and his friends down and kill them, but they'd probably be hard to find, and I'd probably be in the same position I had been in tonight, knowing they were around and that they were a daily menace to my life but still not able to find them.

"Thank you," I said. "Thank all of you. You saved my life. I won't forget it."

"Glad to have had the fun," Frank said. "I'll get back to my tent. We'll start work on that partition in the morning."

Frank left, but Ed stayed, staring down at me and scowling as if he couldn't make up his mind about something. Finally he said, "I think I ought to stay here with you, Jim.

That bunch might be back."

"Not Bailey," I said. "Not if he took the beating you said he did. They're all out of town and ten miles away by now."

"I don't want you staying here," Cherry said sharply to Ed. "I can look after Mr. Glenn. Tomorrow evening you come with a team and wagon and take him home. Until then he's my responsibility."

Ed threw up his hands. "All right," he said. "I'll be here tomorrow evening."

After Ed left, Cherry opened one of her boxes and took out a pillow and some blankets and made her bed on the other side of the tent. She started to blow the lamp out, then drew back and looked at me. She asked, "Can I do anything for you?"

"Not tonight," I said.

"Time is a great healer," she said. "If you need anything during the night, wake me up."

She blew out the lamp, and a few minutes later I heard the steady rhythm of her breathing. She was right, of course. Only time would heal my ribs and head. Here I was, for the first time in my life, sleeping a few feet from a very attractive young woman, and I couldn't even get off the mattress.

The night was a very long one and I began

to think the sun had forgotten to come up. I had never been sicker in my life. Maybe I was feverish, but sometime during the night I decided I was going to marry Cherry Owens. When it was daylight, she stirred and turned on her side, her eyes coming open.

When I saw she was awake, I asked, "Would you bring me a drink of water?"

"Of course," she said.

She got up and filled a dipper with water and brought it to me. She slipped a hand under my head, lifted it and held the dipper to my mouth. I drank greedily, for my throat was dry, my lips cracked. When she eased my head back to the pillow I said, "I'm going to marry you, Cherry."

"What?"

"You heard what I said, but I'll repeat it. I'm going to marry you."

"I thought that was what you said." She was on her knees beside me. Now she leaned forward and looked at me closely in the thin light. "You're feverish."

"Of course I am, but I'll get over it, and when I do, I'll marry you."

"Thank you for your decision, Mr. Glenn," she said, "but don't you think a girl ought to be asked?"

"Oh, I'll ask you," I said. "I just thought

that now ought to be a good time to tell you."

"Do you always approach marriage like this?" she asked.

"I never have before," I answered, "but you're the first girl I ever saw that I wanted to marry."

"I'm complimented," she said, "but I'm not convinced it would be the proper thing to do. Maybe you think you compromised me by sleeping in my tent with me and you owe it to me to marry me."

"No," I said. "I never worry about things like that. It's just that I think you'd be a good wife for me and I'm sure I'd be the right husband for you. After we were married awhile you'd love me and I'd love you."

She laughed. "Oh, you are a romantic one, Mr. Glenn," she said. "I've always wanted a romantic proposal, and this is certainly one I'll remember."

I closed my eyes, thinking I'd boogered everything up, but feverish or not, I'd never meant anything more in my life than what I'd just said. When I opened my eyes a few minutes later, she was gone.

Chapter XVI

The twenty-four hours I spent on Cherry Owens' bed taught me one thing which I guess I had known, but only in an intellectual way, and that's entirely different from knowing something down in the bottom of my belly where the great compelling emotions are born. Time, I discovered, is entirely relative.

I had enjoyed the weeks I'd been in Cheyenne, enjoyed them more than I had ever enjoyed any other equal period in my life, so the days had passed quickly, each one of them equal to about one minute of the night and day I spent in Cherry's tent.

My head didn't stop pounding for one instant, and my chest hurt with every breath I took. If I forgot and took anything but the lightest of breaths, the agony was killing. All I could think of was, "God, get this over for me one way or another."

Cherry was in and out of the tent all day.

She closed her restaurant, pinning a note on the flap of the big tent saying she would be closed until she reopened in bigger quarters, and gave her new address on Eddy Street. I told her she didn't need to do it on my account. She said she wasn't, that she just needed the rest. I decided it was a lie, but I didn't feel like arguing.

She didn't bother me by making me talk to her, and I appreciated that. It made me think more of her than ever. A silent woman, I thought, was a rare person. She fixed some chicken broth for me and brought a bowl to me in the morning and again at noon, but I had trouble swallowing even something as innocuous as chicken broth.

That evening I told Cherry not to bring me any of the broth, that I couldn't eat anything. Not long after full dark I heard a wagon and knew they had come to take me home. I didn't want to go, simply because I hurt like hell if I moved, so of course it would be hell compounded when they moved me to the wagon and from the wagon into my house, to say nothing of the bumping of the wagon on the way. I had made up my mind, though, that I would not keep Cherry out of her bed for another night, so I'd grit my teeth and bear it.

Ed and Frank came in and asked me how

I felt. I lied and said fine. Of course they both knew I was lying. They got me on my feet and held me upright. The tent spun around as if it had gone crazy. I thought I was going to faint, but I never had fainted in my life and I wasn't going to start now. It was touch and go for a while, though.

I groaned. I didn't know until we had almost reached the wagon that I was the one doing the groaning, although I had heard it from the moment they had lifted me to my feet. Cherry walked beside us, and after I was on my back in the wagon she promised to look in on me the following morning.

Somehow I survived the jolting trip home and being hoisted to my feet again and half carried into the house. They helped me lie down, and for a while after that I thought I was going to die and hoped I would. I didn't, but I'm sure that, even though I have suffered considerable physical pain a good deal during my life, I never hurt as much as I did that evening while I was being taken home.

I kept on hurting after I was in my own bed, too. I thought about some of the platitudes I'd heard, that time is a great healer and all that kind of thing. Well, it seemed to me that time was damned slow doing its job. The past twenty-four hours had been a century.

Frank took the team and wagon back to the livery stable and Ed stayed with me that night. I asked him if he wanted to sleep in my extra bed, but he just grinned and said no, he'd brought his soogans along.

"I'll be outside your window," he said. "It's a warm night. I'll sleep in my Tucson bed."

I knew enough cowboy jargon to recognize a Tucson bed as "using his back for a mattress and his belly for a cover." He was right about the night being warm; he probably wouldn't need his blankets. Frank had promised to stop by tomorrow evening and tell me how they had got along with the partition. He said Nancy would drop in, too.

I didn't really care much whether anybody came to see me or not. All I wanted was for time to get at the job of healing me. I guess it got started that night. I slept some, and the dark hours did not drag at quite the same slow rate they had the night before.

When it was daylight Ed came into the house and built a fire and made coffee. He cooked breakfast, but I didn't want anything except coffee. It tasted good, the first thing that had since I'd taken my beating. After breakfast Ed left, saying he'd see me later.

As he went through the door, I told him to let Bully Bailey alone, that he was my meat. He grunted and kept on going, but I knew he was going to hunt for Bailey. I was sure he wouldn't find him, that the three men had hightailed out of town. I was equally sure that I would have one hell of a hard time finding them when I started looking.

Cherry came in before noon, bringing another bowl of chicken broth. This time it tasted good, too, so I guess time was getting in a few licks. Nancy showed up late in the afternoon and poached an egg for me. It was awful. I had never seen a poached egg before. I told her to fry the next one she fixed for me.

She didn't stay long. Later, after Frank had eaten supper, he came in and said they'd got a good start on the partition, that Cherry had drawn him a diagram to show him how she wanted the place arranged. They'd have it finished in less than a week, he thought.

He looked at me a moment, then asked hesitatingly, "What are you going to do after it's finished?"

"Build another house," I said. "I'll be up and working with you in a week."

"Yeah, sure," he said, and grinned.

I wasn't working with him at the end of the week, but I was walking and taking care of myself, and I was able to sit up and talk and not get as tired as I had been. Nancy and Cherry saw me every day, but they didn't run into each other until the last day of the week. Cherry had told me the restaurant would be finished that afternoon. She would lay in her supply of food after that, and she would open the following morning. She cooked my dinner and said I was looking fine, all I needed was a shave. I guess I did look like a grizzly bear, but I just hadn't felt like bothering with anything as unimportant as shaving.

Cherry was ready to leave, but she stood across the table from me. I knew she wanted to say something, but I didn't prod her. I waited, and after a while she blurted, "Jim, you don't know how grateful I am for all you're doing for me. You're the first man I ever met who would do something without any thought of reward."

"Whoa now," I said. "You've got me wrong. I'm going to get my reward."

Her mouth firmed up the way it had that first time I'd seen her. Now that seemed a long time ago and it also seemed that I had known Cherry for a long time, and it surprised me that she took what I said the wrong way again.

She didn't blow up in my face this time, though. She said coldly, "And just what form is the reward to take?"

I still didn't feel well and that may be the reason I reacted the way I did, short-tempered and impatient. Besides, it was plain she was still taking what I said the wrong way, and there really wasn't any excuse for her being suspicious of me now.

"You know, Cherry," I said. "I told you I'm going to marry you."

She relaxed and laughed so hard she had to lean against the wall. Finally she wiped her eyes and said, "I'd forgotten that you were going to marry me. I'll have to wait until you shave before I decide whether I'm marrying you; then I can tell whether you're man or beast."

I sighed and said, "I suppose that right now I look more like a beast than a man."

"That's right," she said, and laughed again. "Well, I've got to go and buy my groceries. I probably won't see you tomorrow."

"I'll be down and test your cooking in a day or two," I said.

"You do that," she said, and turned and almost ran into Nancy Rush, who was coming through the front door.

It was the damnedest thing, almost comical, but ticklish, too, and for a moment I didn't know quite what to say or do. Then I remembered they had never met, so I introduced them. They nodded at each other and said something pleasant in an unpleasant way. Looking at them, I was reminded of two cats who had their claws out, ready to slash each other to bits.

Finally, after what seemed another century, reminding me once more that all time is relative, Cherry turned to me and said, "Don't forget where my restaurant is," and left the house.

Nancy didn't move for another full minute. She stood in the doorway watching Cherry until she was down the street a block or so, then she turned and came on into the house. She didn't say "Good morning," or "Howdy" or anything. She went to the stove and poured herself a cup of coffee and sat down at the table.

"So that's the notorious Cherry Owens," she said in a strange, brittle tone. "She's the woman you slept with, isn't she?"

This made me mad, but I didn't want to make Nancy mad. She was very special to me.

I got my pipe and tobacco out, the way I

always did when I wanted to gain a little time. I packed the bowl of my pipe, lit it and pulled on it, and then I said, "You didn't get that quite right. She slept on one side of the tent and I slept on the other."

She looked right at me and sniffed. Then she leaned forward as she said, "The woman's a fool to miss a chance like that. Don't expect me to stay on my side of the tent if we're ever in a similar situation."

So she was going to make it hard for me, I thought. I said, "Well, it wasn't that Cherry was a fool or missed a chance. She knew there wasn't any use to get any closer. She said the spirit might be willing, but the flesh was weak, and she was right. I didn't even think I was going to live through the night."

"I see." She walked nervously around the room for a time. Then she said, "Don't do it. She won't make you a good wife. Now then, can I get anything for you or do anything?"

"No," I said. "I'm getting along pretty well. I can almost take a good breath, and there are times when my head doesn't ache."

"Good." She returned to the table and looked down at me for a moment. Then she leaned toward me and kissed me.

I've kissed a good many women, but I'd

never had the feeling I did right then. Like all great emotional experiences, it was not a feeling I could describe in words. I didn't know anything about electricity, but I supposed that getting a jolt of electricity would have hit me just about the same as Nancy's kiss did.

After she drew her mouth back from mine, she held her face close to mine for several seconds, her eyes wide and troubled. Then she straightened and said, "Good-by." She walked out of the house without another word.

I knew that if we both continued to live in Cheyenne there would be trouble. I had the utmost respect for the institution of marriage, and I knew that if I were married and another man touched my wife, I'd kill the bastard as easily as I'd kill a mad dog.

In my opinion, any man who would take another man's wife was the lowest kind of a human being and I had no use for him at all, but I also knew it depended on which side of the fence I was on. In this case I was on the wrong side of the fence.

These thoughts ran through my mind as I sat there, my pipe going cold in my hand. Then suddenly a prickle ran down my spine. I could see the pattern that destiny was weaving for us. For the first time in my life I felt that I did not have free will. I was a puppet, and some unseen power was pulling the strings. I was scared then, scared all the way down to the very bottom of my belly.

Chapter XVII

Frank came in that evening after he'd had supper. He wanted to know how I felt and if I'd eaten yet, and after he was satisfied that I was all right and able to take care of myself, he said, "A man came by today wanting to rent the other half of the building for a jewelry store. At least he called it that, but from what he said I guess he'll have other gadgets than jewelry to sell. He wanted some counters built and another room partitioned off in the back."

"Let him have it," I said, "if he'll sign a lease and pay six months rent in advance. I don't care to do all the work he wants done and then have him move out in a couple of weeks."

Frank nodded. "I'll tell him."

"How long will it take you to do the work?"

Frank shrugged. "I don't know. Most of the week, anyway."

"All right," I said. "Now, as soon as you get it done, you'll start on another house on that lot I own on the corner of Hill and 22nd Street. I want the house to be about the same size as this one — two bedrooms, a kitchen, and a living room. When you get it finished, you and Nancy are to move into it. You'll pay me whatever rent you can afford. Nancy tells me you're saving all the money you can to build a church. That's fine. Go right ahead and build, but I'm going to have a house for you two to live in."

He sat down and stared at me. He wiped his face, pretending that he was sweating. It was a fine warm evening, but not that warm, so I thought he was probably wiping his eyes. Finally he said, "I don't savvy this, Jim. You could have your choice of a dozen renters before the house is finished."

"Sure I could," I said, "and you and Nancy are my choice."

He shook his head. "No, there's more to it than that. Somebody else could afford to pay you more rent than we can. Now suppose you tell me why you're doing this for us."

I didn't want to tell him that he was an absolute fool for making Nancy live in a tent, although I'll admit I was tempted to. I puffed on my pipe for a time and thought about my answer for several seconds, then I took my pipe out of my mouth.

"I owe you a hell of a lot, Frank," I said. "More than I'll ever repay. For saving my life when Bailey and his pals jumped me, and taking over the responsibility of the building while I'm laid up. That's enough reason."

"You don't owe me anything," he said. "I'm glad to have the work."

"There's another reason," I said. "I guess it's the main reason I'm doing it. Nancy can't spend the winter in a tent, as cold as it gets here. It's not safe, either. We'll have hundreds of plug-uglies when the end of track gets here. A woman like Nancy will get raped sure if she's living in a tent, with you being gone as much as you are."

He stiffened and stared at the floor, his face going pale. As ridiculous as it sounds, I don't think he had thought of either the cold weather or Nancy's safety. He asked without looking up, "Has Nancy com- plained to you?"

"Not a word," I said, "and I'll bet she hasn't complained to you, either. She's not the complaining kind, but I know more about the winters here than you do. I think I know more about the toughs who'll flock into Cheyenne from Julesburg, too."

He sighed, still staring at the floor. He looked as guilty as hell. I didn't know what was bothering him until he said, "I suppose you think I ought to build a house to live in instead of a church."

"No, I don't think that," I said. "It's up to you. It's not my business to tell you yours. Right now building houses is my business. I want you and Nancy for renters. It's that simple."

"No, it's not that simple," he said. "I'm not like Ed Burke, who seldom has a serious thought in his head. I keep thinking about my eternal soul and what I owe to the Lord and what He wants me to do. I think about these hard cases I see in Cheyenne who are going to hell at a gallop. I've got to build that church, Jim. I've learned I can't do any good preaching in the saloons, and I can't get a congregation if they have to stand in the hot sun or out in the cold weather in front of my tent while I'm preaching. On the other hand, I realize I owe something to Nancy, too."

"Damn it, Frank," I said, "I'm not trying to tell you what to do. I just know what I want to do."

"I know, I know." He rose, walked to the door and stood staring into the twilight. After a long silence, he said moodily, "It's

194

not easy to make decisions like this, Jim. I guess that's what I'm trying to say. You see, when we were first married, we had a little church in eastern Kansas. Nancy didn't like living there. The ladies in the church didn't like her, either. Maybe they were jealous, her being as pretty as she is and all. There wasn't one of the other women who came close to being as pretty as Nancy is. It didn't take me long to figure out we had to move. I'd always wanted to be a missionary and it seemed to me this was a good field, so I came here and I fetched Nancy with me." He shook his head. "It's not a good life for her, though, not a good life at all."

I didn't say anything. I couldn't. I agreed with him that it wasn't a good life for Nancy, but I knew he wouldn't like to hear me say it. I puffed on my pipe and he stared at the street in the fading light. Several minutes passed; then he turned to me and said, "All right, we'll take you up on your offer. I'll tell Nancy. I know she'll feel better when she hears. Good night."

"Good night," I said.

After he left, I sat there thinking about Frank and the ways a man should serve the Lord. I guess it's something we all have to decide in our own way and our own time, but I was damned sure that letting your wife freeze to death in a tent or run the risk of being raped by some tough was not the way to do it. The more I thought about what a fine woman Nancy was, and what a short-sighted man Frank was, the more patience I lost with him.

She came by the next day to thank me for the house and to see if I needed anything. She only stayed a minute. After she left, I was convinced more than ever that she wasn't happy with Frank. She never said a word against him or even anything that was critical, but I sensed that something was being left out of her life. After that day I didn't see her for a long time.

As soon as I felt like walking I went downtown to my building and met Jorgens, the jeweler who had opened his store a few days before. Then I went into Cherry's restaurant. She'd found an old man to wash dishes and had hired a woman to help out, although Cherry still did most of the cooking and liked to wait on her customers too, if she had time. It was early in the afternoon and her dinner crowd had left. The place smelled of new lumber and paint along with the stew and whatever else she had cooked.

When she saw me come in, she called, "Welcome, landlord. I wondered how soon you were coming down to check on your investment."

"I'm not here to check up on my investment," I said. "I just got hungry."

"Good," she said. "Come on back to my room. I haven't had dinner yet. We've been busy, and the crowd just cleared out a few minutes ago."

The other woman was cleaning up the counter. She was a big rawboned Swede, older than Cherry and not particularly attractive, but that wasn't important. She looked capable and strong, and that was important. Cherry introduced me to the woman, and then to the old man who was washing dishes. He had one short leg and must have been close to seventy. There wasn't much work for a man like that in a boom town, and I suppose he was glad to find a job that gave him a living.

Cherry had me fill my plate with stew and take a couple of biscuits and a cup of coffee, then led the way to her room. It was neat and clean, not big enough maybe, but it seemed adequate for her bed and bureau and several boxes she had not unpacked. She pulled a chair up to one of the boxes and motioned for me to sit down.

"A poor table," she said, "but it will have to do. Making things do is something I've got used to."

She sat on the bed and used the other side of the box for her table. The stew was good and I ate with relish. The truth was I had been getting mighty tired of my own cooking. Cherry watched me eat, smiling as if pleased, and sent me back to the kitchen for a second helping.

"It's a pleasure to see you eat like that," she said when I returned. "You were downright picky the last time I fixed something for you to eat."

"I'm glad I'm able to eat," I said. "I don't know how close I came to cashing in my chips, but I felt like I was going to. Now I think I can pick up a hammer in another week or so."

We talked about her business and she wanted to know what I was going to do next and how soon the end of track would be in Cheyenne. When I got up to go, she wouldn't let me pay. "Next time," she said. "This time I wanted to have you visit with me and just . . . well, just be company."

I started to leave; then I turned back and looked at her. She was a very attractive young woman, her gaze fixed on me, her moist red lips parted a little. I said, "Cherry, will you marry me?"

She gave a start and rose from the bed, her lips coming together, the smile going out of them. She opened her mouth to say something and shut it, then she said, "Jim, are you really serious this time?"

"I was never more serious in my life," I said.

She shook her head sadly. "You don't love me, Jim. I think you're just lonesome."

"You're right about me being lonesome," I said. "I don't love you the way the love stories tell about, but I learned to know you pretty well when I was flat on my back. The important thing is that I can take care of you and I admire you. Love will come, the right kind of love that makes a home. A lot of families start with less."

She nodded, the small smile returning to the corners of her mouth again. "You're a very honest man, Jim, and I admire you for it, but it's not enough. Not yet anyhow. Ask me again someday."

"All right, I will," I said.

When I got home, a man was sitting on the porch waiting for me. He was dressed up like a dude, with an elk-tooth charm dangling from a chain that was stretched across his vest. He was wearing a black derby hat and one of the biggest diamonds I ever saw in a ring on his right hand. He had a fine short beard, a carefully trimmed mustache, and he smelled of bay rum. He shook hands with me and said his name was Lucky Sam Bellew.

"I'm a land speculator," he said. "It's like playing poker. You've got to outguess everybody else in the game. Right now here in Cheyenne I'm trying to outguess the government and the railroad. I'm betting on the Union Pacific making Cheyenne one of the major cities on their main line. I want to buy your lots."

"They're not for sale," I said. "Not yet anyway. I'm playing a little poker with them myself."

"That's your right, of course," he said. "You were smarter than most. You got in on the ground floor and bought them cheap from the railroad. Now I may be a fool, and there is no sure way of knowing when land values will level off. I'm a little scared that I'd lose on these lots, with the end of track just a few miles east of town. They may shove the end of steel right on over Sherman Hill and winter in Laramie. Cheyenne might wind up a little burg of fifty people."

He irritated me. I'd told him plain enough that the lots were not for sale. I said tartly, "Mr. Bellew, I just got done telling you —"

"I heard you, but you haven't heard me," he said. "I'll give you a thousand dollars a lot. That's one hell of a big profit for you, if you stop and figure it."

The offer boggled my mind some. It was twice as much as I had been offered before, and I'd thought five hundred was a good offer. I was tempted. I sat there looking at him for about thirty seconds, thinking that I had twenty-five lots I could and would sell. I'd still have two more I intended to keep on Eddy Street because they were good business sites and I wanted to build on them and have additional rental property. I'd have twenty-five thousand dollars, which was more than I had ever expected to have in my entire life.

Then I decided that if Lucky Sam Bellew intended to gamble, I could too. I shook my head and said, "No. They're not for sale."

Bellew nodded and shook hands and left. I stayed on my front porch for a time listening to the saws and hammers that were working all around me. I wasn't sure whether I'd been a fool or not, but I didn't worry about it. I still had the lots, and I could still sell them for a profit even if nobody else paid me a thousand apiece.

I started thinking about Cherry. She'd marry me in time — I was sure of it. I was also sure she'd make a good wife, which was important, but I couldn't help thinking how different it would have been if Nancy were free and I had asked her to marry me. I would have said flat out in the plainest words I could manage that I loved her. I couldn't say that to Cherry. I wanted to marry her, though. I wanted to very much, but I guess my motive was questionable, to say the least. I thought that if I married Cherry, I wouldn't get into trouble with Nancy.

Chapter XVIII

Steel reached Cheyenne on November 13. We knocked off work and walked down to the railroad grade to watch the rails being laid through town. Frank stopped at the tent and persuaded Nancy to go with us. I dropped by the restaurant and talked Cherry into going, too. I told her she wouldn't lose any business, that every man and his dog would be down there along the grade.

All the way to the grade Cherry walked beside me and Nancy walked beside Frank, and I don't believe either woman said a word to the other after the first cool greeting. When we arrived, we found that I was right. Every man and his dog were there, particularly the dogs.

Laying the rails was as interesting a show as I had been told. The surveyors, bridge builders and graders were all working miles west of Cheyenne. There had been a good deal of Indian trouble, even though soldiers out of Fort D. A. Russell were constantly patrolling the route the railroad would take.

Most of the men employed by the Union Pacific were Civil War veterans who worked with their guns close at hand, but we were constantly hearing of brushes with the Indians, particularly among the surveyors, who had to work far out ahead of everyone else. They were the most likely men to get killed, and many of them were.

The Casement brothers, General Jack and Dan, were responsible for laying the track, and much of the grading, too. Jack Casement had been a prominent general during the Civil War and had put together a well organized, disciplined group of men. Most of them were Irish, a tough, brawling, hard-working bunch of men who might have been very hard for someone else to manage, but the Casements handled them well.

As I stood in the crowd and watched the rails being put down, I was amazed at the proficiency and speed with which the job was done. A light car pulled by one horse came up to the end of steel, the car loaded with rails. Two men grabbed the end of a rail and moved forward. Other men took hold of the rail by twos, and when it was clear of the car, the men went forward on the run.

At exactly the right second someone yelled a command to drop the rail. They did, being careful to put it into place right side up. Another gang of men was doing exactly the same thing on the other side of the track. I held my watch on them several times, and noted that it took about thirty seconds per rail.

As soon as the car was empty, it was tipped to one side while the next loaded one moved up; then the empty car was tipped into position again and was driven back for another load, the horse galloping as if the devil was right on his tail. The gaugers, spikers and bolters kept close on the heels of the men dropping the rails.

Just a few minutes watching these men gave me an admiration for them I had never felt for a group of laborers before. I had not seen anything like it, and I never saw anything like it afterwards. It was co-operation at its best.

Then the thought came to me that I was going to make a fortune out of my lots and I owed it to these men who were putting the rails down and spiking them into place, along with the graders and bridge builders and surveyors. Of course, I owed something to the Union Pacific company and General

Dodge and the Casement brothers, but the men on top were making good money. The Irishmen who did the sweating and ran the danger of getting an Indian bullet or arrow in their briskets weren't getting rich.

There was a hell of a lot of banging as the end of steel moved past us. I did some quick calculating as I watched. Three strokes to the spike. I counted ten spikes to the rail. Somewhere I had heard it took 400 rails for a mile of track. About that time I quit calculating, but one thing was sure: those sledges were going to swing a lot of times before the line was finished between Omaha and Sacramento.

We walked back to Cherry's restaurant in a kind of daze. The whole operation was incredible. Sherman Hill lay west of Cheyenne, then the desert, which offered a different kind of resistance, with the Wasatch Mountains on beyond the desert. Of course the Central Pacific, with its Chinese labor, had even a worse kind of terrain to cover, with the Sierras making an almost impenetrable wall.

Cherry invited all of us to dinner. At first Nancy said she had some things to do and couldn't stay. Then Frank said something in a low tone. I couldn't hear the words, but from the sound of his voice I knew it was something harsh, perhaps bitter. She said something back, her face turning red, but she went in and sat down at the counter, Frank on one side of her, a carpenter on the other.

Cherry's hired woman had dinner almost ready. We ate hurriedly because we'd heard that the first train to Cheyenne would arrive that afternoon, and of course the whole town would be down there on the tracks to welcome it.

It was a historic occasion, the day we had been waiting for, and I'll admit I had an uneasy feeling in the bottom of my belly every time I thought about turning Lucky Sam Bellew down when he'd offered me a thousand dollars for each of my lots. I just wasn't sure whether I had made a mistake or not.

I'd heard and read some wild tales about Julesburg. Early in the summer, or maybe it had been in late spring, there had been only about fifty people in Julesburg. By the end of July it had exploded to about four thousand, with streets of mud or dust depending on when it had rained last.

The prices the merchants had been able to charge for their goods were outrageous. Apparently it was the grab for money that had made Julesburg the town it had become, but the absence of law and order was what worried me. I think all of the businessmen of Cheyenne felt the same way.

We simply did not want Cheyenne to become another Julesburg, which had had more than its share of whorehouses, dance halls, gambling places and saloons. The women, so I had been told, walked around town with derringers carried on their hips. They would rob a man by putting something in his drink, but he would not be allowed to take proper measures against them after he came to.

One reporter wrote that Julesburg had people who would kill a man for five dollars. I believe it. Dead men had been found in town or close to it every day, their pockets emptied of whatever they were carrying, and yet the bulk of the people in Julesburg apparently were indifferent to what was happening.

All of this ran through my mind as I ate. I didn't say much to Cherry, who sat beside me at the counter, but the thought kept nagging me that Nancy wasn't safe in her tent and Cherry might not be safe in her restaurant if we allowed Cheyenne to go the way Julesburg had.

In the end, it was the good women like Nancy and Cherry who built the towns and brought civilization to the frontier, not the whores, who too often worked hand-in-glove with the sneak thieves and murderers who had made Julesburg a literal hell. Now that Cheyenne was the end of track, Julesburg would cease to exist as a town, and it would happen overnight.

I knew what Ed Burke would say if I told him what I was thinking. As we hurried back to the track I decided he was right — a vigilance committee was the answer. I knew he was right when the train pulled in, with the cars banging and the bell ringing and the whistle shrieking.

One of the men on the train yelled, "Gentlemen, I give you Julesburg." That was exactly right. While everyone else was whooping and hollering as the passengers left the train, I just stood there as if I was paralyzed.

Frank nudged me in the ribs and asked, "What's the matter with you, Jim?"

I shook my head and came out of it right away. I managed a weak holler, but it was easy to see that the train was carrying the frame shacks and poles and tents that had made up much of Julesburg, along with the barroom equipment and gambling devices that had given it the reputation of being the most notorious city of sin in the West.

Along with the railroad men, mule skinners and hunters who were on the train, there were the whores and the pimps, the professional gamblers and con men. Within a matter of hours Cheyenne would be a city of sin that would match the Julesburg of yesterday. It struck me that this historic occasion was not what I had expected it to be.

Cheyenne had planned a huge celebration, with a platform for speakers and big signs that read, "The Magic City of the Plains greets the trans-continental railway" and "Old Casement, we welcome you" and "Honor to whom honor is due." I wanted no part of it, and I couldn't help wondering if progress always meant that you had to swallow the bitter with the sweet.

I'd had more than enough. I said, "Cherry, let's get out of here."

She nodded. As we walked back along Ferguson Street she glanced at me and asked, "What's the matter, Jim?"

"It's a funny thing," I said, "how it is when you actually see something that you knew was coming. Cheyenne will be the hell on wheels that Julesburg has been and it scares me. Have you got a gun?"

"We've got three," she said. "I knew this was coming and I've been scared, too, so I bought three pistols the other day. I gave one to Olga and one to old Pete and I kept one. We'll use them if we have to."

"Good," I said. "If you need any help from me, get word to me as fast as you can."

She laid a hand on my arm and squeezed it. "Thank you, Jim," she said.

I left her at the restaurant and went on home, more worried and upset than I wanted to admit. We had policemen, and we had a civilian auxiliary police force, in which I had very little confidence. I knew damned well that our official law enforcers simply couldn't handle the number of toughs who had come in on that train. To make it worse, more would come. I had no doubt of that.

Frank stopped in later and said it had been a festive day. Then he gave me a close look and wanted to know why I was so glum. I told him, adding, "If you're looking for souls to save, a lot of them came in on the train today. I guess the people who have been in Cheyenne from the day the first settlers arrived haven't been angels, but we've been pretty close compared to the riff-raff that was on the train."

He frowned and scratched his chin. Then he asked, "How do you know the train was carrying people like that?"

"I saw enough of them to know," I said.

"That kind is never hard to identify. We also saw the stuff they were bringing with them from Julesburg. Besides, we've known all along that Julesburg would pick up and move here as soon as Cheyenne became the end of track. I don't know of any way to keep the undesirables out. All we can do is control them once they get here."

He hadn't even thought about it, I guess. From what Nancy had said, and from what I had observed about him, he was that kind of man. Now he nodded and said, as if only half-convinced, "I guess you're right."

"Has Nancy got a gun?" When he shook his head I said, more sharply than I intended, "Damn it, Frank, get her one. You'd better stay with her every evening until we get your house finished."

He nodded again. "I guess I had."

I knew he wouldn't. If one of these hardcases ever so much as touched Nancy, I'd kill him, no matter what Frank said or did. I was plain disgusted by the naive way he looked at the situation, but killing a man after it was too late wouldn't help Nancy. I wished they'd move in with me, but I knew better than to ask them after what Nancy had said the last time I'd suggested it to her.

I had a visitor that night after it was dark,

a man named Jess Munro. I'd seen him in town and knew him by name, but I had never actually met him or talked to him. One thing was sure: he was the kind of man you'd notice in a crowd.

He was about thirty, I judged, a dark-faced man with a black mustache and beard, and black hair. His eyes were dark brown, his jaw square, the kind of jaw you'd expect to see on a forceful man. He was stocky in build, with large hands and muscular shoulders. He'd be a hard man to whip, I told myself.

Munro carried himself with a straight-backed military stiffness and precision that I associated with an army man. I suspected he had been an officer on one side or the other during the war, probably with the Union because his speech gave no indication that he was a Southerner. I had never seen him without a gun on his hip. He had one now, and I wondered about it because he claimed to be a dealer in real estate and had an office on Ferguson Street.

He shook hands with me, his grip very strong. He pinned his gaze on my face as if making a judgment about me, then said, "Ed Burke tells me you're a tough hand. I saw you operate the night Frank Rush tried to preach in the Head Quarters Saloon. You saved his life. I think you'll do."

"Do for what?"

"You saw what the train brought in this afternoon," he said, ignoring my question. "Not that it is any surprise. The police can't do the job, even with the help of some of us who have been appointed law officers on a standby basis. You would have been contacted if you hadn't been laid up." He shrugged and added, "I guess we would be of help in case of a riot, but that's about all."

"I was laid up for a while, but I'm all right now," I said. "I've been working a full day for a week or so. I had thought about volunteering for police duty, but hadn't got around to it. I've been as concerned as anyone about what's going to happen."

"Good," he said. "Then you'll be willing to serve on the Vigilance Committee we're organizing. Some men, just four as a matter of fact, will act as chiefs. That's what we want you for. You'll have fifteen men under you to carry out any job that the Central Committee decides on. Will you do it?"

Here it was at last, laid right on the line. I had to make a decision one way or the other — now! I hesitated, looking straight at Jess Munro. I remembered all my old doubts and fears of the Vigilantes that had plagued

214

me when I'd lived in Black Hawk, but this was a different situation. Something had to be done fast if Cheyenne was to be saved.

Still I hesitated, saying, "I've always been leery of vigilante rules. They operate outside the law. It can become mob rule very easily."

"That's right," he said grimly, "but we intend to take steps to safeguard against that happening here. I have appointed myself Chairman of the Committee for the simple reason that I've had some experience with vigilance committees and somebody has to get the ball rolling. Of course, I will be subject to removal by a majority of the Committee."

He paused, scratching his chin, then added, "Glenn, damn it, we just don't have much time. This bunch of toughs will be in control of the town before we know it if we don't do something. We've got to get on the job and do it quick."

It seemed to me that I had no choice, doubts or no doubts. I said, on impulse I guess, "I'll do it."

"Fine," he said. "We're meeting in the hall over Miller's store tomorrow night at eight o'clock. Don't mention this to anyone. Just be there."

"I will," I said.

We shook hands again and he left. I still wasn't sure I had done right. I wasn't even sure that Jess Munro wouldn't use the Vigilance Committee for his own purposes. So the old doubts were still there, but again it seemed I had no choice.

I couldn't just sit on my hind end and let the plug-uglies rule Cheyenne. I could do more to control the Committee by belonging than I could as an outsider, particularly if I was what Munro called a "chief." Tomorrow night I would know for sure.

Then my thoughts returned to Jess Munro. He was the type who enjoyed giving orders. Was he doing this just so he'd be in position to give orders, as he had as an officer in the army? I didn't actually know he had been an officer, but I thought it was a pretty safe guess.

Was he really a real estate dealer? Or was he on somebody's payroll? I had to admit that I might never know the answers to these questions.

Chapter XIX

We hadn't been working more than half an hour the next morning when a man came by and told us there had been two killings the night before. A railroad man had got into a brawl with one of the new gamblers named Tate Horn in the Head Quarters Saloon and Horn had shot him to death.

The other killing was plain murder any way you looked at it. A second railroad man apparently had been visiting one of the whorehouses — at least, the murderer wanted everybody to believe that was the case. The man had been stabbed in the chest and his pockets emptied. The body had been left back of one of the whorehouses.

My two carpenters did a lot of talking about it during the day, but Frank didn't say much. I hoped he was thinking about Nancy. I didn't say much either, but the doubts I'd had about the Vigilance Committee disappeared in a hurry.

I figured the first thing we'd do was to run Tate out of town. I didn't know whether he'd started the fight or not, but we didn't want him in Cheyenne and I was sure everyone who had lived in Cheyenne any length of time would agree with me. It was impossible to guess how many others he'd kill if we let him stay.

I climbed the stairs to the big room over Miller's store five minutes before eight that night and found that most of the men were there ahead of me. Three men sat at a table at one end of the room: Jess Munro, a banker named Fritz Thiessen, and the speculator, Lucky Sam Bellew. I didn't have any way of knowing who had been working with Munro to organize the Vigilance Committee, but I'll admit I was surprised to see a respectable banker and a land speculator joining Jess Munro.

For a time I stood just inside the door looking around. I knew a good many of the men. Some had been here before I'd come to Cheyenne; others had arrived about the same time I had. All of them had been here for quite a while, and all of them that I knew were men I would call solid citizens.

I saw Ed Burke standing on the right side of the room beside a window. I walked over to him and punched him in the ribs and said, "Howdy, Ed."

He turned, saw who it was, and slapped me on the back, a big grin stretching across his face. "Well, by God, I didn't know if Jess would talk you into joining up or not."

"I hesitated," I admitted, "and last night I had plenty of doubts, but this morning I figured it was the only thing to do."

The grin faded. "Hell of a note, ain't it? Two men killed the first night after the Julesburg bunch hits town."

Munro was on his feet and pounding on the table. When the rumble of talk died, he said in a loud, commanding voice that carried the length of the room, "Gentlemen, the meeting will come to order. As you all know, I'm Jess Munro. I'll serve as Chairman of this meeting." He motioned to Thiessen and introduced him, then Bellew, and added, "We are the self-appointed Central Committee of the Cheyenne Vigilantes, organized for the purpose of keeping law and order in Cheyenne. We appointed ourselves for the simple reason that someone had to get this group started."

He stopped, his dark eyes sweeping the room as if trying to decide how we felt, then he went on. "You all know what happened last night. I guess there won't be any argument about the necessity for speed, but I do want to assure you of one thing. Whenever our actions do not satisfy you, any five members of the Vigilance Committee can call for an election and we can be removed by a majority vote of the organization."

He picked up a sheet of paper. "First I'll read to you the by-laws of the Cheyenne Vigilance Committee. I wrote them, but I claim no credit for them. They are based upon the by-laws of similar committees."

The document was a short one, stating the purpose of the Vigilance Committee, giving the method of removing the Central Committee as he had just stated, and saying that at no time would violence be used to keep the peace unless extreme conditions demanded it.

I was still thinking about that and telling myself that somebody, probably Munro, would have to decide what those extreme conditions were, when he laid the sheet of paper on the table and picked up another one.

"I will now read the oath we are asking all of you to take," Munro said. "We want you to know what it is before you take it. If any of you feel you cannot honestly take this oath, you will leave now. But remember one thing: you are not to inform anyone of the identity of the men you saw in this room. If you do, you will be dealt with in a manner that will make you regret you had ever opened your mouth."

I realized this was necessary, but again I wondered who would decide the manner in which the informer would be dealt with, and once more I had a notion it would be Jess Munro. We could be in for a bloodbath if he were a brutal man, and he could well be that kind. It was the old doubts that simply would not die.

Munro waited a good thirty seconds. When no one left the room, he read the oath. It stated that none of us would inform the regularly appointed law officers of our actions or of the actions of any other member of the Committee if he was doing Committee business, that we would not under any circumstances let our personal feelings or reasons enter into making our decisions as members of the Committee, and that at all times we would be reasonable and just in acting to preserve law and order in the city of Cheyenne.

After he had read the oath, Munro waited for another thirty seconds before going on. Still no one had left the room. Munro said, "Very well, I assume you are all satisfied with the by-laws and oath. Are you ready to take the oath?"

We said yes, a great rolling rumble of sound that came from all corners of the big room. Munro said, "We don't have enough Bibles for you to lay your hands on, but you will take this oath as a sacred obligation, fully as sacred as if you had placed your hand on the Bible. We will start by saying, 'I, John Smith,' or what your name is, 'do hereby swear,' and then you will repeat after me the oath word by word, and finish by saying 'so help me God.' If any man who takes this oath breaks his word, then God help him, because none of us on the Committee will."

If anyone had dropped a pin, I guess it would have sounded like a ten-penny nail. The room was that still, except for the heavy breathing of the sixty-odd men who were assembled here. We went through the oath just as Munro had outlined it for us.

I would have said it was impossible to get that many men to take anything with the deadly seriousness that we were taking this oath business, but I would have been wrong. The killings of the previous night had had the same effect on every man here that they'd had on me, I guess. Anyhow, there was no horseplay, no shuffling of feet, no laughing, no whispering.

When we finished with "so help me God," Munro nodded, smiling that brief half-smile of his, and said, "Good. The criminal element will never take control of our city."

Munro picked up a third sheet of paper. "Gentlemen, I will give you your teams. The Central Committee along with the four chiefs will constitute what we will call the flying wedge of the Cheyenne Vigilance Committee. We will undertake the drastic work that must be done and done quickly. There will be occasions when we will have to strike hard and fast after a vicious crime has been committed, before the crime has been forgotten by the people of Cheyenne.

"However, we need every man here to give us the appearance of strength that we must have if we are to function effectively. So tomorrow night all of you will gather at the town jail before eight o'clock. Bring your rifles and gunnysacks with holes cut in them for your eyes. We will parade along Cheyenne's principal streets. I have seen this done on a number of occasions, and I assure you it makes an impressive warning to the criminals. Many of them will leave town immediately."

He glanced at the sheet of paper in his hands, then went on. "The men who will serve as chiefs are Jim Glenn, Ed Burke,

Charley Williams, and Bronco Stead. I will read Glenn's team first. When I finish reading the names of the four teams, I will designate the corners in which each of you will meet."

He read the names, then asked the chiefs to come to the table for the lists of names. We did, and again, and for no logical reason, I wondered how Munro had selected the chiefs. Williams owned the Star Saloon, and Stead operated the Western Livery Stable.

I understood how he had picked Ed Burke. Certainly Ed had been pushing the idea of the Vigilance Committee for weeks. I could understand why he picked me, with Ed recommending me, but I was puzzled over his choice of a saloon keeper and a livery stable operator. I shouldn't have been, I guess, because a saloon keeper and a livery store operator could be solid citizens the same as anyone else, but just the same I wondered about it, perhaps because I didn't know either man.

Munro designated the corners for each team to assemble, then gave us fifteen minutes to get acquainted with our men. I shook hands with the members of my team. I knew several of them and I made an effort to pin the right name to the right face of the ones I didn't know. I would not make a good politician because I always had trouble remembering men's names if I didn't have much to do with them.

Munro called us to order presently, asking, "Are there any questions?"

Apparently there were none, so Munro said, "I want the four chiefs to come to the table as soon as we adjourn. Remember, you are to assemble at the town jail with gunny sacks and rifles tomorrow evening at eight o'clock. No absence short of violent sickness will be accepted."

He paused, his dark eyes seeming to bore into every man there. Then he said slowly, and with considerable emotion, "Gentlemen, the one quality which every Vigilance Committee must have is loyalty to its officers and the willingness to obey their commands. Meeting adjourned."

The men left the hall without talking, a grave and unusual silence for so many men. I don't know why the questions about Munro kept popping into my mind, but there was no doubt about the real meaning of his words, although he never actually stated it. What he intended to say, and I was sure of it, was that the man who did not obey his commands would be punished. Was he the one to decide what the punishment would be? To my way of thinking, murder inside a Vigilance Committee for disobedience was just as bad as murder by one of the criminal element we were trying to control.

The four of us who had been appointed chiefs moved forward to stand across the table from Munro. As we faced the men who were on the Central Committee, it struck me that both Thiessen and Bellew were a little nervous, but Jess Munro was not. I wondered if Thiessen and Bellew were thinking along the same line I had been.

There was no doubt about one thing. This was Jess Munro's party and he was enjoying every minute of it. I knew then beyond the slightest doubt that before the Vigilance Committee was disbanded I would be knocking heads with Munro. We both might be sorry that he had picked me as one of the chiefs.

CHAPTER XX

Munro waited until everyone had left except the members of the Central Committee and the four chiefs. Then he reached under the table and lifted out a wooden box. When he raised the lid, I saw that the box was filled with revolvers.

"We've got an ugly job to do tonight and I thought you might not be armed," Munro said, "so I brought these. Any vigilance committee's effectiveness depends upon how quickly and violently it reacts to a crime. Two murders were committed last night. We do not know the identity of one killer, but we do know the identity of the other. We are going after Tate Horn."

As soon as he had handed out the revolvers, he reached into the box again and took out a coiled rope with a hangman's knot on one end. There was no doubt about his intentions. He expected us to help him hang Tate Horn.

I looked at the three men standing beside me and then at the two men seated beside Munro. I sensed that they were as uneasy about this as I was, but I didn't see the slightest indication that any of them were prepared to challenge Munro. Either we'd play dead and roll over or I'd buck him, and I had no intention of rolling over and playing dead. I knew very well that if we went along with Munro and hanged a man, we'd be tarred with the same brush, and from then on Munro would have his way on everything.

"What are you going to do with that rope?" I asked.

He stared at me as if I were an idiot to ask such a question. Then he said, "We're going to hang Horn with it."

I said, "No."

His expression changed. I guess he knew he wasn't looking at an idiot, but I don't think he was sure just what he was looking at or how far I'd go in opposing him. He glanced at the other men, then brought his gaze back to me, a hint of caution in his dark eyes.

"What do you mean by 'no'?" he asked.

"There are seven of us who will take part in the hanging," I said. "Who beside you decided that Tate Horn is going to hang?"

That seemed to shock him. I don't think the thought had entered his mind that anyone would oppose Horn's hanging, and he had promised himself the pleasure of seeing the man swing. Now he was sore, just plain mad, and I was certain that my previous suspicion of Jess Munro being a cruel man was correct.

I had always known that there were a good many people who enjoyed a hanging, that there were still places in the United States where people brought their lunch and made a public spectacle out of an execution, but it was a kind of recreation I had no stomach for, and I couldn't understand how any human being could be that way. From that moment on I had no real respect for Jess Munro.

Munro's face turned red right up to the roots of his hair. Several seconds passed before he managed an answer, but he finally got it said. "Nobody."

I was sure that had been the case, but before I could push the matter he demanded, "Why should there be?"

"Because you're one man," I answered, "and one man out of seven has no right to involve all of us in a hanging that might get us into trouble up to our necks. The law would call it murder. If this flying wedge as you called it is going to function as it should, all seven of us will make the decisions, not just you or any one of us."

Bellew said, "That's right, Jess." Thiessen nodded agreement. I couldn't see the faces of the men who stood beside me, but I had the feeling they were supporting me.

Munro couldn't speak for a moment. He sat back in his chair and glared at me. I believe he would have killed me on the spot if he'd thought he could. I'm convinced he had not expected resistance from any of us, and he found it hard to believe he was actually getting it.

"Well, by God," Munro said finally, "I didn't think you or anybody would object to hanging a man like Tate Horn. This is the way we scare the living hell out of every tough in Cheyenne. When they wake up in the morning and find Horn's body swinging from a cottonwood limb down by the creek, they'll be running over each other getting out of town." He stopped, glaring at me, then said, "Well?"

"I understand that," I said, "but the point is I don't know anything about Tate Horn or his fight with the man he killed or why he killed him. The murdered man may have been responsible for what happened. Just because he worked for the railroad doesn't put him in a class above Horn."

"No, but he was a working man and Horn is a gambler," Munro said, as if being a gambler was enough on the face of it to convict Horn of murder.

"I'm in favor of running Horn out of town," I said, "and that would be a warning to the rest of them who came to town yesterday, but if he killed the other man in self-defense, I'll have no part in hanging him."

"That's what he did," Bellew said. "I should have spoken up sooner. I was in the Head Quarters when he did it. His girl came from Julesburg with him. They call her Red Rose. She's a redheaded young woman who stands behind his chair when he's playing poker. He claims she brings him luck.

"Anyhow, the Irishman, a fellow named Mike Mulligan, came up and started talking to Rose. He'd been drinking and he was plenty ugly. He carried a gun, all right. I saw it under his waistband before the trouble started.

"Rose asked him to leave her alone, but he started to pat her on the shoulder. Then Horn told him to leave her alone. He just laughed and began feeling of Rose's breasts. She hit him a good wallop on the nose and started it bleeding. He backed up and went for his gun. I don't know whether he intended to shoot Rose or Horn, but Horn killed him before his gun was half leveled."

"Why hell, Jess," Ed Burke said, "we can't hang a man under those circumstances. I'm like Jim, though. I'm for running him out of town."

The rest of them agreed with that. Munro sat there fuming, the corners of his mouth working as he fought his anger, but by then there wasn't much he could do except give in. He nodded and got to his feet.

"All right," Munro said. "We'll go get him and tell him that if he's in town tomorrow night, we will hang him. If he is there, we'll have to do it. You savvy that?"

I didn't much like it, but it seemed a reasonable compromise, and I figured Horn would pull out without any more trouble. He'd be a fool if he stayed, and a man who makes his living playing poker couldn't be a fool. We all nodded our agreement. Munro reached into his box again and pulled out seven gunnysacks.

"We'll put these on, though sooner or later our identity will be known," Munro said. "We're going to have to expect that, and we'll probably have some attempts made on our lives. Sam, you lead the way because you know Horn by sight." Then Munro fixed his gaze on me. "Glenn, you'll back his play. The rest of us will string out behind you. If anybody pulls a gun or a knife or jumps either of you, we'll shoot him. We'll draw our guns when we go into the saloon."

We pulled the gunnysacks over our heads. Mine didn't smell good and it was rougher than a cob, but I could put up with it for a while. Munro blew out the lamps and we left the hall, with Munro still carrying the rope. I don't know why he kept it unless he wanted everybody in the saloon to see it. Or maybe he thought something would happen that would persuade us to hang Horn after all. Anyhow, he had it and kept it in plain sight.

We went into the Head Quarters, Bellew leading the way. I was two steps behind him, the other five behind us. We had our guns in our hands. It was almost comical to see the shocked expression on the men's faces as we came in. Within a matter of seconds the noise in the big room had stopped, and the silence was so complete that when someone coughed the sound was like thunder booming into a still summer day.

Bellew went straight to Horn's table. The man was a common type among gamblers, lean and thin-faced, with a neat black mustache and slate-gray eyes that told you nothing about what he was thinking or feeling. Red Rose was standing at his back, and she was, as Bellew had said, a young redheaded woman.

"Come with me, Horn," Bellew said.

For a moment the gambler didn't move. He stared at Bellew, then at me, and finally at our guns. He laid his cards on the table and rose, his gaze turning to the five men between us and the door. One of the men at the table said, "You're busting up our game, Mr. Gunnysack. We know what you're trying to tell us. Now get out."

Bellew hit him across the top of the head with his gun barrel, a short down-striking blow that knocked the fellow cold. He fell sideways out of his chair and lay motionless on the floor.

"All right," Horn said. "I'll go with you. Let's not have any more trouble."

"That suits me," Bellew said.

Horn walked to the door, his head high, his shoulders back. If he saw the rope in Munro's hand he gave no indication of it. Red Rose started to follow him, then stopped when I said, "Stay here."

We marched Horn into the street, no one else raising a hand to help him. The other five eased out behind us, Munro calling to the men in the saloon, "Sit pat if you want to stay healthy."

He stood in the street facing the door. When no one followed, he said, "We'll take him to the creek."

We walked him to Crow Creek, going down the middle of the street and across the railroad tracks so that anyone on the boardwalks could see what was happening. We stopped when we reached the first big cottonwood.

"I've got a right to a trial," Horn said. "I killed the fool in self-defense. Anyone who saw it will tell you that."

"We know," Bellew said, "so we're offering you a deal. If you will get out of town pronto, we won't hang you."

"If you're in town tomorrow night at this time, you'll swing," Munro said.

The light was so thin that I couldn't see his face, but I could almost feel the relief that rushed through him. "I'll be out of town before sunup," he said, and wheeled and ran.

We stood motionless until we couldn't hear his footsteps. Then Munro laughed shortly. "He will be, too," he said. "Remember. Tomorrow night. Bring your guns and gunnysacks."

We broke up then, with Lucky Sam Bellew falling into step beside me. We didn't say anything for a block; then we took the gunnysacks off our heads. I rubbed my face and said, "Feels good to get the damned thing off. Makes my skin itch."

"It does for a fact," Bellew said. "Thought any more about selling your lots?"

"No," I said. "I'll hold them for a while yet. I'm not going to sell all of them anyhow. I'm a builder, not a speculator."

"Give me first crack at them when you do decide to sell," he said. "I might raise my previous offer."

So he didn't think the market for town property had topped off yet. I felt good about that. I'd been uneasy about not selling, but now I was satisfied I had done right.

"I'll do it," I said.

We walked in silence for another block. Then he said in a low tone, "You had guts to stand up to Munro. He's a hard man to stand up to — I know from experience. I likewise know I should have spoken up about how Tate Horn happened to shoot the Irishman, but I was afraid to buck Munro. I would have, though. I mean, before we actually done the hanging."

He paused, then added doubtfully, "I think I would have. Anyhow, from now on Munro won't be quite so anxious to decide everything by himself. You've heard the saying about how total power corrupts totally or something like that. Well, I guess Munro had total power until you challenged him. If you hadn't done it just when we're getting started, no one could have stopped him."

I was glad to hear him say that because I wasn't sure how the others felt about what I had done, even though they had supported me. I asked, "What does the man do? He claims he deals in real estate. Does he?"

"No," Bellew said. "I'd know if he did. It's just a cover-up. Nobody knows for sure who's paying him, but there's a rumor he's a troubleshooter for the railroad. It might be true — I don't know. Well, I turn off here. I'll see you tomorrow night."

I walked on home thinking about it. The rumor made sense and I was inclined to believe it. The railroad men didn't want Cheyenne to become another Julesburg, and this might be their way of stopping the toughs before they took control. In any case, I had made an enemy out of Jess Munro.

CHAPTER XXI

Tate Horn kept his word. He was out of town before sunup. At least I assumed he was, because no one in Cheyenne saw him the next day or any other day that I heard about. I would have heard about him, because news like that spreads in a hurry. By mid-morning the next day everybody in Cheyenne knew what had happened in the Head Quarters Saloon, and that made Tate Horn the best-known name in town.

I guess most folks expected to find his body swinging from a limb of one of the big cottonwoods. When it wasn't found, they assumed he had been murdered and his body hidden somewhere out on the prairie. Of course, none of us who had taken Horn out of the Head Quarters had anything to say.

He may have shown himself to some of his cronies after we let him go, but they kept mum about seeing him if they had. Apparently he took Red Rose with him because she disappeared that night, too, although there were some people in town who speculated that the Vigilantes had murdered her.

Any way we looked at it, his disappearance was almost as big a warning to the criminal element as his hanging would have been. It was interesting to listen to some of the talk around town. The police, of course, denounced the Vigilantes, saying they could handle any crime that was committed and that Horn's killing of Mike Mulligan had been investigated and was found to be an act of self-defense, and therefore it had not been a crime.

There were others who feared Vigilante rule as much as they feared rule by the criminal element, and they said so frankly. On the whole, though, I think the people of Cheyenne approved of us and what we had done and slept a little sounder because of it.

I thought that Frank Rush and the two carpenters looked at me a little speculatively, as if wondering whether I had been involved in the Vigilante doings, but they didn't ask and of course I didn't volunteer anything. The carpenters talked frankly about favoring the Vigilante activity, saying that maybe their wives would be safe now and they could go home from a saloon at night without worrying about being knocked in the head and robbed.

Frank only said, "Whenever you take the power to enforce the law out of the hands of the duly appointed officers, you run a risk of exchanging one set of rules for another one that's worse. Who can say for sure which set is best?"

I agreed with him one hundred percent. It was the exact reason I'd had so many doubts about joining the Vigilance Committee and why I had challenged Jess Munro. I said nothing to Frank or the carpenters, however. They could make up their own minds about the matter, and I was afraid that anything I said would make them think one way or the other about my involvement.

It was, of course, the kind of problem in which I was damned if I did and damned if I didn't. My very silence might give me away. In any case, I was not in the habit of being confidential with the carpenters, and Frank never questioned me about it, so I didn't have to commit myself.

The next day we paraded exactly as Munro had planned. At eight o'clock we assembled at the town jail on Thomes Avenue. Every man was on hand. Munro organized us the way he wanted us, then we moved in a solid mass to Eddy street, marching in columns of four, each team making a solid block of sixteen men in four lines. Munro, Bellew, and Thiessen were out in front. My team came next. I was on the right end of the first line, the same position that was occupied by the chiefs of the other three teams.

Nearly all of us had been in one or the other of the two armies during the Civil War, so marching was not new to us. From what I heard the next day, we put on a formidable show, our faces covered by gunnysacks and our rifles very much in evidence. After that we were known as "the gunnysack brigade," a facetious name perhaps, but one that put fear into the hearts of the undesirables.

We marched practically the full length of Eddy Street, took a cross-street to Ferguson and went along it, back on Hill, and then we returned to the jail. We scattered after that, taking off our gunnysacks in the darkness and circling to our homes. It was inevitable that some of us would be identified, but as Munro had said, that was to be expected, and I don't think any harm came from it.

I had a jolt as I approached my house. The lamps had been lighted in the front room and the blinds had not been drawn, so someone or several someones had moved in on me. I was sure Cherry wouldn't do it, and I doubted that either Frank or Nancy Rush would. There had been a rash of claim-jumpers in the last few weeks — lot-jumpers would be a better term, I guess — and I assumed I had a house-jumper on my hands just as I'd had when I returned to Black Hawk after my hitch with the First Colorado Volunteers.

I ran then, right into the front room with my rifle on the ready, so furious that it's a wonder I didn't start shooting the instant I saw anyone. But fortunately I didn't entirely lose control of myself. The moment I cleared the door, a woman sang out, "There's our man." And a second one cried, "It's Jim, all right."

I stopped and looked and swallowed, and I wasn't sure I was seeing what I thought I was seeing. Rosy and Flossie Martin had moved in on me. I wouldn't have been surprised if it had happened the first month I'd been in Cheyenne — in fact, I had expected them. But they hadn't showed up and I'd just about forgotten them.

The next minute they were all over me, hugging me and kissing me and acting as if I was their long lost sweetheart. I finally got my rifle laid down so I could cooperate, then I shoved them back and asked what they were doing in Cheyenne.

"Doing?" Rosy stared at me as if I had to be stupid to ask a question like that. "We're going into business as soon as you can build a house for us."

"Of course we're going into business," Flossie said. "We sold out in Black Hawk."

"We damned near starved the last month or so," Rosy said, "and we kept hearing about all the activity up here in Cheyenne, so here we are."

"We're going to get rich as soon as you build our house," Flossie said. "We had our driver bring us right here. Everybody knows you, so we didn't have any trouble finding the house."

"We'll live with you until our house is built," Rosy said.

"We'll use just one of your bedrooms," Flossie said, "except for the times you need us."

"We'll cook for you and keep house for you," Rosy said.

"Of course we will," Flossie said. "You'll have all the comforts and happiness of a husband and none of the responsibilities."

I sat down in my rocking chair and held my head. "My God," I said, "don't you think you'd better ask me about some of the things you're talking about?"

"Oh, we knew you wouldn't object."

"Of course not," Flossie said indignantly. "You're not the kind of man who would refuse an offer like this."

"Well, I can and I do," I shouted. "Now get out of here, both of you. Go to the hotel and get yourself a room. Tomorrow we'll talk business about the house you want built."

"Why, shame on you, James Glenn," Rosy said, pointing an accusing finger at me. "You wouldn't turn two innocent girls out into the night, would you?"

"To be attacked by wicked men while we walk the street?" Flossie demanded. "No, you wouldn't do that, Jim."

I looked at one and then the other, and damned if I could tell from the hurt expression on their faces whether they were pulling my leg or not. Of course they were, but they were still serious about it. This was the way they always had been. There were times when I thought they were idiots and other times when I knew they were the smartest whores I had ever run into. Either way, they were a weird pair.

"Did you say innocent?" I asked. "And did I hear you call yourself girls?"

"Now don't get nasty, Jim," Rosy said.

Flossie shook her head at me reprovingly. "It isn't becoming of you, Jim. It really isn't like you."

I got up and faced them. I said, "Now look here, both of you. You are not going to make a whorehouse out of my place. Do you understand that?"

They nodded, suddenly subdued. "Yes," they said together. "We understand perfectly."

"And another thing. I have a good friend who is a preacher. I'm fond of both him and his wife. I wouldn't for the world have them know I was harboring two women like you."

"Oh, we wouldn't tell him you were harboring us," Rose said.

"And we wouldn't tell him what kind of women we are," Flossie added.

"And there's a third thing," I said, ignoring their remarks. "I've met a girl I intend to marry. If she ever found out I'd had any truck with you two, she'd throw me overboard so fast it'd make my head swim."

Rosy drew a cross over her heart. "We won't tell her."

"We promise," Flossie said. "We'll even lie for you."

"Now about the house," Rosy said. "We

understand lots are expensive and hard to find."

"And that good carpenters are hard to find, too," Flossie said. "But we were told that you have some good men working for you and that you're one of the best builders in Cheyenne."

"I'd say that was all true," I agreed, thinking I was finally going to get rid of them. The red-light district was beginning to shape up on Eighteenth Street and I owned a lot in that block. "I'll sell you a lot for one thousand dollars and I'll build the kind of house you want on the lot. We'll work out the plans tomorrow when I can get to the hotel, probably early in the afternoon. I'm almost finished with the house I'm on, so I can start . . ."

I stopped. I thought I'd won and I'd be shoving them out of the house in another minute, but damned if they hadn't pulled the blinds and locked the front door as I was talking, and now they started to undress.

"What the hell are you doing?" I yelled.

"What does it look like?" Rosy asked. Before I could answer, she said, "We're going to bed — that's what. We've had a long day on the stage getting here from Denver and we're tired."

"We looked at your bed and it's big enough for all three of us," Flossie said. "Now get your clothes off and come to bed so you won't keep us awake any longer than you have to."

Every time I knocked heads with these two women I felt as if I were punching a feather bed. Of course I couldn't put two naked women out into the street. It was easier just to go to bed.

Chapter XXII

I got Rosy and Flossie out of the house at daybreak the next day. I knocked off work in the middle of the afternoon, found them in the lobby of the hotel, and took them to the office of Judge Eli Saunders, a lawyer I knew and trusted. They thought this wasn't necessary, but they didn't argue about it. Saunders drew up a contract, the women paid me one thousand dollars for the lot, and I promised to get started on their house by the middle of the following week.

That night after supper Lucky Sam Bellew called on me. The evening was a cold one, so we sat close to the heating stove and smoked, talking small talk that didn't amount to anything. We agreed that the town had been quiet after the Tate Horn business and that it was colder than hell and probably snowing hard on Sherman Hill and that chances were the railroad would be stopped in its tracks within a few days.

I thought he had come to talk Vigilante business, but he seemed to have trouble getting to it. I saw him knock his pipe out into the coal scuttle and slip it into his pocket. I heard him clear his throat and I watched him get up and walk to the other side of the room and finally turn and go to the stove. For a time he stood there with his hands jammed into his pants pocket, scowling as if there was something he had to say and couldn't find the words. By that time I had a pretty good idea he wasn't here on Vigilante business.

"Glenn," he said finally, "I asked you about selling your lots and you said you were going to keep them for a while. Now I'm not a man to push you, and you sure as hell have the right to do whatever you feel you should, but I'm going to make you an offer that sounds ridiculous. Maybe it is. Maybe I'd be better off if you turn me down flat.

"I can't even guess how high town lots are going. We do know that the Union Pacific is going to make a town out of Cheyenne, it being a division point and all, with a branch line running south to Denver. So the lots will always have some value. They won't go back to cow pasture like the lots in Julesburg."

He cleared his throat again. It seemed to me he was taking a roundabout way to get to what he meant to say, and I wondered about it. I decided he was so uncertain about Cheyenne's future that he had to talk himself into making an offer. I just sat there and pulled on my pipe and waited for him to dig his own grave, which he proceeded to do.

"You don't spend your time down on Ferguson and Eddy Streets playing poker with town lots," Bellew went on, "and that makes you smarter'n I am. My trouble is I don't have any lots to play poker with. That's why I'm making you this offer. As you said, you're a builder, not a speculator. On the other hand, I'm a speculator, not a builder, and I've got to have some lots if I'm going to sit in on the game."

He got his pipe out, filled it and lighted it. He still hadn't made any offer and I was convinced that he felt he had to try to buy my lots but the logical part of his brain was trying to put the brakes on telling him the lots weren't worth it and he might end up holding an empty sack. I still kept my mouth shut and waited.

After he got his pipe going, he said, "I'm not as good a gambler as I thought I was when I came to Cheyenne. The stakes are

250

too high. I've got a pretty good sense of values and I know that the damned speculators — and I don't mean me — have bid the lots up until they're clear out of sight. I should warn you that they may go still higher and maybe you'd be smart to inquire around before you take my offer." He took the pipe out of his mouth and stared at it, his forehead furrowed by thought. "Has anybody come to you lately to buy?"

I nodded. "Several of them, but they struck me as fast-talking boys I didn't trust and I gave them no encouragement whatever. They just never got around to making me a firm offer. I guess I didn't let them."

"You haven't given me any encouragement either," he said, putting the pipe back into his mouth, "but I'm going to make you a firm offer anyhow. I'll give you a check tonight for part of it and I'll meet you at Judge Saunders' office at nine o'clock in the morning. We'll complete the deal there and I'll write you another check for the balance."

By that time my patience had worn out completely. I got up and waggled a finger under his nose. "My God, Bellew," I said in what must have been a threatening tone, "either do your job or get off the pot. What is your offer? You act as if you don't really want to make it."

"I don't," he snapped. "I'm scared to make it. Like I said, the stakes have gone too high, but I've got to have some property or I can't do any business. You own the best bunch of lots in town that haven't been built on. If I can buy them, I'll be back in business."

He took a long breath and gritted his teeth like a boy about to dive into a water hole for the first swim in the spring. "I'll give you twenty five hundred for all the residential lots you'll sell, and three thousand for the business lots."

My knees gave way and I sat down again. I couldn't believe he'd said what I'd heard. He must have gone completely crazy. I had expected an offer of maybe twelve hundred, or fifteen hundred at the most.

"I'll take it," I said quickly before he could change his mind. "I'll let twenty residential lots go and five business lots."

He nodded, still nervous, and walked to the table, sat down, and asked for pen and ink. I brought them to him and he wrote out a check for ten thousand dollars drawn on an Omaha bank. Then he said, "Tomorrow morning at nine in Judge Saunders' office."

"I'll be there," I said.

He walked to the front door, stopped and looked back at me. He said, "Two days ago a couple of women named Martin looked me up and asked about the price of lots and how much it would cost to build a house. Then they quizzed me about you. Did they ever find you?"

"Yeah, they found me," I answered, "but there's something wrong in what you just said. They didn't get to town until yesterday."

He shook his head. "I remember exactly when it was. It was day before yesterday. They'd been in town a day or so then."

"What did you tell them a lot was worth?"

"I said it was worth whatever you could get somebody to pay, but I thought any good lot would fetch around twenty-five hundred." He turned the knob, then asked, "What kind of work do they do?"

"They're whores."

"I'll be damned." He scratched his head. "They don't look like it. I was pretty well impressed with them. I thought maybe they were business women of some kind."

"Oh, they are," I said. "They're business women right down to their big toes."

He laughed shortly. "You never know. Usually I can spot one as far away as I can see her, but they fooled me. Well, I'll see you in the morning."

He went out, shutting the door. I looked at the check and then I thought of all the money I was going to get in the morning and I just didn't believe it. I wished my father could see this check. He'd given me some pretty good advice that had turned out better than either of us had guessed.

I was a rich man, and I hadn't turned my hand to earn it. I'd just invested my money and hung on for less than five months. Now I was looking at a check for ten thousand dollars, and in the morning I'd have another one for fifty-five thousand. I looked at the check again and told myself that when my father was alive, we had thought that ten thousand dollars was a fortune.

Then all of a sudden I thought of what Bellew had said about Rosy and Flossie being in town for two days at least before they had seen me. They had plain out lied to me. More than that, they knew the lot they were buying was worth two-and-one-half times what they were paying. The good feeling went out of me and I was furious.

I went downtown on the run, stomped into the hotel, and banged up the stairs. I pounded on their door. When it opened, I was looking at Rosy, who had pulled a red robe over her gaily flowered nightgown.

"Why, it's Jim, Flossie," Rosy called. "He's come to see us."

"All you had to do was to send for us," Flossie said. "We can't do it here in the hotel —"

"I didn't come here to do anything but wring your god-damned necks." I pushed past Rosy and shut the door. "You sons-of-bitches lied to me."

They stared, their mouths sagging open. Then Rosy began to cry and Flossie dabbed at her eyes. Rosy whispered, "Honey, why are you calling us names?"

Flossie came up to me and put an arm around my waist. "Darling, I'm ashamed of you, calling us son-of-bitches. Now you know that isn't true. We've always been good to you."

"Of course we have," Rosy said between sniffles. "You remember how it was in Black Hawk when we got you started building houses."

"You learned a lot on our house," Flossie said, "and we never complained once because you were slow and had to do some of your work over."

Rosy lay down on the bed and cried louder than ever, but somehow she managed to say, "We've always loved you, Jim. You're not like any other customers we ever

255

had. You're special."

"You certainly are," Flossie said. "You're very special."

She kissed me, and then Rosy sat up and pointed a finger at me. "Why are you treating us this way? We don't deserve it at all."

"No we don't," Flossie said. "It makes me feel so bad that I think I'll . . . kill myself."

It was a hell of a good show, but calling me "honey" and "darling" and telling me they'd always loved me didn't really change anything. I said, "You told me you'd just got in on the stage, but the truth is you'd been in town at least two days."

"Of course we lied to you, silly," Rosy said. "Don't you know why?"

"He wouldn't know why," Flossie said scornfully, "so I'll tell him plain out. We wanted to sleep with you and we knew you wouldn't let us stay unless we could make you think we'd just got to town and were tired."

I knew damned well they were twisting me around their little fingers into a good tight knot, and after I was gone and the door shut they'd probably laugh their heads off at how they had fooled me, so I said, "And another thing. You knew the speculators had run prices for town property up to twenty-five hundred dollars, but you only paid me one thousand for my lot."

"But honey," Rosy protested, "you made the offer."

Flossie nodded. "Now wouldn't it have looked funny if we had said, 'No, Jim, we won't give you your price of one thousand.' "

They had me. They were right as rain. It had been *my* offer. It wasn't their fault that they knew more about property values than I did. I swallowed, pulled the door open and began to back into the hall. "I'll tell you what," Rosy said. "We'll make up that fifteen-hundred-dollar difference in trade."

"Sure we will," Flossie said heartily. "You won't lose a penny and you'll enjoy yourself every minute."

"I accept your offer," I said, "but I'll be an old man before I pick up fifteen hundred in trade."

"No you won't," Rosy said.

"You'll be the best old man in the territory," Flossie said, "and it will always be waiting for you to come and get it."

"Are we forgiven?" Rosy asked.

"We've got to know or we won't sleep a wink tonight," Flossie said solemnly.

"Sure, you're forgiven," I said, and backed on out of the room and pulled the door shut.

I went down the stairs and across the

lobby to the street, not sure why or how it had turned out the way it had. I should have known better than to go storming up the stairs to their room the way I had. I just wasn't any match for them.

When I went into the street it was snowing hard, the wind driving the flakes against me and stinging my face. I hurried home, my collar pulled up against my throat. I had a sour taste in my mouth, knowing I hadn't accomplished much. All I'd really succeeded in doing was to punch the feather bed again.

Chapter XXIII

I didn't sleep much that night. I had a funny feeling that I'd just had a pleasant dream and I'd wake up in the morning to find that Lucky Sam Bellew hadn't been to see me at all and I didn't have any check for ten thousand dollars. But when I woke up, the dawn light only beginning to touch my bedroom windows, there was the check on my bureau just where I had left it the previous evening. I was a rich man and I was going to be richer.

I got to Saunders' office five minutes early, but Bellew was already there. We finished our business before noon, so I had time to eat dinner and catch the east-bound 12:30 train, this time with a second check in my pocket for fifty-five thousand dollars.

Even after I was on the train with both checks in my wallet I couldn't get rid of the horrible feeling in the bottom of my stomach that it couldn't really have happened.

259

Maybe the checks would bounce. Maybe Bellew didn't have that much money in his account.

He did. My worries fizzled out; I had no trouble cashing the checks. Then I got cautious, thinking that one of the banks in Omaha might go broke and it might be the bank that had all of my money, so I divided it, depositing it in three different banks, keeping out five thousand dollars, which I carried in a money belt buckled around my waist. All the way back to Cheyenne I fretted about being robbed.

As soon as I reached Cheyenne I went to Fritz Thiessen's bank, wading through six inches of snow that had accumulated on the ground since I'd left, and deposited most of the five thousand. I owed a big bill for building materials, and this would give me enough to get squared away and still have some cash left in the bank.

Thiessen was in his private office when I deposited the money. He happened to see me and called me back into his office. He shut the door and waved me into a chair, then he sat down behind his desk and leaned forward.

"Do you know where Munro, Burke, Williams and Stead went to?" he asked.

"I just got back to town from Omaha," I

said. "I didn't know they had gone any-where."

"They have," he said solemnly. "I don't like it. They saddled up and left about sunup, riding west. Bellew told me about it. If you've been out of town, they couldn't have told you if they'd wanted to — but damn it, they should have told me. If it's Vigilante business, we should be informed. All of us."

I nodded agreement. "Bellew doesn't know?"

"Not a thing. He's a man who always gets up early, and he'd just finished breakfast and had left the restaurant when he saw them riding out of town. He hollered at them, but they kept going, pretending they didn't hear him."

This made me about as uneasy as it had made Thiessen. Still, if something had come up since I'd left town, they couldn't have consulted me, and I could see why they hadn't told Thiessen and Bellew. Both men were soft, and I doubted that they could stand a hard ride if that was what the four men had in mind. I didn't feel like telling Thiessen that, but I agreed that he and Bellew should have been consulted.

"Maybe they aren't going on Vigilante business," I said.

"Maybe," he grunted, "but the odds are that's exactly what they're up to. You may not have heard about the holdup. The Denver stage was robbed south of the Colorado line yesterday. The guard was killed and the driver wounded. The robbers got away with the strongbox and cleaned out the passengers. I heard there was three of them."

Thiessen leaned back and shook his head. "The trouble is it isn't within the jurisdiction of the Cheyenne officers. By the time the Colorado lawmen got on their trail, the outlaws were out of the country. A hard wind blew all of last night, so any tracks that were in the snow were covered up before morning."

I hadn't heard, but it struck me right off that the four men had left Cheyenne to run down the outlaws. I didn't try to argue with Thiessen. I just spread my hands and shook my head. "I don't know what to say, Fritz. Chances are Ed Burke picked up some information and told Munro. You know Munro wouldn't let a chance like that slip by."

"We'll have it out with them when they get back," Thiessen said angrily. "I thought you set Munro straight the other night, but maybe he's so bullheaded he can't learn."

262

"He's a bullhead, all right," I said.

It was late in the afternoon when I left the bank. I built a fire when I got home and cooked supper, but the house was cold and I couldn't get it warmed up for quite a while. I thought about what Thiessen had said. In fact, I didn't think about anything else for a while.

I could guess what Munro would say when we jumped him. For one thing, he'd claim that the holdup had been on the other side of the line and wasn't the proper business of the Cheyenne Committee. He could also argue that he had a majority of the seven with him, so if we'd had a meeting and taken a vote, he had the four votes he needed for whatever action they had taken; the other three of us might as well save our wind. He could also have said, as I'd thought when I was talking to Thiessen, that I was out of town and he knew Thiessen and Bellew couldn't make the ride.

These were all facts we couldn't deny, but there was another aspect of this business that bothered me. I knew Ed Burke well, and by this time I felt I had Jess Munro sized up. I didn't know Stead and Williams very well, but it was my guess that they were four of a kind, tough men who would hang stage-robbers without hurting their conscience. Munro would have his hanging, and now he could do all the talking that he wanted to about making an example of these outlaws as a warning to the others.

In spite of all I could say to myself about the validity of Munro's arguments, the old doubts were right back in my mind again. Not that I was against hanging men who would hold up a stage and kill the guard and wound the driver. It was just that I would have to be absolutely sure of their guilt before I'd have any part of a hanging, but I was convinced that Jess Munro would hang men he *thought* had committed the crime just to get the warning over to the hardcases he wanted to get rid of.

Frank Rush dropped in after I'd finished my supper. He said the house was finished and he and Nancy would move in tomorrow morning. Barely in time, too, with the cold snap here and the snow on the ground. He was grateful to me, of course, for making the house available, and he was sure Nancy was too.

He didn't look at me while he said this. I wondered if he knew how I felt about Nancy, and that it was only my concern for her comfort and safety that had forced me to make the Quixotic gesture that I had. I knew very well I could have rented the house ten times and had cash coming in, and I knew equally well that I'd get little cash for the rent from Frank.

I'm not intimating that Frank meant to be dishonest about it. Rather, he felt impelled to put his money into his church building. He probably told himself that later on, after the church building was finished, he would see that I got all the rent that was coming to me.

I would not, of course, make an issue out of it and I told him so. I said that he had done fine work for me and he was not to worry about the rent. Then I said, "I've got a contract to build a house on that lot I own on Eighteenth Street. We'll get started on it in the morning. I guess it's not too cold to work."

"No, it's not too cold." He cleared his throat, swallowed, and finally blurted, "I'm sorry, Jim, but I've got to start on my church. I'm going to have to quit working for you."

I guess I should have seen this coming, but I hadn't, and it struck me that he was being disloyal, that he should stay with me as long as I had work that was pressing. I didn't say anything, though. I took time to fill my pipe and light it, something I had learned long ago to do when my temper began crowding me.

Before I struck the match, the thought occurred to me that Frank knew what the house on Eighteenth Street was going to be used for and he didn't want any part in building it. For some reason the notion comforted me and took away the feeling that he was disloyal.

"Good luck with it," I said. "I hope you'll come back and work for me after the church is finished."

"I hope I can," he said.

He rose and we shook hands. He never did work for me after that. As a matter of fact, I didn't see much of him after that, because I didn't go to church and he didn't come to see me. When he had scraped some rent money together, he sent it over with Nancy.

Nancy was ashamed and apologized for being so far behind in the rent. It hurt me to see a proud woman like Nancy brought down to the position where she had to apologize for Frank. I told her not to say anything about it, that I had been determined to get her out of the tent and into a house, and that it was all right with me if I never got a nickel of rent.

She stood at the door and looked at me, and I looked at her. I wanted to tell her that the only reason I had built the house was that I loved her and couldn't stand the thought of her freezing to death in that damned tent and being in danger of getting raped every night by the hardcases who roamed the Cheyenne streets, in spite of all that the police and Vigilantes had done.

I didn't say any of it because I knew she understood that, even though I had never actually said it. I was convinced she loved me for it, even though she had never said that either. She turned and walked away. I went to the door and watched her as long as she was in sight.

I'm not sure of the exact thoughts that were in my mind as I looked at her, but I don't think I ever, at that or any other time during those months, entertained the hope that someday I would have her. I despised men who butted into another man's marriage — an attitude that never really changed.

Frank's leaving me didn't hurt as much as I was afraid it would. I was lucky enough to find another carpenter the next day, but now I stayed on the job almost all the time, whereas before, I had known that Frank would do a good job of overseeing the work if I wanted to go somewhere. Now I had to do it, so I was tied down far more than I had been.

Less than a week after I returned from Omaha, Munro and the other three man rode back into town. The weather had warmed up and most of the snow had gone off the ground, so we had mud, which was what had held them up, according to Ed.

He came into Cherry's restaurant as I was eating supper and told me they'd just got in. He ordered a steak and I sat beside him at the counter and drank coffee until he finished. Then he walked home with me. I built up the fire and offered him a drink and a cigar, and when we were comfortable I said, "I want to hear about this trip you and Munro and the other men made. Thiessen and Bellew are sore because they weren't informed."

"Is that so?" He seemed surprised. "Hell, Jim, it just wasn't any of their put-in. If it had been Cheyenne Vigilante business, we'd have told them, but this was out of town. I got wind of what had happened through one of the outlaws who knocked the stage over. He came by for a horse and told me the other three had hightailed for Dale City and had holed up there. I rode into town as soon as I could and told Munro. He asked Williams and Stead to go with us because we needed at least four men."

"You knew they'd go, and you knew they wouldn't kick about hanging three outlaws," I said.

He was surprised again. He pulled on his cigar for a moment, then said, "That's right . . . You know, it never occurred to Munro that Bellew and Thiessen would feel that way. I'll tell him and he can talk to 'em. He's a tough bastard, that Munro, but he'll keep Cheyenne clean. You can count on that."

"I believe it," I said, and I sensed then that my trouble with Jess Munro wasn't over by a long shot. I'd known all the time, but for some reason I was reminded of it right then very forcibly.

"You know," Ed said, "I'm guessing that the railroad is gonna have to stop work for a while on Sherman Hill. We seen a lot of snow up there on top."

Dale City was a little burg about forty miles west of Cheyenne, so I understood why they'd been gone so long, what with the snow and then the mud. I just waited, figuring that he'd get around to telling the whole story if I gave him plenty of time.

He never did get around to telling the whole story, though. I guess I didn't give him enough time. What he said next set me off. "We surprised 'em. They probably figured they were so far from Cheyenne that nobody from here would bother 'em, and being in Wyoming, they didn't count on nobody chasing 'em from Colorado. We got 'em under our guns and we took 'em down to a railroad trestle and strung 'em up."

He stopped and looked at me, grinning. "You know who it was? Well sir, you wouldn't guess. I was surprised because I didn't think they had it in 'em. It was your old friend Bully Bailey and his two side-kicks."

I was stunned. I blinked, and the blood began to roar in my head. Before I knew what I was saying, I yelled, "You son-of-a-bitch! Bailey was my meat. You knew that. Why did you hang him?"

He'd looked as if he thought I'd be pleased with what they'd done, but what I said wiped the grin off his face. He stood up and jammed his hands deep into his pockets.

"Jim," he said, "if anybody else had called me a son-of-a-bitch I'd have cleaned his plow for him good, so don't repeat it. But I will say one thing to you. You are a ████-damned fool. Bailey would never have faced you in a gunfight. Sooner or later they'd have come into Cheyenne and dry-gulched you. They'd have killed you the other time by kicking you to death if me and Frank

270

Rush hadn't saved your life. You're too much of a gentleman or a fool — I ain't sure which — to have shot Bailey in the back, and that's the only way you could have killed him. Now you're safe and you call me a son-of-a-bitch for doing you a favor."

He got up and stomped out. He was dead right and I knew it, but I couldn't find enough guts to tell him until Sunday, when I rode out to his ranch and told him. He laughed and said, "Get off that horse and come inside. I've got a bottle that needs killing."

That's the kind of man Ed Burke was.

Chapter XXIV

Those of us who had been prophesying that the railroad would mire down in the snow on Sherman Hill were proved right. Chief Engineer Dodge had named Fort Sanders on the western side of the Black Hills as his objective, but he didn't quite make it.

Any way you looked at it, Dodge and the Casements and the others had to be given "A" for effort. They must have done the greatest job of railroad building the world had ever seen. At Cheyenne they had built 517 miles from Omaha, and 87 miles had been laid in the last three months. Besides that, there was always extra work to be done, such as putting in the sidings and switches.

The distance from Cheyenne to the start of the climb was fifteen miles, with the summit of the Black Hills another fifteen miles farther west. Dodge's goal, Fort Sanders, was only twenty more miles downhill from the summit.

They reached eight thousand feet on the pass and there the snow stopped them, still ten miles from the summit and thirty miles short of Fort Sanders. But the Union Pacific had laid 240 miles of track in 1867, and if any of us in Cheyenne had been asked, we would have said it was a hell of a good job.

Even though the laying of track had stopped, a lot of work was done through the winter months for the big final push to Ogden and beyond. All kinds of materials were piled high along the track and the Casements' warehouse in Cheyenne was packed with stores ready to be used the following spring.

Tons of iron rolled in; ties were piled up like young mountains, and more were being cut in the Black Hills and Medicine Bows. All of this was fine for business, and for a few months Cheyenne prospered. But we had our headaches, too: before we knew it we were a city of ten thousand people.

Rosy and Flossie were crying for their house to be finished. They were losing money every day, they said, and I knew they were. I hired two more men and we rushed it through. From the night they opened both women were kept busy with crowds of Irish graders and track-layers who had been

273

called in from the end of steel, and the new men who were pouring in on every train from Omaha.

Again I was reminded how the things that happen to us are never unmixed blessings, and that the pill of success may be sugar-coated, but the pill can be mouth-prickling sour when the sugar is gone. It was fine to have so much business in Cheyenne, so much money to spend, but there was the other side of the coin: lots and building costs too high, crowds on the streets twenty-four hours a day, rents too high, people living in tents and shacks that were a health hazard and a disgrace to Cheyenne, and an increase in the criminal element along with the booming population.

As soon as I finished the Martin women's house, I started a new business building, this one on Eddy Street. I could have rented it a dozen times over if I'd had it finished, but first the house for Frank and Nancy Rush had delayed me, then the Martin house, and the upshot of it was that I simply didn't get my building done in time to cash in on the big boom.

Still, I didn't complain. I had sold my lots to Lucky Sam Bellew at close to the top of the market. The boom price of lots had leveled off, although I think some of the corner business lots did bring as much as thirty-five hundred after I sold to Bellew.

I don't know how Bellew came out. Within a month from the time he bought my lots he sold out and left town. Probably he ended up about even, the slump not coming until early in the spring. I suspect he put every nickel he had into my lots, knowing, as we all did, that when the boom was over prices would drop as fast as they had sky-rocketed. The question was not *if*, but *when.*

I think Bellew found the game too much for his nerves, so he probably got out when he could by selling for about the same figure he had paid me. He didn't go broke, though there were plenty who did. Later in the year I was able to buy back some of the lots I'd sold to Bellew for five hundred dollars apiece.

Speculators had given me a fortune, and for that I was thankful, but I had no reason to lose sympathy on the ones who lost their shirts off their backs. It was the same in any gamble — they knew the possible consequences when they sat in on the game. Some won and some lost, but when the slide came, the ones who did lose lost big.

As I said, we had an increase of the criminal population with the boom in the overall population. We had more whores, more pimps, more con men, and more sneak thieves. There was no way to keep this element out of town, but I don't know what would have happened to Cheyenne if we had not organized the Vigilantes.

I still had some doubts, I still kept my eyes and ears open waiting for Munro to go off half-cocked, but to my knowledge he never did. Somehow we kept the lid on. I'm not saying we didn't have some murders and robberies. We did, of course, and we had men mugged and rolled and beaten, but Cheyenne did not become another Julesburg. Most of the stories written about Cheyenne's lawlessness were exaggerated by reporters who, when the facts failed to give them a good story, simply made one up.

I was busy and so was Cherry, and for that reason we didn't see each other as much as I would have liked. Maybe Cherry wanted to see more of me than she did — at least, I wanted to think that. Many times when I dropped into her restaurant for supper she only had time for a quick smile when she saw me. Later in the winter she did sometimes invite me back into her living quarters to eat supper with her, or more often simply to have a cup of coffee with a piece of cake or pie she had set aside for me.

From the day the first train from Julesburg had arrived with all the toughs who were moving to Cheyenne, I had worried about Cherry. Now, with the bridge-building and track-laying crews called in for the winter, conditions were far worse.

As far as I know, there was only one time when she had any serious trouble. By sheer good fortune I was on hand to save her from what might have been a tragedy. I had worked late that evening. Then, to make me still later, Munro had called a meeting of the Central Committee along with the four chiefs, so I hadn't had time to get any supper.

Munro called these meetings at least once a week and sometimes oftener because he had spies among the hardcases. Ed Burke seemed to know what the plug-uglies were planning, too. Munro always put before us the names of men he thought should be run out of town. He gave us chapter and verse along with the names. If we all agreed that they had to leave town, and we practically always did, they were warned. They usually pulled out before their time was up and that was the end of it.

The way we operated was to locate our man, usually in a saloon when he was drinking at the bar. Then one of us would go into the saloon and tap him on the shoulder and say, "You're wanted outside." Or, "There's a man out here who wants to talk to you."

When we got him into the street, we'd escort him around the saloon building to the alley, where a bunch of us would be waiting, and tell him to be out of town before sunup. All of us except the Vigilante who had gone into the saloon would be wearing our gunnysack masks.

If our man was still in Cheyenne after we delivered our warning, we'd go after him a second time. We would show him a rope, then give him a hell of a beating. After that he'd pull up stakes as soon as he was able to travel. It didn't fail once, so the bad ones were on the move out of town almost every day, and the others heard about it and stayed inside the law. They knew they'd be next if they didn't.

I didn't take part in any of the hangings, though there were some. And I never knew for sure that Munro or any of the Vigilantes were involved in these hangings. I always believed that the toughs were the ones who were responsible, doing it to get rid of their rivals. Of course, they expected the blame to fall on the Vigilantes, which it did.

Anyhow, I was hungry that evening. I

wouldn't have been surprised if Cherry had locked up and gone to bed, but she hadn't; she was still looking for me to drop in. The evening crowd was gone and she had sent her help home, so she was alone, except for a big red-bearded bastard who'd had enough to drink to make him mean.

He should have gone to a whorehouse, as horny as he was, but he'd lingered over his coffee, watching Cherry as she cleaned up. Finally she told him to leave. That was what triggered him. When I came in he had her backed into a corner and was trying to kiss her. She was fighting him off, but he was too strong for her. In the fracas before I took a hand, he had torn her blouse clear down across her right breast.

I seldom lost my temper — I mean, lost it to the place where I had no control over myself. But this time I lost it completely. I guess I was a madman when I tackled the fellow. He didn't know I'd come in, he was that busy with Cherry. If I hadn't showed up, I'm convinced he would have raped her right there on the restaurant floor, and perhaps killed her.

I caught him by a shoulder and yanked him around. He was so surprised that he released his grip on Cherry. She ducked away from him and backed into the kitchen, trying to hold her blouse together. I hit the man in the mouth, knocking his front teeth out, cutting his lip, and flattening his nose so that blood spurted in a fine red stream.

He went back and down, his head hitting a corner of a table. I jumped on him, my knees driving the wind out of him. I got a handful of hair and banged his head against the floor. I wasn't doing any thinking. Afterward I couldn't remember what I had done, but Cherry told me I was hammering a tattoo on the floor with the back of his skull. Once in a while, for good measure, I'd slug him on the jaw with my free hand.

I don't know how Cherry got through to me, but she finally did. When I realized what I was doing, I stood up and stared down at the man. His face looked like a piece of raw beef. I got him by the feet and dragged him into the street. The night was a cold one, and I knew that if he laid there awhile he'd freeze to death. I didn't give a damn if he did.

For a moment I stood in the doorway and watched him. I guess the cold air revived him — or maybe it was the snow. Anyhow, he got up on his hands and knees and started to crawl away. He spilled out flat on his belly, then struggled up to his hands and knees again and crawled a few more feet before he fell again.

I turned and closed the door. Cherry was standing motionless, one hand clutching the front of her torn blouse, her eyes on me as if she had never seen me before in her life.

I went to her, asking, "Are you all right? Did he hurt you?"

"I'm all right," she whispered. "You got here just in time."

I put my arms around her and kissed her long and hard. I'd kissed her before, but never like this. When we finally drew apart, I said, "Cherry, marry me. Marry me right away. I don't want you to take any more chances staying here by yourself."

She looked at me, her moist lips quivering. "I'll marry you," she said, "but not right away. I've got to think about it some more."

"Why?" I demanded. "You've had all winter and part of last fall to think about it."

"I'm afraid, Jim," she said. "Afraid of what you might do sometime. You'd have killed that man if I'd let you alone."

It was my turn to stare at her. "Sure I would," I said. "He deserved killing."

"I didn't know you had a temper like that," she protested. "It scares me."

It didn't make any sense to me. I'd saved her from a raping. Very likely I saved her life. I turned on my heel and strode to the door. I was afraid to stay there — I'd have lost my temper again if I had. She was scared of me because I'd lost my temper. I guess she thought I could come in and see her being abused and beat hell out of that bastard and be my cool, calm self while I was doing it.

Before I slammed the door behind me, I yelled, "Lock up."

"Wait, Jim," she cried out. "Don't go."

But I didn't wait. I shut the door with a hard slam and walked home through the snow. I built a fire and cooked my own supper, then I sat at the table and smoked my pipe. I felt as if I had eaten a plateful of rocks. After a time I calmed down and my stomach felt better.

When I could think straight again, I began to wonder if I really wanted to marry Cherry. I wasn't sure right then. I wasn't sure at all.

Chapter XXV

I didn't sleep much that night. Cherry crowded into my thoughts and refused to leave. I knew I had to make a very important decision. Either I was going to marry Cherry or I wasn't, but if I was, I had no patience with her stupid remark that she had to think it over some more. She'd had all the time in the world to think about it, and if she still had her doubts, then marrying me wasn't the thing for her to do.

Nothing had changed for me. I knew, as I had all along, that I didn't love her. I had never told her that I did. It was a simple proposition for me of having reached the age in which I felt a need to settle down and raise a family. I needed a wife, I needed a housekeeper, and I needed a woman to entertain. Good business required entertaining, and I was very much aware that when Cheyenne settled down to a town's normal routine, I would have to answer many demands that weren't evident now.

From my point of view, I had a great deal to offer a woman. I could give Cherry a comfortable home and a life with far more luxuries than she was used to, more than the average woman had. I had big plans for the future. I would do more building as time went on and Cheyenne grew on a permanent basis.

The Indian problem on the plains was far from settled and wouldn't be for a long time, so I was convinced that Fort D. A. Russell and Camp Carlin would be here for years. The army was going to need beef and wood and hay, and I intended to get my share of the contracting business. I didn't know anything about it, but I could learn just as I had learned to build. Other men had grown rich dealing with the army, and I saw no reason why I shouldn't, too.

I had spent a lot of time in the last few months dreaming about the future. Now I had the money to do anything I wanted to. I could hire crews of men to cut wood and hay and haul them to the fort. I could buy a herd of cattle in Colorado and hire cowboys to drive it to the fort. Once a man has money to deal with he can turn a dream into reality, and that was exactly what I aimed to do.

Before this I'd never allowed myself to dream big because I didn't have the money I needed to work with, but now the sky was the limit for my dreams, and I needed a woman to fill out the dreams, to share my good fortune. I'd lived long enough by now to realize that the really fine things of life do not come to men who live alone.

I considered myself a practical man, and love is always a part of being practical. I had offered Cherry a proposition, a fair exchange. I was sure she understood. But if she kept her part of the bargain, she had to trust me. The fact that I had lost my head and almost killed a man should not make her afraid of me. I resented it. No wife could be an adequate wife if she was afraid of her husband. I had seen wives who were afraid of their husbands, and she had hurt my pride when she had said in effect that that was the way it would be with us. Men like that were bullies, and I hated them.

By the time it was dawn I'd made up my mind to have it out with her. We'd make our rules; we'd know what to expect out of each other. If these rules didn't suit her, then by God she wasn't the woman for me to marry.

Apparently I was in a daze that day as I worked. One of my men asked me if I was sick, and another remarked that I must have been up all night tomcatting around. When it was supper time I went to Cherry's restaurant and sat down on a stool at the counter. Apparently the waitress had told Cherry, because she came out of the kitchen within a minute or so from the time I sat down. She walked behind the counter until she came to me.

Leaning forward, she whispered, "Jim, come back to my room. I want to talk to you."

The Irishmen who sat on both sides of me snickered and winked at each other, but I slid off the stool, ignoring them, and followed Cherry to her room. She closed the door after me, then turned and put her arms around me and kissed me.

It was the first time she had ever made the first move, and it knocked my plans right out of my head. I wanted her. This was the first time for that, too. I guess I had never thought she wanted me physically, but now I felt she did.

Then when she drew back and whispered, "I've been looking for you all day, Jim. I'm so glad you came tonight."

I looked at her, puzzled, and not quite knowing what she expected. From the expression on her face I wasn't even sure she knew what she had done to me. Then, quite suddenly, the feeling came to me that she hadn't wanted me that way at all, that she was seeking forgiveness and letting me know she didn't want to lose me.

Whether I was right or wrong about what was in Cherry's mind, I decided I couldn't say any of the things I had intended — things I would have said if I'd been talking to Nancy Rush and she had been free to marry me.

Nancy would have known exactly what was in my mind, and the same hunger would have been in her that was in me. But Cherry was different. In some strange way she seemed to live apart from the ordinary human world of passion and love and all the other strong human feelings that make life worth living for most of us.

"I'll get our plates," she said, and disappeared into the kitchen.

She returned with two plates of stew, went back after bread and butter and coffee, then brought two slabs of dried apple pie and set them on the bureau. We didn't talk much as we ate, but as soon as we were finished she took the dirty dishes back into the kitchen, then returned and pulled her chair close to mine. She reached for one of my hands and held it as she talked, squeezing it now and then to emphasize what she was saying.

"I want to apologize for last night, Jim," she said, "but first I must thank you for saving me perhaps from a fate worse than death. I mean that literally, not as a joke as people so often make it. I would rather be dead than to have been violated by that man. The part I want to apologize for was saying I was afraid of what you might do. I'm not afraid of that at all. I can only say I was so worked up — I mean just plain scared — that I didn't know how it sounded."

She took a long breath that was really a sigh. She was close to crying when she went on: "Jim, you are a fine man; I'm proud to be asked to marry you. Just give me a little more time. I've hated men all my life. My father was a monster and my mother hated him. She taught me to do the same and I guess I saw my father every time I looked at a man. I'm getting over it. You've helped me get over it, but I still need more time."

I saw tears running down her cheeks. She brushed at them impatiently with her free hand. She said, as if angry at herself, "I'm sorry, Jim. I hate bawling women and it isn't often it happens to me. It's just that I want you to understand and I'm not sure you can. I'm not like any other woman in the world. I don't want to be different, but I am."

She was silent then for a full minute or more, staring at the wall in front of us. Then she burst out, "Of course I don't want to be like some women. I mean, like the ones on Eighteenth Street who sell themselves to men. They're animals. A man buys a woman and she sells herself like a . . . a piece of merchandise. I have no sympathy for those women."

"They're still people," I said. "It's just that they've chosen that way to make their living."

"Are you defending them?" she demanded.

"No," I said. "All I'm saying is that they're people."

"They're animals," she snapped. "They chose that way of making a living because they are too lazy to work. I've had trouble hiring help, but there have always been plenty of those creatures in town who have not wanted to work." She took another long breath. "I never intended to get on that subject. I know you're not the kind of man who has anything to do with them, and of course you've known all the time I'm not that kind of woman."

I didn't tell her about my relationship with

Rosy and Flossie Martin, and I hoped she would never find out. She was too innocent to understand, I thought, and of course once we were married I wouldn't need them and I'd never see them again.

"Well then," I said, "are we still getting married?"

"Oh yes," she said quickly. "Of course we are."

"When?"

"I don't know," she answered slowly. "I told you I still need a little time. Part of it, I think, is to prove to myself that I can make my own living, not just when there's a boom on, but during ordinary times when we have to scratch for a living."

I couldn't and wouldn't press her, but I wasn't really satisfied by her explanation of why she wanted to wait. I thought she just couldn't bear to pin the date down, that what she had said about hating men was probably true, and that this had been responsible for some of her attitudes and actions.

Now I remembered how suspicious of me she had been at first. She had been kind and compassionate when I had been beaten up by Bully Bailey and his friends, but I had been helpless then. When I looked back over these last months, I was struck by the time it had taken me to wear down her suspicions.

"I'll buy you a ring tomorrow," I said. "I'll stop in about the middle of the afternoon when you aren't busy."

The following day I took her next door to the jewelry store and bought her the biggest diamond in the place. She liked it and admired it, but somehow I was disappointed in her reaction to it. I'm not sure why, except that I had an idea she was saying all the right words but wasn't really feeling what she was saying.

That evening when I ate supper she was nowhere to be seen. I didn't ask about her. I thought that if she wanted to see me she'd make herself known. I walked home through the twilight, wondering why she had stayed out of sight.

The sky had cleared and the stars were beginning to come out. The air was biting, with a hard wind driving down from the Black Hills across the prairie and drifting the snow in places up to my knees or higher.

I was chilled when I went into the house. The instant I opened the door, the warm air rushed at me. I stepped inside quickly and shut the door. Then I saw Nancy sitting in a rocker beside the window. It was the first time I'd seen her for nearly two months.

She had brought the rent money in February and now it was almost April.

"I didn't want to sit here in the cold," she said, "so I built a fire. I made some coffee."

I pulled off my sheepskin and hung it up, then slapped my hat onto a nail beside the front door. I said, "I'm glad you did. Do you want some coffee?"

"No, I had a cup just now," she said, "but I'll pour you some if you —"

"I just left the restaurant," I said. "I'll have a cup after while."

"The rent is on the table," she said bitterly. "I don't know whether it's in advance for April, or whether Frank is paying some of the back rent. He didn't say."

"It's all right," I said. "I've told you that."

"No, it's not all right," she said. "I've always paid my own way, but now I'm forced to live on your charity. On Zach Dunlap's, too. We have a big bill at his store . . . I don't know, Jim. I don't think I can stand it much longer."

"How's Frank?" I asked.

"Fine," she answered, the bitterness still in her voice. "You know he's working for Fred Stallcup?"

"I'd heard that he was," I said.

Stallcup was the biggest builder in Cheyenne and probably paid better wages than I did. He was a man who would appreciate a good worker like Frank Rush. I was a little put out with Frank for not coming back to work for me, but I guess I didn't have any right to be.

Probably Frank hadn't been sure I'd do any more building. As a matter of fact, I wasn't either. It was only a matter of days until the railroad would send its crews out again and Cheyenne's boom would peter out. Frank probably thought he had a better chance to have a permanent job with Stallcup than with me.

"His conscience hurts him," Nancy said, "so he's afraid to face you, owing rent like he does. That's why he has me bring it to you. But the church is almost finished, so maybe he'll do better in the future. I'd like to get a job, only Frank won't let me. But if he doesn't pay you off, I will get a job, no matter what he says. I'll see that you're paid."

"Nancy, don't . . ."

I stopped. I could go on telling her a dozen times not to worry about the rent, that I didn't need the money, but it wouldn't have done any good. It seemed to me that nothing could do any good for her as long as she lived with Frank. He would never change.

I had purposely stayed away from Nancy because I did not trust myself. Now that I was engaged to Cherry, I had still more reason to stay away from Nancy. Still, I found myself walking toward her, slowly, not by choice, or by any decision on my part — I was moved by some compelling force that had not been willed by me.

From where I stopped, close to her, I could see only the side of her face. She was a beautiful woman — Frank Rush did not deserve her. He did not even realize how great a treasure he had. She was not cut out to be a preacher's wife. She had known that for a long time, but I don't think Frank did. He probably hadn't thought about it any more than he had thought about Nancy's safety when the Julesburg crowd had rolled into Cheyenne last November.

Then for the first time I was aware that in one way Frank was like Cherry. Neither had any understanding of the world in which they lived — Cherry, who hated men, and Frank, who thought of very little except the saving of men's souls.

"Divorce him, Nancy," I said. "Don't go on bruising yourself this way. There's no future for you living with Frank."

Slowly she tipped her head back to look at me. I saw misery in her face, complete and absolute misery such as I had never seen on the face of any other human being. She said, "I know that, Jim, but I can't divorce him."

"Why?" I demanded. "Why, when you know —"

"Several reasons," she interrupted. "One's enough. He's a kind and gentle man who would never injure me in any way. He lives the best he can with the understanding he has. He would never know why I divorced him. It would kill him."

She rose and walked to the door, then turned to look at me. "Jim, the Bible says it's as great a sin to think adultery as it is to do it. That makes me a great sinner."

What she said startled me. Before I could say anything, she had added. "Good-by. I just wanted to see you for a few minutes."

"I'll walk home with you," I said.

"No, it isn't dark yet," she said. "I'll be all right." She turned the knob and pulled the door open, her gaze still on me. Then she asked, "Are you going to marry Cherry Owens?"

"I think so," I answered. "I bought her a ring today."

"Don't do it, Jim," she said. "She's the wrong woman for you."

"Why?"

She stepped outside and shut the door, not answering. I stood at the window and watched her until I couldn't see her any more. I didn't have any idea why she had said that about Cherry.

Chapter XXVI

During the winter General Dodge had been called back to New York to confer with the top men of the Union Pacific. Get to moving in the spring as fast as you can, the top men had said, comfortable in their heated offices and homes. Hang the expense! Push the end of steel on west with all possible speed.

Time! That was all that counted. Beat the Central Pacific to Ogden. Get as close to the California border as you can. Maybe we can shut the Central Pacific out of the rich trade of the Salt Lake valley. To hell with anybody else. We'll take every nickel we can.

This was the law of the jungle. On beyond the Black Hills was the Laramie Plains, then the Red Basin and the Bitter Creek country, and finally the snow-covered Wasatch Range. After that, of course, there was the Utah and Nevada desert — if the Union Pacific could lay track fast enough to beat the Central Pacific and get there first. The reward was to the swift, not to the honest, the compassionate, or the idealistic.

To the fat and comfortable planners and plotters in New York, it made little difference how many surveyors and bridge builders and graders and track layers froze to death or were killed by Indians or died from exposure or drinking bad water in the Bitter Creek desert. The old mountain-man legend said that a jack rabbit had to carry a canteen and a haversack to make it across that desert. True or not, it made no difference to the big men in New York. Get the rails laid any way you can. Time! Nothing else counted.

So General Dodge gave the surveyors their marching orders. They left Cheyenne late in February and crossed the Wasatch Range in sleds, the snow so deep that it covered the tops of the telegraph poles. Spring came slowly that year, so slowly that much of the equipment and many of the animals were lost. The miracle was that any of the men survived.

When April 1 came, the army of graders, bridge builders and track layers that had wintered in Cheyenne moved out, even though the ground on Sherman Hill was still frozen as hard as cement, too hard for the picks and shovels of the graders to work.

It took a month for the railroad to reach Laramie, near Fort Sanders. For a time Laramie was the end of steel, and many of the problems that we had faced in Cheyenne all winter simply moved west to face the people of Laramie. Later Benton, on the edge of the Red Basin, was hell on wheels, then Rawlins, and after that Green River and Bryan, which was thirteen miles away.

Within a matter of days we saw Cheyenne change from the roaring boom town to a quiet city scattered along the Union Pacific tracks, the tents and many of the shacks gone, fifteen hundred people instead of ten thousand. Most of the fifteen hundred who remained were solid citizens who had made a decision, many of them months ago, to cast their fortunes with Cheyenne — win, lose, or draw. I was one of them.

Early in April Jess Munro called the leaders of the Vigilance Committee together in his office. There were six of us, the same men with the exception of Lucky Sam Bellew, who had persuaded Tate Horn to get out of town last November.

I had not seen much of Jess Munro for several weeks. The first impression I had of him as I stepped into his office was that he had not changed from the time we had taken Tate Horn out of the saloon and told him to leave Cheyenne. He was as tough and tight-lipped as ever. He leaned back in his chair and looked us over. It seemed to me he was almost smiling — as close to smiling as I ever saw him.

"Gentlemen, our job is nearly finished," Munro said. "From now on, with one exception the police can handle the problems that come to Cheyenne. I think we have done very well, and the town owes more to us than anyone knows."

Then he leaned forward, the ghost of a smile gone from his lips. "However, you will continue to serve as Vigilante officers until such time as I disband you. That will not be for some time, not until I know the danger of lawlessness is gone . . . The fact that the mass of laborers has left Cheyenne does not mean that peace and harmony will prevail. We have had some organized crime, and we will continue to have it for a while. That is the exception I mentioned which the police will not be able to handle."

Munro sat back in his chair. "Believe me, gentlemen," he went on in a subdued voice, "I am better informed on this matter than any of you, because I have contacts among the undesirables who will sell information to me for a price. The reason I asked you to

300

come here tonight was to tell you to be prepared for a call to duty at any time, even though you may think the need for our organization is passed . . . We will not, of course, make a show of force as we did last November. You men are the key to our success. I expect you to respond when I need you. The call may not come for several weeks, but it will come. Now are there any questions?"

"I've got a problem," Bronco Stead said, "although I'm not sure anybody can help except to give me some advice."

"Let's hear it," Munro said.

"I've bought about a dozen Kentucky horses," Stead said. "In a few weeks I'll be leaving Cheyenne to bring them here by train. They're worth a fortune. Fact is, I'm spending a fortune for them. They're mostly brood mares, though I'll have three studs in the herd. I expect to make a good deal of money selling them to some of the Englishmen who've started cattle ranches around here. They have more money than sense, and they appreciate good horseflesh. My problem is how to keep them from being stolen. Some of the organized crime you're talking about is horse stealing, and if I'm any judge, horse thieves never turn down an opportunity like this."

Munro nodded as he reached for a cigar, bit off the end and lit it. He didn't say anything for a time, but he looked at us as if thinking some of us were the horse thieves Stead was talking about. He pinned his gaze on me, then on Ed Burke, and went on along the half-circle of men who faced him.

"What do you men think?" he asked finally. "Have you got any advice to give Bronc?"

We didn't. At least, we didn't have anything to say. Munro took the cigar out of his mouth. "I told you we have had some organized crime in this country in spite of all we could do. The truth is we haven't done a damn thing so far to smash the organization. All we've done is to cut off a few limbs, but the roots are as sound as ever."

Munro waggled a finger at Stead. "I'll tell you one thing, Bronco. These horses you're bringing in will tempt the same outlaws who have been robbing the stages."

"I know, I know," Stead said sharply, as if insulted because Munro was telling him something he already knew. "If they can get my horses across the line into Colorado, they can drive them into Denver, and I'd have one hell of a time finding them, let alone proving ownership."

302

"All I can tell you is to keep a heavy guard on them as long as they're in Cheyenne."

"How heavy is heavy?" Stead asked.

"Whatever you want to pay," Munro said. "Good men will cost you money, and you're the only one who can decide whether you can afford to hire enough men to guard them adequately."

"I can't afford not to," Stead said in a tired voice. "I wish now I'd waited for a while, but I've made my deal and I've got to go through with it."

We broke up a moment later. I walked out of the building with Ed Burke, more troubled by the meeting than I liked to admit. When we reached the boardwalk, I said, "Ed, I had a bad feeling about Munro. Looked to me like he suspected some of us of being in cahoots with the outlaws."

Ed laughed shortly. "Sure he did. Still does, probably. He looked at you first, then at me, which got me to wondering if you're his Number One suspect and I'm Number Two."

"He's got no grounds to suspect us," I said, getting more angry by the second as I thought about it. "For all we know he's into it up to his neck. This might be his way of turning suspicion to one of us."

We reached the door of the Head Quarters

303

Saloon and stopped. Ed pulled thoughtfully at an ear, then said, "That hadn't occurred to me, but you could be right. I'd sure like to turn the tables on that bastard." Then he shrugged, as if dismissing the thought. "Come on in, I'll buy you a drink."

"Thanks," I said, "but I'll get along and see if Cherry's still up. Maybe she'll have some coffee on the stove and a piece of pie put away for me."

"You're a lucky man, Jim," he said in what struck me as a tone of envy. "I see she's wearing your ring. She'll make you a good wife." He hesitated, then added, "I guess you didn't know it, but I've been purty sweet on that girl myself." He shook his head. "Hell, you had the inside track all the time. I should of known that."

"I'm just lucky," I said, and went on along the street.

He'd given me quite a start. I had known, of course, that Ed took his meals in Cherry's restaurant when he was in town, but I hadn't known that he'd ever given her a romantic thought. He'd never even hinted at it to me.

Cherry's restaurant was still open. She was glad to see me, as she nearly always was when I dropped in. She locked the front door and told me to come on back to her room. She brought coffee and pie, and I enjoyed myself until I remembered what Ed had said, so I asked her about it.

She looked at me, troubled. "I'm surprised he mentioned it to you," she said. "He's proposed a dozen times. Just a day or so ago he wanted me to leave the country with him. He said he had plenty of money for me to live in style."

"He's lying," I said angrily. "He's never made a nickel on that ten-cow spread of his. He plays some poker, but he's not a very good player and I never knew him to win any big pots."

"I thought he was lying," she said, "and I thought it was funny he tried to persuade me to leave with him, knowing I'm engaged to you and being a friend of yours and all."

"It's funny, all right," I agreed.

But it wasn't laughing funny. I thought about it as I walked home. I couldn't make it out. I'd never understood Ed anyhow, though there wasn't any mystery about that I never understood people who didn't work and were as happy and easygoing as Ed. The point was it didn't seem like him to try to steal my girl, especially after she had started wearing my ring. It might have made sense if Cherry had been the flirty kind, but there wasn't a flirty bone in her body.

I lay awake a long time that night, but I couldn't make it add up right. Before I dropped off to sleep I told myself I'd ask him plain out the next time I saw him, but I didn't have a chance. I never saw him in town again.

Chapter XXVII

Through the following weeks we had to adjust to a changed Cheyenne — no crowd on the streets, plenty of room in the hotels for transients, very little crime, and not much business. All of us, I think, were glad to see the tents and the worst of the shacks go. We noticed more soldiers in town, too. Actually there weren't any more, but before they had been a small minority. Now we were aware of them simply because fewer people were on the streets or in the saloons.

The red-light district was cut down to a few houses on Eighteenth Street. Of course, one of them belonged to the Martin women. I still dropped in about once a week, sometimes just to talk. They were always glad to accommodate me, whether it was business or talk. They cried poormouth to me about how their business had gone downhill.

I told them to move to Laramie, but they refused to do that. They were comfortable here, they liked the house I had built for them, and they claimed their trade was from the best businessmen in Cheyenne and the best officers from Fort D. A. Russell and Camp Carlin.

Maybe they were lying to me, but I let them enjoy their lies, even to telling me how much they thought of me. They said they wouldn't leave here unless I married Cherry, and if I wasn't going to marry her, how about marrying one of them?

I didn't take them seriously, but I liked them, and I usually wound up at their place Saturday night and often slept there until late Sunday morning. Cherry never wanted me to stay with her after ten or eleven o'clock.

I didn't know what Ed Burke was doing, but I didn't see him. I thought maybe he didn't come to town any more, or maybe he did come and I just never ran into him. Anyhow, he didn't look me up the way he used to. Possibly he was hurt because he hadn't got anywhere with Cherry. I didn't think he was that sensitive, but then I hadn't thought he was in love with Cherry, either.

A couple of times I dropped in on Nancy and Frank Rush, but I didn't feel comfortable with them. Nancy was quiet and withdrawn, and Frank never looked at me while we were talking. He always looked past me for some reason, so I decided I wasn't really welcome there.

Perhaps it was exactly as Nancy had said — Frank's conscience hurt him. He wasn't working, because Stallcup had quit building and there weren't many good jobs in Cheyenne. Frank had finished his church and had good crowds most of the time, so I supposed he was busy with his congregation.

Cherry attended Frank's Sunday morning service and told me about it. She accepted his brand of religion without question. This was something we seldom talked about, and I was very much aware that it would be an issue between us if we had any children. I would never under any circumstances allow my children to go to a church that was as strong on hellfire and brimstone as Frank's was.

I refused to worry about it, though. The truth was I had just about given up on marrying Cherry. I didn't press her any more to set the date. It was up to her. Maybe she wanted to be begged, but I had made up my mind I wouldn't do it.

I spent a good deal of my time at Fort D. A. Russell. I knew most of the officers and I had started to dicker with them for a wood contract — or hay, though I preferred a deal in wood. We hadn't quite come to terms. The truth was I had to feel my way, this being something new for me. I wasn't real sure how much I'd have to pay men to cut wood and then haul it to the fort. The situation was a good deal different from hiring carpenters to build houses.

When my second business building was finished, I rented it to a man who started a saddle and harness shop. He said now that the railroad boom was over, Cheyenne would become a center of cattle raising, and I thought he was right, though maybe a little premature. I built a room in one corner of the building and used it for an office. I furnished it with a desk and several chairs, so it was comfortable enough, but I didn't spend much time there.

Like most of the other businessmen in Cheyenne, I was on the streets or in the saloons more than I was in my office. Of course, we kept tabs on the progress of the railroad. The end of steel had gone past Laramie and was now moving across the Laramie Plains.

Then near the end of May, Bronco Stead returned from Kentucky with his horses. They were in the corral behind his livery stable, and as soon as the word spread every man in town except Frank Rush hurried to the corral to get a look at the horses we'd heard so much about.

They were fine animals and I would have loved to have owned one, but I was never a fool over horses as some men are and I had no intention of spending a fortune for one of them. I suppose they were worth their weight in gold, though Stead got cagey when anyone asked what he wanted for them. My guess was he hadn't decided what to ask, perhaps because he didn't know how much he could get out of the Englishmen.

That night they were stolen. I never heard all the details, although I'm sure that if Stead had put an adequate guard on his corral, as Jess Munro had told him to do, it wouldn't have happened. I assume he was trying to save money. Or it might have been a trap for the thieves. That seemed a crazy idea, using a fortune in horses to trap a gang of thieves. I was inclined to accept it as a possibility, though, knowing how anxious Jess Munro was to get the deadwood on the men who were involved in what he called "organized crime."

Anyhow, Stead and two men were guarding the horses when they were surprised by the outlaws. Stead claimed there were a dozen men in the outfit, but when the sheriff looked the ground over he said he doubted that the gang had over four men. In any case, they got the drop on Stead and the two guards, slugged them with their gun barrels, and drove the horses off, leaving the three men lying on the ground beside the corral.

I tried to go down there that morning as soon as I heard about it, but the sheriff had several deputies and city police guarding the place, so no one could get within fifty feet of the corral gate.

Jess Munro saw me and came to me. He said in a low tone, "Be ready to ride tonight. We're going after those horses."

"Not me," I said. "We've got a sheriff and a police force. They're paid to enforce the law."

"Glenn, sometimes I wonder how smart you are," Munro said contemptuously. "You know what'll happen. The sheriff will snort around here till noon talking and getting ready. Finally he'll ride out with a posse and get as far as the Colorado line; then he'll be back, all tuckered out and saying he didn't have any authority to go over the line."

"Which same is true," I admitted, "but he can wire the Colorado lawmen and —"

"We won't be held up by any line," Munro interrupted. "I need your help, Glenn. You took an oath. What do you think I've been staying around Cheyenne for? I aim to get those bastards and you're going to help me."

"So you'll get your hanging after all," I said sourly.

That remark didn't set well with him. His eyes narrowed and his lips squeezed together and his face got red. He said, "I don't have to ride all night to manage a hanging — I can go to Laramie and have a dozen. I'm going to bust up this gang of outlaws. I knew they couldn't pass these horses up."

"All right," I said. "I'll be ready if it works out with the sheriff the way you say it will."

It did. I should have known it would. This kind of thing was old business to Jess Munro, and he was an expert at it just as he was in judging men.

I had finished supper and gone home when Munro showed up with Stead and Williams and a half-breed named Red Buck. I'd seen Buck around town and had talked to him a time or two, but I didn't know him well.

After the exodus around the first of April, Buck had stayed out of town. At least, I hadn't seen him. He claimed to be half Cheyenne and half French, and maybe he was. He was a tall, very thin man, with a dark face and black hair and the high cheekbones of a Cheyenne.

He was an excellent horseman and a good tracker, but I was surprised when Munro said, "Saddle up, Glenn. Red Buck knows exactly where the horses are. If we can get there before dawn, we'll have 'em. We'll get our men, too."

I didn't feel any great obligation to help recover Stead's horses, and I felt even less obligation to keep my oath, because I figured the time that bound me to it was past, but I was interested in breaking up the gang of thieves. If I continued to live in Cheyenne, which I intended to do, I wanted it to be a law-abiding town and I wanted a safe road between Cheyenne and Denver.

I had built a small shed on the back of my lot. I kept my sorrel there instead of at the livery stable where I had left him when I first came to Cheyenne. I saddled him and rode into the street within a matter of minutes.

"Where's Ed Burke?" I asked. "He always wants in on a deal like this. We could use another good man."

"We could at that," Munro agreed. "We'll stop at his place. It's not out of our way."

It was dark by the time we crossed Crow Creek. The weather had turned cold in the afternoon and now a chill wind was driving down from the Black Hills. We were all wearing coats. It was hard to talk above the wind, so we didn't try. The sky was clear and the stars gave us some light even though there was no moon.

We reached Ed's place sometime before midnight. I stepped down as Munro said, "See if he's home, Glenn. The last time I was out here he was gone."

I opened the door and yelled, but no one answered. I struck a match, found a lamp, and held the flame to the wick. I looked around, appalled by the dust that had drifted in around the door and windows. I went into the bedroom and realized immediately that he hadn't been here to stay for a long time. He had cleaned out the things he'd need if he was traveling. He hadn't left much in the house, not even any grub in the kitchen.

I blew the lamp out and went back to the waiting men. "He's not here," I said. "Looks like he hasn't been home for a while."

"That's the way it looked to me the last time I was here," Munro said. "Mount up and we'll get to moving."

We rode southwest. I'd never been in this country and I had no idea when we crossed into Colorado. The wind continued to knife us. Still no one tried to talk, maybe because of the wind, or maybe because we all knew we were taking on a dangerous job. If it went as expected, men would be hanged, and I didn't think anyone except Munro would enjoy it.

We didn't stop to rest our horses until almost dawn, when the word came back from Red Buck, who was leading the procession, that we were almost there and we'd leave our horses here. We stepped down and tied our mounts.

In the darkness I couldn't make out exactly what the country was like, but there were willows here and I heard water running a short distance from where I stood. We followed Red Buck for a quarter of a mile. I had a feeling we were in a narrow ravine, with very steep sides. It would make a good place to hole up, the walls likely hiding the corral and what buildings there were from anyone who might be riding by.

Presently Red Buck stopped us. He said in a low tone, "The outlaws are asleep in that shack. The horses are in a corral behind the shack. At least, that was the plan. They're heading out for Denver as soon as it's daylight if nobody stops 'em."

I had no idea how he knew this, but I didn't ask. Munro said, "We'll stop them. We'll move up to the shack, easy and quiet.

Bronco, you and Glenn take the far side. The rest of us will stay on this side of the door. We'll wait till one of them shows himself. Bronco and Glenn will handle him. The rest of us will go in after whoever is inside. Red tells me there should be only three men."

I could see the first hint of dawn in the eastern sky. In a few minutes there would be some early light, enough for the outlaws to spot us if they woke up and looked out through the windows. But maybe there weren't any windows and maybe Red Buck knew that. He did seem to know a great deal about these men, so much that I began to wonder if he had helped steal the horses.

We made it to the front of the shack. Stead and I moved past the door and slipped around the far corner. I'd been right about the windows. There were none, at least on the front and east side of the building. We waited for ten, perhaps fifteen minutes — it's hard to say because time drags in a situation like that. Presently a man inside the shack coughed. Then I heard him cross to the door, a board in the floor squeaking under his weight.

He stepped outside to relieve himself. We waited until he was done and had turned back toward the door, one hand buttoning his pants. I wasn't showing much of myself, just enough to watch him. I punched Stead with an elbow, then rushed the man, getting a hand over his mouth as I pulled him back around the corner of the shack.

In spite of all I could do, the man made a strangled kind of grunt. One of the men inside called, "What's the matter with you, Hamp. It ain't time —"

The three men outside the door lunged through it. The man I'd nabbed wasn't as big or strong as I was. I had him on the ground face down, one hand on the back of his head, his face in the dust. He flounced around, trying to get me off his back. Finally I drew my gun and rammed the muzzle into his neck. When he felt the gun, he quieted down in a hurry.

"I've got him," I said to Stead. "Go inside. They may need you."

They didn't. There were only two men inside the shack. They were out of their bunks and had their revolvers in their hands, but they didn't have time to use them. Munro and Red Buck, the first through the door, got them before they could fire a shot. Munro slugged his man with his gun barrel. Buck didn't touch his. He said, "You're covered," and the man froze.

A moment later Stead was back with me. "No trouble," he said. "Like taking candy from a baby."

I got off my prisoner and stood up just as Munro came out of the shack. He and Williams were carrying a man. The sun wasn't up, and the light was still very thin, but there was enough of it for me to see that their captive was Ed Burke.

CHAPTER XXVIII

I was stunned. For a few seconds I just stood there, staring at Munro, then at Ed. As soon as I found my voice, I yelled at Munro, "What's the matter with you? That's Ed Burke. You know him as well as I do."

They laid Ed down in the grass. Munro said to Red Buck, "Get the ropes." Then he turned to me. "I guess I know him better than you do, Glenn. He's the brains of the wolf pack we've been trying to run down. Now we've got the deadwood on him and we're going to hang him."

"Oh no you're not," I said. "Are you out of your head? He's got a ranch. We stopped there tonight. He's been in and out of Cheyenne ever since I've been there. You appointed him a Vigilance Committee officer. You act like you've forgotten all of this."

Munro shook his head. "No, I haven't forgotten it, and I'll admit that appointing him a Vigilante officer was the biggest mistake I've made for a while. I wasn't onto him then. He used his position to know what we were planning and to give me some bad advice. Like hanging the three men at Dale City. He was one of the outlaws who robbed that stage, but by blaming the other men and getting them hung he got suspicion turned away from him and his friends."

"I don't believe it," I said. "Anyhow, he's my friend. You're not going to hang him."

"You try to stop it and you'll get yourself beefed," Munro said. "Go take a look at what's in the corral. You'll find the horses there." When I hesitated, he snapped, "Go on. We won't string them up till you get back."

I ran past the shack to the corral. There was enough light for me to see that Stead's horses were there all right. I ran back, not knowing what I was going to do, but dead sure I was going to stop the hanging. Even if Ed was as guilty as hell — and it looked to me as if he was — I aimed to see that he had a trial.

When I got back to where Munro and the others were waiting, Ed was conscious. Then he saw me and said, "Well, so you caught up with me too, Jim. I shouldn't have come back from New Mexico, but I kept thinking of those damned horses that

Munro and Stead had been waving in my face. I had to show 'em we could take 'em. We did, too."

"And you got yourself caught," Munro said roughly. "Now you'll hang."

"It wasn't you that caught us," Ed said. "It was that ███-damned double-crossing bastard over yonder." He motioned toward Red Buck. "How come you're dealing with a man like him, Munro? He'll sell you out just like he did us if he gets a chance."

"He won't have a chance," Munro said. "I'm paying him off and he's getting out of the country pronto. If he doesn't, I'll see he winds up in the jug."

"You're getting purty low," Ed jeered.

"Not any lower than I ever did," Munro said smugly. "I've always had spies among the toughs. You know that. It's not hard to find men who'll sell out for a price."

I glanced at Red Buck. The sun was almost up now and the light was good enough to see the expression on his face. He wasn't ashamed one bit. I guess a man like that is never ashamed of what he does. He was scared, though. Maybe he thought Munro wouldn't keep his bargain and would end up hanging him too.

Stead and Williams were standing a few steps behind me, holding their guns on the other two horse thieves, who looked like any of a hundred hardcases I'd seen come and go in Cheyenne all winter. I'd get no help from either Stead or Williams. I didn't know how I could buck four men of the caliber of these four, particularly Jess Munro, who was just about as hard as they came. I had to do it someway. I kept telling myself that Ed Burke was not going to hang.

Ed and Munro were still jawing back and forth, Ed needling Munro about being so low he could crawl under a snake's belly with his hat on for dealing with a double-crosser like Red Buck, and Munro, as smug as a cat lapping up cream, saying he didn't mind being that low as long as he got his man.

"We couldn't have found either the horses or you," Munro said, "if it hadn't been for Red Buck, so he turned out mighty useful."

"He helped us take the horses," Ed said. "He's as guilty as any of us. He was in that stage robbery that we strung Bully Bailey up for. He's been in most of the robberies and killings that I know anything about, and you admit you're using him."

"Sure I'm using him," Munro said. "He comes pretty high, too, but he's worth it. With you out of the game, your pards will hightail out of the country."

"Most of 'em are over in Laramie now," Ed said. "You'll have it all to do over again."

"Not exactly," Munro said. "I don't often run into a man like you, sitting out here on a little spread innocent as all hell and pretending to be an honest rancher and doing your best to get the Vigilantes organized. You were cute, Burke, cuter'n a scheming female trying to get her man. You even fooled Jim Glenn there."

All the time they were gabbing, Munro taking the opportunity to brag a little and Ed just using up time in the hope that something would turn up, I was thinking about Ed and how he had managed to fool me. I had thought of him as a friend, but now I wondered if he hadn't just used me for his own advantage.

He was the first man I'd met in this country. He'd put me up for the night almost a year ago and he'd ridden into Cheyenne with me the next day. He'd helped me when I'd started to build. He'd saved my life when he and Frank Rush jumped Bailey and his friends, and even though I'd been sore about the hanging of Bully Bailey, everything he'd said had been true. If they hadn't strung Bailey up, he would have dry-gulched me sooner or later and I'd be dead.

On the other hand, Ed had lied to me and pretended to be something he wasn't. I'd always had a certain amount of respect for an outlaw who didn't deny what he was, but I had damned little respect for a man who claimed to be an honest rancher and was robbing stages and killing people all the time. He'd even tried to steal Cherry while she was wearing my ring.

Well, I didn't respect Ed, who was a first-class hypocrite, but I liked him. He had saved my life — nothing could change that.

"Let's get on with the hanging, Jess," Stead said.

"All right," Munro said. "We've wasted enough time. There's several limbs on those big cottonwoods that are stout enough to hold a man. Toss the ropes over them and then fetch up the horses."

"There'll be no hanging," I said. "We're taking these men to Cheyenne for trial."

"Well, by God," Munro said as if he didn't believe he'd heard right. "You never learn, do you, Glenn. Well sir, you're bucking me for the last time. I'm running this show and don't you forget it."

"You always give a condemned man one last request, don't you, Munro?" Ed asked.

Munro looked at him, the almost grin coming to his lips again. "Sure, Burke," he said, "but we're not taking time to build a fire and cook you a meal. You're going to have to swing on an empty stomach."

"That ain't my last request," Ed said. "I want to talk to my friend Jim. I've got some advice to give him about not throwing his life away for a no-good piece of scum like me."

"All right," Munro agreed. "That's more sense than I expected to hear from a man like you, but remember that Red Buck is going to have his gun on you all the time. If Glenn tries to hand you his iron, you're both dead."

"I believe Buck would do it," Ed said. "I've seen the bastard kill a child just to watch him die. Compared to him the rest of us are angels."

Munro had turned to the cottonwoods and was ignoring Ed as he gave Stead directions about the ropes. Ed was on his feet, reeling a little. His head must have been splitting, but he came on to where I stood halfway between the shack and the cottonwoods.

When he reached me, he said in a low voice, "That was right. I meant what I said while ago. You're a good man, Jim. You'll take care of Cherry. Better'n I could. Don't give 'em any excuse to kill you. Munro hates you from your boot-heels right on up to the top of your head. You keep bucking him and he'll have the best time of his life killing you."

"Why didn't you put guards out?" I asked. "You wouldn't have been surprised if you had."

"Because I never thought that damned, sneaking Red Buck would sell us out," Ed said. "We was figuring on moving out early this morning and I didn't dream Munro would have any dealings with a bastard like Buck. If he hadn't guided you here, Munro wouldn't have found this place for a week. By that time I'd have been in New Mexico." He paused, then added, "Stupid, wasn't it? You should always figure the worst from a man like Buck."

He was about three feet from me, blood trickling down his forehead. Buck stood ten or twelve feet from us, close enough to hear most of what Ed was saying, but he gave no sign he was insulted or sore over what Ed had said about him. He had the same impassive expression on his dark face I've seen a lot of Indians have. They can hate you enough to kill you, just as if you were a bug to step on, but you'd never know it from the way they look at you.

Suddenly Ed's knees gave way and he fell

against me. I grabbed him, and as I eased him to the ground, he whispered, "Dig in front of the manger in the first stall in the shed at my ranch. Give the money to Cherry. It's all I've got to leave her."

He acted as if he'd fainted, going loose all over and closing his eyes. I pulled my gun and I lined it on Munro. "You heard what I said a while ago," I told him. "We're taking these men in for trial. If one of the others shoots me, I'll get you before I hit the ground. That's a promise."

Munro chewed on his lower lip, then said, "Glenn, you're either a hero or a fool. You're not holding a good enough hand to play your bet out."

"I'm neither a hero nor a fool," I said. "You know I believe in the law handling cases like this. I've had my doubts about the Vigilantes all the time, particularly because of bastards like you who enjoy hanging men. Now have a couple of your boys saddle the horses that belong to Ed and his friends and we'll start back for Cheyenne, just like you said."

"I kind of admire you even if you are a fool," Munro said. "I've been in this business for a long time. I've belonged to several Vigilance Committees and I've done my share of hanging, but I never met a man before who was a stickler for law the way you are, and who was willing to back up his beliefs with his life. You've got a big future in Cheyenne if you live."

That was the point, I thought. Munro had no intention of letting me live. Red Buck would have shot me in the back if Ed hadn't got to his feet and rushed him. At least Stead told me that later, though at the moment I couldn't take my eyes off Munro to look around to see what had happened.

I heard the shot and started to move to one side so I could keep my gun on Munro while I figured out what was going on behind me. If I'd known, I'd have smoked Munro down. As it turned out, I didn't have a chance to find out what was happening.

I got around just enough to see Buck standing there looking surprised, smoke from his gun barrel drifting away into the early morning stillness. Ed was bending forward, one hand gripping his chest; then he toppled over on his face. The next instant the roof fell on me and I dropped into a bottomless well, turning head over heels as I fell. It lasted only a moment; then there was nothing but complete and absolute darkness.

Chapter XXIX

I don't know how long I lay there, but when I came to I was immediately conscious of two things: a headache that threatened to split my skull right down the middle, and the bright sunlight in my eyes. I sat up and rubbed my face, turning so that my back was to the sun. Then I opened my eyes, and I saw them.

Munro had done his job, all right. Ed and his two friends were dangling from cottonwood limbs, swaying just a little in the breeze that came down the ravine, the limbs groaning as the ropes scraped against the wood. I'd seen men after they'd been lynched and it always made me sick. The sight of these three would have made me sick even if Ed hadn't been one of them.

I suppose it was the complete loss of human dignity that came to a human body when death was from hanging that gave me that feeling. I never felt the same when I saw a man who had been shot to death; shooting never gave a body the grotesque, macabre look that hanging did: the twisted head, the gaping mouth, the purple face. Maybe, too, I have always felt that hanging was a horrible way to die.

Whatever the cause, I was sick. I got up and staggered toward the shack, the ground turning in front of me. It seemed to have waves, like the surface of a lake when it is driven by a hard wind. I almost fell before I reached the shack. When I did reach it, I put a hand against the wall to steady myself, and then I began to retch.

It went on for what seemed a long time. I continued to do it long after there was nothing left in my stomach to come up. When it finally stopped, I went to the stream, lurching back and forth like a seasick man. I got down on my hands and knees and washed my face and took a drink of water, but it was quite a while before I felt like getting back on my feet.

I knew what I had to do, whether I felt like it or not. Jess Munro had left the bodies here for the magpies to peck at, but I couldn't. I cut them down and removed the ropes from their necks. I wasn't sure about Ed — he didn't look like the other two. He had a bullet hole in his chest, and I wondered if he was dead before they had put the rope on his neck. It would be like Munro, I thought, to hang a dead man because that was supposed to be the fate of a horse thief.

I hunted around the shack and the shed behind it and finally found a pick and shovel. I spent most of the day digging the graves. They weren't as deep as they should have been, but I was too tired to dig any deeper. I found a tailgate in the weeds back of the shed. I carved Ed's name on it, birth-date unknown, and below that: *May 30, 1868.*

Not that anyone would ride by here and look at the graves, or read what I had cut on that tailgate, but I felt better doing it. I guess I thought it was the least I could do for Ed Burke. I hadn't saved his life. I hadn't even been able to get a trial for him, but I had done all I could and I could not blame myself for what happened to him.

I rolled the bodies into the graves and shoveled the dirt on them. I set the tailgate into the earth at the head of Ed's grave, and then I stood there for a while, thinking I ought to sing a hymn or pray for them or maybe recite some scripture.

I didn't, because I couldn't. It wouldn't make any difference to them anyhow, but I got to thinking about Frank Rush's brand of religion and how he thought he was saving men's souls. I wondered if he had ever tried to save Ed's. I asked myself if Ed was bad or good, and how could I tell if any man was bad or good, including myself. I could think of a lot of good things to say about Ed.

On the other hand, if he had held up that stage and killed the guard and wounded the driver, then he was bad by almost any standard. But then maybe he hadn't been the one. Somebody else, a man like Red Buck, might have done the shooting. Somehow I just couldn't see Ed Burke ever shooting a man he didn't have to.

Munro had left my horse in the corral, which surprised me. I saddled up, so tired and weak I didn't think I'd ever make it into the saddle, but I did. I hadn't had anything to eat all day, but I couldn't have eaten if a banquet had been spread before me. My stomach was still too queasy.

The sun was almost down by this time, but I figured I'd find Ed's ranch by dark. I wondered if Red Buck could have heard what Ed had whispered to me as he fell against me. If he had, Ed's money would be gone. Or, even if he hadn't heard, he might have suspected what Ed was telling me.

Maybe he was hiding out somewhere around Ed's place, waiting to get the drop on me and make me tell him where the money was.

I didn't feel like riding hard, so I didn't get to Ed's place as soon as I thought I would. The sun was down and the dark was moving in fast when I reined up beside his shed. I swung down, looking around and listening while I hung onto the horn. I think I would have fallen on my face if I hadn't.

I didn't see or hear anything out of line. As soon as my dizziness left me, I opened the door and led my horse inside. Then I closed the door and listened some more. It was all right, I thought. Probably, Red Buck was twenty miles away by now.

Ed had always kept a lantern hanging just inside the door. I found it and lighted it. Then I led my horse into the second stall, tied him and offsaddled, and decided to wait until morning to hunt for the money.

I lay down in the straw of the first stall, thinking I was probably lying on the loot that Ed had hidden there. I'd take it to Cherry when I found it, just as he had told me to do. There was no way of finding out who it belonged to, and I certainly had no intention of keeping it.

I couldn't go to sleep for a long time after

I blew the lantern out. I woke up several times before dawn; I just couldn't get rid of the feeling that Red Buck was around there somewhere. If he had heard what Ed had told me, he wouldn't tell Munro. He'd take Munro's money and say he was leaving the country; then he'd come out here and wait for me to show up.

I kept my gun in the holster, knowing that if I pulled it out and laid it beside me I wouldn't be able to put my hand on it if I needed it right away, and then I'd be in a hell of a fix. I don't know how many times I woke up and listened and dropped off into a light sleep again. I had some wild dreams, and maybe it was the dreams that kept waking me up. I thought I was gunning Red Buck down, and then I was trying to find Jess Munro and shoot him.

When I woke the last time I saw that the first light of dawn was showing through the knotholes and the cracks between the boards on the east side. The next instant my heart began to pound. I heard the hinges of the door squeak. Someone was opening it very slowly and carefully.

I have never made any claims about being a seventh son, or the seventh son of a seventh son, but I think I had known all the time that Red Buck would try this. I eased my gun out of the holster. Then I caught a man's movement as he slid through the door. I had no intention of lying there and being shot to pieces, or having that bastard get the drop on me and shoot off my fingers and toes until I told him where Ed's money was. He was enough Indian to do exactly that.

As soon as I could pinpoint the man's position, I started shooting. I didn't wait to see if it was Red Buck. I put the first slug just about where I figured his chest was and I lowered each shot a few inches so my fourth one would drill him in the belly.

I held the last shell in my gun so I'd have one more load if I needed it. I moved quickly to one side and then I listened. The man was down, all right, but I couldn't tell whether I'd killed him or not. When I didn't hear any groans or hard breathing, I figured I'd got him, so I edged toward him, keeping close to the wall of the shed. Holding my gun in one hand, I fished a match out of my pocket. I struck it and moved it so the light fell on the man's face. My breath went out of me the same as if someone had bit me a hard blow in my belly. It wasn't Red Buck at all. I had shot and killed Jess Munro.

I blew out the match and sat back on my

heels and tried to figure out how this could have happened. Munro had been too far away to hear what Ed had said to me. Buck was the only man who could have heard, so how had Munro found out?

One thing seemed certain: Red Buck wasn't a man to give anything away. The more I thought about it, the more sure I was that Buck had sold his information to Munro and left the country, figuring that getting a few dollars from Munro was better than taking a chance on staying around.

Anyhow, I had to think that Munro had come here to get the money for himself. For some stupid reason, maybe selfish, I was gratified to think that he was as big a thief as anybody when the chips were down. I could only guess, of course, but I figured that Munro must have thought that I'd remain at the other place and bury the bodies, and then I'd be too tired to ride, so I'd stay there until morning.

He was a smart man and he had me pegged right. I hadn't felt like riding so far, and I wouldn't have done it if I hadn't been afraid that Red Buck would beat me to the money if I spent the night at the hideout.

One thing I did know: I was in trouble if anyone found out I had killed Munro. He wasn't a man who made many friends, but he was respected in Cheyenne. If he had been working for the railroad, I'd have somebody on my tail in a hurry.

I led his horse inside the shed, tied him in the last stall, and shut the door. I watered my horse, looking around and listening as my horse drank and wondering if Munro had come alone. No one seemed to be around. I'd have known it by now, because whoever had been with him would have heard the shooting and made a try for me. Anyhow, if Munro had bought the information, he wouldn't be likely to share it with anyone.

As soon as I could, I got my horse back into the stall, tied him, forked hay into his manger and gave him a bait of oats. I closed the door and lighted the lantern. Using a shovel Ed had left in the corner beside the pitchfork, I started digging.

It didn't take me more than ten minutes to find a metal box. I lifted it out of the hole, flipped the lid back, and looked at more money than I had ever seen in one place in my life before. No sense in counting it, but I judged the box contained at least $10,000. I wondered what Cherry would do with so much money.

I hunted around the shed for something to put the money in, and ended up by emptying the half-sack of oats. I moved the money from the box to the sack and tied it. Then I stood looking at Munro's body for a while and a happy thought struck me. I'd bury him where I'd found the box. It would make him happy, I thought, to share the same hole with the empty box.

I don't know what had got into me. Maybe all the things that had happened in the last twenty-four hours had made me a little crazy. Or maybe it was because my head still ached and my stomach was still queasy. I hadn't eaten anything for about thirty-six hours, but I don't think a meal would have stayed down if I had eaten one.

Sometimes I am convinced that people's emotions bring about their sickness. I hurt worse, and had been hurting even before I'd been slugged, than any time I could remember, at least since I'd had the beating that Bully Bailey and his friends had given me. To find out what Ed Burke really was, and then try to save his life or at least get a fair trial for him, to fail and end up by cutting him down and burying him — all this did more to make me sick than the whack I'd received on my head.

Somehow I found the strength to enlarge the hole until it was big enough to hold Munro's body. I dropped him into it, then lifted his head and shoved the empty box under it so it served as a pillow. After I filled the grave and raked litter over it, I didn't think anyone would suspect that a man was buried there.

I tied the sack of money behind my saddle, led my horse outside, and went back after Munro's horse. Halfway between Ed's place and Cheyenne I turned Munro's horse loose. Someone would find him and bring him in, or just keep him.

In any case, I didn't know what else to do with him. I couldn't see that finding Munro's horse would lead anyone to his body. Even if it did, it wouldn't throw any suspicion on me unless Cherry did some unnecessary talking, and there was no reason for her to do that.

When I reached Cheyenne, the first thing I did was go to Cherry's restaurant. It was close to noon and the smell of cooking food was just about more than I could stand, but I went on back into the kitchen, trying to ignore my stomach's announcement that it had been empty for a long time.

Cherry was standing beside her big range frying meat. She smiled when she saw me and spoke a greeting. I said, "I've got a present for you."

She frowned as she looked at the gunnysack. "I haven't got time to look at it now, Jim, but if you'll —"

"You'd better take time," I interrupted. "Ed sent it to you."

"Ed Burke?" She turned to a woman who was working for her and handed her a fork, motioning for her to watch the meat. As she led the way to her room she asked, "Why didn't Ed bring it?"

"He's dead," I said.

She whirled to look at me, to see if I was telling the truth. "What happened?"

"He had an accident."

"What kind of an accident?"

"He dropped off his horse."

"How could he drop off a horse?"

I didn't want to tell her what had happened, so I lied a little. I said, "I mean he fell off his horse."

She closed the door as I dumped the money on the bed. I said, "Ed asked me to bring this to you."

She froze, her lips parting, her eyes wide as she stared at the money. She walked slowly to the bed, then fell on her knees and began fingering the greenbacks and the gold and silver pieces as if she didn't believe they were real.

All she could say was, "My God, Jim, look at all this money. Just look at it!"

I turned around and strode out of her room. I went home and put my horse up, then walked into the house and made coffee. I was plenty hungry, but I didn't think I could keep anything down yet, so I didn't try to cook.

After I drank two cups of coffee I fell asleep in my chair. I slept a few minutes, then woke enough to stagger into my bedroom, take off my boots and gun belt and fall across the bed. I slept the clock around, and when I woke up it was dark.

I cooked a meal, my stomach having settled down to where I could eat, though I was careful not to eat very much. I thought about Jess Munro, and how I had killed him. It surprised me to discover I did not feel at all guilty. My feelings were quite the opposite, in fact. I was struck by the thought that by accident a strange sort of justice had been brought about, with Munro meeting his death by trying to steal Ed Burke's stolen money.

If I had known it was Munro, not Red Buck, who was slipping into the shed, I probably would not have fired. But I didn't know, so Jess Munro had died.

CHAPTER XXX

Sometimes I've had the idea that my life has been marked by different periods, periods that were determined by events more than by time.

For instance my childhood while my mother was alive, my growing-up years with my father, the wood-cutting and building era in Black Hawk, interrupted by the brief interlude with the First Colorado Volunteers, then my move to Cheyenne and my engagement to Cherry. This chapter, at least my engagement to Cherry, came to a final end on the second Sunday morning in June, 1868. Not that it was any surprise. But I had not wanted to make the absolute and complete break. Cherry did.

After leaving the money with Cherry, I decided not to go back. I felt that the next move was up to her. I'll admit I had been irritated by the way she'd acted when I gave her the money. Apparently she had been hypnotized by it. She hadn't even said, "Thank you." "Why did Ed want me to have it?" The ugly thought occurred to me that she had agreed to marry me because she knew I had some money, and now she was indifferent because she had enough money of her own to do what she wanted.

I was aware that she might have been temporarily knocked off her moorings when she saw the money, but she could have come to my house later to talk about it. But I didn't see anything of her. The chances were that I'd have been home if she had come, because I stayed pretty close for several days. I simply didn't feel like doing anything.

I had gone to Bronco Stead's livery stable and talked to him. That was when he told me that Ed had seen what Red Buck was aiming to do and had got to his feet and jumped between us, so that he took the bullet which was meant for me.

Stead also said that he was the one who had knocked me cold with his gun barrel. He said it was better for all concerned than killing me, which is what Buck or Munro would have done if I'd stayed on my feet and kept prodding them about a trial.

He was more than likely right, because Munro had had all he could stand of me and sooner or later would have given Buck the signal to try again. Stead went on to say that killing me would have created some problems, as well known and liked as I was in Cheyenne. He also claimed he was the one who had persuaded Munro to bring my horse up and leave him in the corral. How much of this was a lie was more than I could tell.

I asked Stead why Munro had insisted on me going along. He said they wanted to be sure I knew why they were hanging Ed. Unless I had actually seen Stead's horses in the corral with my own eyes, they knew I would never believe Ed had helped steal them. They were dead right about that, but they hadn't guessed I'd raise so much hell about Ed and the other two getting a trial. The reason they missed their guess on this, I think, was that Munro would never admit he couldn't handle another man, no matter who he was.

Finally, Stead told me that Munro had left Cheyenne for Laramie to help the Vigilantes there. When he failed to show up, I guess they wondered what had happened to him, but as far as I know his body was never found, so his disappearance remained a mystery.

Aside from going to Stead's livery stable

and the grocery store and the post office, I stayed at home. It was not so much that my stomach still hurt, or that I was tired. I recovered from my physical ailments, but I didn't get over my mental and emotional problems so easily. I simply could not get the picture of Ed Burke swinging from a limb out of my head.

Knowing as much as I did about Ed, I realized he was a paradox, both good and bad, and I wasn't at all sure he took Buck's bullet to save my life. The more reasonable explanation was that he wanted to avoid a hanging. Being shot to death was certainly better than hanging. Still, what he had done saved my life, along with Bronco Stead knocking me cold.

In any case, Cherry did not come to see me. I had decided not to see her, so our relationship was one hell of a failure as far as romance went. As I thought about it more, it occurred to me that Cherry would have left town with Ed if she had known he had as much money as he had. I may be doing her an injustice, but I had expected her to come to see me, and when she didn't I was hurt, and then angry.

When I thought about her dropping to her knees and fingering the money, and the greedy expression that came to her face, I sensed that she had given up any serious thought of marrying me and that it was only a question of time until something happened to make a formal break.

Oddly enough, I felt relief. I didn't want a wife and family enough to beg her to marry me, even if she was the only woman in Cheyenne I knew who was eligible and I would consider marrying. The formal end came the Sunday morning I've mentioned, a little before eleven o'clock.

I'd gone to the Martin house the night before and had stayed there, as I did quite often. Rosy and Flossie had welcomed me, as they always did, telling me I was their favorite customer and asking why I'd stayed away so long. They'd cooked breakfast for me. After we'd eaten I remained at the table, smoking and talking to them while they did the dishes. The truth was I hated to go home to an empty house and I didn't have anything else to do.

I found myself thinking of Nancy Rush and how pleasant it would be to go home to her, and then I considered how it might have been with Cherry if we had really loved each other, or even if she had welcomed marrying me and wanted to be my wife, as I had first thought she did. I had to face the truth that I had expected too much of her.

The way she had kept putting me off and saying she needed more time was ample proof that she had not wanted to marry me at any time.

Finally I got so churned up just thinking about Cherry that I couldn't sit there and listen to Rosy's and Flossie's chit-chat about nothing of importance. I got up and walked out of the house and down the path to the street. For some reason, my father's old saying about the sun being on the wall came back to me.

It was the first time I had thought of that statement in months. I felt guilty. I had all this money and so far I hadn't done much with it. I remembered the parable about the three servants whose master had given them varying amounts of talents. I knew I had to find something to do.

I didn't see Cherry until I reached the boardwalk that ran parallel to the street. I almost collided with her. She stood motionless, staring at me, her face so white I thought she was deathly sick and was going to faint.

I said, "Good morning, Cherry."

She pointed to the Martin house with a trembling finger. "Jim, you . . . you didn't come out of there, did you?"

She knew damned well I did. She couldn't

have helped seeing me walk down the path. I was just plain sore because she was so quick to condemn me for something she didn't approve of when she had postponed marrying me as long as she had.

"You bet I came out of there," I said, my tone sharp. "Those women are my friends."

She jerked my ring off her finger and shoved it into my hand. "I never want to lay eyes on you again," she said and, whirling, ran back the way she had come.

I suppose she had been headed for Frank's church and, being a little late, had come this way because it would save her a block or so. By walking fast, she had probably assured herself it wouldn't contaminate her.

I stood there staring after her, feeling quite satisfied now that it was over. Actually, it had been over for quite a while — maybe it had never really started. I knew one thing for sure: this was better than getting married and then having our marriage turn out a failure, as I was sure it would have done.

Cherry's holier-than-thou attitude toward whores had got to me before. I had a notion that for all of their sinning, Rosy and Flossie were better human beings than Cherry was.

Turning, I walked back into the house. I called, "Break out the champagne. My engagement is over. Finished. Done."

"Glory be," Rosy cried as she ran out of the kitchen. "That does call for champagne."

"It calls for a real celebration," Flossie said. "What do you want to do, Jim?"

"Oh, I don't know," I said. "Drink the champagne and then go home."

"I've got a better idea than that," Rosy said. "Let's go back to bed."

"Of course," Flossie said. "That's lots better than going back home. There's nobody waiting for you there."

That was exactly what we did.

The following Monday morning I saddled up and rode out to Fort D. A. Russell. I signed a contract that afternoon to cut and deliver two hundred cords of wood by November. The next morning I hired a crew. By noon we were on our way to the Black Hills.

CHAPTER XXXI

Even now I do not know any more than Pilate did exactly what truth is. I've read that the knowledge of truth comes from inside a man. If so, then this is the truth. If Cherry were telling the story, the events of the past year would be different. I mean, they would appear to be different to a third party. The same thing would be said if Nancy or Frank Rush were telling what had happened. I am convinced that no one can tell his life history and be completely objective.

I would not ask anyone to believe I was innocent of all wrongdoing. I have read and talked and listened about free will, yet I am not certain how much free will we have. On the other hand, I do not believe that all the events of our lives are planned before we are born, that we move through life as so many puppets while some great, unknown power pulls the strings. Perhaps we act from instinct, driven by some inner compelling power of which we are not fully aware.

Still, I am sure we make our own destiny. Only the foolish ask, "Why did this happen to me?" Only the foolish deny their responsibility for the fate that comes to them — good, bad or indifferent. So, inadvertently, I chose my destiny. It may seem strange, but if I were given the opportunity of living the months of September and October over, I would not do anything different than I did, even with the wisdom of hindsight.

Through the summer I worked as hard, probably harder, cutting and hauling wood to the fort, than any of my men. This being my first contract, I wanted to meet my deadline with time to spare. I was sure that a satisfactory performance would bring additional contracts. I always left my sorrel at the fort, so after I had pulled into the fort on Saturday afternoons with my load, I would unharness my team, saddle my sorrel, and ride into Cheyenne.

This was the routine I had followed every Saturday from the time I had started hauling wood early in the summer. In Cheyenne I would get my mail, take care of whatever items of business were pressing, and then heat water and bathe before I went to bed. I was always sweaty and dirty, and I always felt thoroughly gummed up by pitch, which seemed to cover my clothes like a suit of sticky armor.

We'd had some rain during the summer, but nothing like the gulley-washer that hit Cheyenne not long after dark the evening of the first Saturday in September. Lightning started flashing just about the time I put my sorrel away. I heated the water, as I did every Saturday, poured it into the washtub, which I had brought into the kitchen from the back porch, and added a couple of buckets of cold water. I undressed and tossed my pitch-stiffened clothes across the room, then stepped into the water and lathered my body, enjoying the muscle-relaxing heat of the water. That was when the storm hit.

I had known the storm was coming for an hour or more, judging by the black clouds that had rolled up over the Black Hills and then moved eastward, and the slashing lightning and booming thunder that I'd been hearing for the past hour. I was thankful that I was in for the night and had not been caught in the open with my team and load of wood, or in the saddle between Fort D. A. Russell and Cheyenne.

Not that I thought I was sugar or salt and would dissolve in the rain. It was just that it would have been damned uncomfortable —

that's all. I'd been out in storms like this one both in Colorado and Wyoming, and I avoided one every time I could.

It's not only getting wet. It's the wind and the sudden sharp drop in temperature, along with the searching fingers of lightning, which act as if they are actually trying to touch a man and fry him to death. I've had lightning hit trees very close to me, suddenly, without warning, giving the impression of an exploding shell. It is, to say the least, mighty damn scarey.

When I stepped out of the tub and started toweling myself dry, I saw a flash through a kitchen window that must have hit very close. Immediately after, I heard the jarring blast of thunder that rocked the house. A moment later the back door opened and Nancy Rush stepped into the kitchen. She shut the door and leaned against it; then she closed her eyes and seemed to freeze there.

Never in my life have I seen a more thoroughly soaked person than Nancy, or one who had a more woebegone expression on her face. Water ran down her cheeks, strands of wet hair were plastered against her forehead, her dress clung to her body, and she was shivering violently. More than that, she was scared. I wasn't sure whether she was shivering from fear or the cold.

For a moment I stood motionless, staring at her, as completely surprised as I ever had been in my life. She looked at me, but I had the feeling she didn't really see me or know that I was absolutely naked.

She tried to say something and couldn't, and then closed her mouth. She was breathing hard. I suppose she had been running, but I don't think her failure to speak was due to being out of breath. I guessed that a combination of the cold downpour along with that close flash of lightning had completely unnerved her.

I came out of it in a moment. I threw the towel down and ran to her. "Get over to the fire," I said. "You've got to take your clothes off. Come on, I'll help you."

Water ran down her legs and off her shoes onto the floor. She wiped her face with her wet hands, and this time when she tried to speak, she said in a tone that was barely audible, "I got caught."

"You sure did," I said.

I took her hands and led her to the stove. I ran into the bedroom and returned with a clean towel. She was trying to unbutton her dress, but she was still shivering so much that her fingers were all thumbs and refused to obey her mental commands. There was no doubt about her being caught in the storm, but why she had started out in the first place was the part I wondered about.

"Let me do it," I said, and handed the towel to her.

She dried her hands and face and wiped her hair with the towel while I unbuttoned her dress. My fingers weren't much better than hers, and she must have been carrying ten gallons of water that had been soaked in by her dress and petticoats and long drawers. Somehow I got all her clothes off her chilled body, then rubbed her with the towel until her skin was pink.

She was still shivering when I pulled a couple of chairs up to the stove. I wrung as much water as I could from her clothes, then hung them over the chairs to dry. I took one of her hands and led her into the bedroom. She went willingly and without protest.

I threw back the blankets and helped her into bed. As soon as she lay down, I got into bed beside her and pulled the blankets over us. I put my arms around her and drew her to me and held her against my warm body. It must have been at least ten minutes before she quit shivering.

"I take long walks every evening," she said. "Sometimes in the middle of the day, too. When I left home this evening, the clouds didn't look so bad. It was warm then. Real pleasant. As soon as I realized the storm was coming, I started to run, but the rain caught me and then the lightning struck. Just a block or two north of here, I think. I was so scared I couldn't keep running, so I came in here."

She giggled and I knew she was feeling all right again. "Excuse me for bursting in on you when you were taking a bath. I didn't intend to embarrass you."

"You didn't," I told her. "As a matter of fact, I've spent a good deal of time daydreaming about a situation like this, but I never expected it to be anything more than a daydream. Now you're here in my arms, I'm not so sure about that. Maybe I really did expect it to happen."

"Oh Jim, I know, I know," she said. "I tried to keep it from happening, but I knew it would. Someway, somehow."

Then she kissed me and the door swung open for us. It was an experience I cannot describe any more than I can describe a brilliantly colored sunset to a man who has been born blind. I have known of only a few human experiences that are beyond words. This was one, the spirit soaring to the mountain top, the total feeling far greater than any human being could experience from his five senses.

It has been said that when all conditions are right, the physical level of feeling transcends the usual mundane experience of life and becomes spiritual, that in reality the physical and spiritual are very close and all of life is one.

Some of the great lovers of the ages have discovered this. If they were poets, they have recorded it, saying in effect that only stupid people divide life into separate categories and contend that they always remain separate. If a person is filled with nothing but lust, or has a compelling appetite for food and drink, or is driven by an insensate hunger for power, this might be true. It was not true of either of us. We didn't lie there and exchange sentimental words of love, but the love was there. We both knew it without the words.

Nancy slept for a few minutes. I held her in my arms all the time she was in bed with me, thinking how I had hated men who took other men's wives. It had been a foolish judgment, because I had not understood how it could happen without guilt, without blame. Now, with her warm flesh close to mine, I knew what Frank would think if he ever found out. Still, I felt no guilt. If he had truly and properly loved her, she would not have been in bed with me.

She woke with a start and threw the blankets back with a violent gesture. She sat up, looking around and breathing hard. I said, "You're all right, Nancy. You're safe and you are loved."

She took a long breath and said in a tone of wonder, "Why, it is true, Jim. I thought for a few seconds I had been dreaming again."

"It really happened," I said.

"I've got to go," she said. "I want to get home before Frank does."

"It's raining," I said, "and your clothes are probably still damp."

"It's not raining so hard now," she said, "and I won't be in my wet clothes very long."

She got out of bed and ran into the kitchen. She started to dress. I followed her and stood in the doorway watching her, not wanting her to go but knowing it would be wrong to try to keep her. I wondered if she would ever come back, and again I knew it would be wrong to urge her, that it was a decision she had to make.

She smiled as she slipped on her dress. She said, "Thank you, Jim. I'll sleep tonight. I haven't slept well for a long time. It is something Frank has never understood. I have tried to explain it to him, but he won't listen. I don't try any more."

My fists were clenched so tightly the nails pressed into the flesh of my palms. It was hard for me to breathe. I felt as a man must feel who has had a very brief glimpse of Paradise and then sees the curtain pulled together in front of him, cutting off the view.

I asked, "Where is Frank?"

"Calling on the sick," she said bitterly, "or just visiting members of his flock. He has time for them even though he may not have time for his wife. He has become a successful minister and there are many who love him."

"Divorce him, Nancy. Marry me."

Right or wrong, the words came out of me in a kind of desperate cry. I could not let her go, so I tried to keep her. She shook her head at me, smiling again, the bitterness gone from her. "I can't, Jim. It's something else he could never understand. It would destroy him. I just can't do it."

She walked to the door, put her hand on the knob, then turned to me. "You are my love," she said. "I'll be back."

"Saturday night?"

She nodded. "Next Saturday night."

She left, closing the door behind her. I

looked at the wet spots on the floor where she had stood when she had first come in. The puddles the rain had made had not dried up, but they would soon be gone. They could not last, and I knew, too, with deep regret, that this new relationship with Nancy could not last either.

Chapter XXXII

Nancy kept her promise and came to my house every Saturday night through September and October, but she seldom stayed very long. She would usually sleep a little while and then lie in my arms for a few more minutes. After that she would get up and dress and hurry home, saying she did not want Frank to come back to the house and find her gone.

We never talked about ourselves and the future. I had a strange feeling of unreality during those weeks. I wanted it to last through eternity, but my rational mind kept reminding me that it was the most futile of hopes, that each Saturday night might be the last one.

After she left, I would continue to feel her presence. I would sit by the stove and smoke and think of her, of all that had happened while she had been with me, of every word she had spoken, and then how transient this relationship was.

She would never be my wife no matter how much I wanted it to be that way. I knew this with the same certainty that I knew the sun would come up in the morning. I accepted each Saturday for what it was — a few minutes, an hour or two — and I accepted the inevitability of the fact that soon I would have only memories.

It was not until the middle of October that Nancy stayed most of the night with me. We got out of bed near midnight and I built up the fire and made a pot of coffee. We drank and I smoked, and I looked at Nancy with the heart-sinking feeling that this might be the last time she would be here. I don't know why the feeling was so strong that night, unless it was the fact that our relationship had lasted longer than I had thought it would and I could not believe it would continue much longer.

We sat in silence for a long time, and then I burst out, for no reason except that I wanted her to know, "Nancy, do you know how much I love you?"

"Yes." She put her coffee cup down on the table and reached out and took my hand. "Do you know how much I love you and how long it has been?"

"I know how long," I answered. "From

that first evening when Frank had me to supper and you cooked a good dinner over the fire in front of your tent."

She nodded. "Except that through all of that evening and all the other times I have seen you I resolved not to let my love overcome my honor. I married Frank for better or for worse. I had every intention of keeping my marriage vows. I would have succeeded if I hadn't been caught in the storm that night."

I got up and walked to the stove, not as sure of that as she was. For some reason I had a crazy notion that what had happened was inevitable, that if the storm hadn't brought us together, something else would. I lifted a lid and knocked my pipe out and replaced the lid. Then I said, "Nancy, I have always condemned men who slept with other men's wives. To me they had no honor, but it was a judgment I should never have made."

"Don't have any guilty feelings," she said quickly. "I owe you an explanation."

"You don't owe me anything," I said, "and I don't have any sense of guilt. Even if I had a choice and could live these last six weeks over, I wouldn't change anything we have done. It's just that when I consider how I used to feel I get pretty damned humble. I guess it bears out what the Bible says about not judging."

"Yes, I guess it does," she said. "Anyhow, I want to tell you one thing about Frank. I loved him very much when we were married even though I wasn't interested in being a preacher's wife. I was willing to try and I did the best I could. No matter how hard I tried, I was constantly criticized for doing too much or not doing enough or wearing the wrong dress or flirting with one of the men of the church when I hadn't done anything more than to say good morning."

She poured another cup of coffee and sipped it for a moment. "I think I could have stood that if everything had been right between me and Frank. I have never understood why he feels the way he does about a man's and woman's physical love. He never comes to me until he has to just for enough relief to go to sleep . . . It's always over in about ten seconds — then he goes to sleep. That's why I told you the first night I was here that I could sleep. It was the first time since I married Frank, and it's why I take the long walks I do — but walking doesn't do any good. Frank believes it is wrong unless we do it to have children. It's immoral. It's . . . it's surrendering to the flesh and the devil. Well, I've given up any hope of having children."

She sat staring at her coffee, tears running down her cheeks. She asked in a low tone, "Why does he feel that way, Jim? Why?"

"I don't know," I said, "except that it is an old teaching which is part of the Christian dogma. It was Adam's and Eve's original sin in the Garden of Eden, they say, a carnal sin that comes from man's lower nature. I say it is a false doctrine. I don't believe they sinned and I don't believe we have sinned."

"Neither do I," she said, "but I do know we can't keep on. It's got to the place where I'm afraid to look at Frank for fear he'll guess about us. If I continue to come here, he'll find out sooner or later."

"I've asked you to divorce him," I said. "I'll tell him if you want me to."

"No, Jim," she said. "I can't do it."

We were silent again for a while. Then I remembered a question I had been wanting to ask her and just never thought of it when I had a chance. "Why did you tell me not to marry Cherry?"

"She's too tight-lipped. She won't make any man a good wife." Then Nancy laughed. "Well, it was more than that. I was jealous. I didn't want you to marry anyone else."

"But if I can't marry you . . ." I began.

366

"I'm just a dog in the manger," she said, "and I hate myself for being that way."

Later, as she was getting ready to go home, she told me that Frank was sitting up with Grandma Carruthers. The old lady had been one of the most steadfast members of Frank's flock. For a month or more she had been bedfast; then about a week ago she had taken a turn for the worse. She couldn't die and she couldn't get well, and she had to have someone to take care of her all the time. Her daughter, with whom she lived, was completely worn out, so Frank was taking the nights and Nancy spent part of each day with her.

"We can't go on much longer," Nancy said. "We just can't last. Frank has had very little sleep for a week." She stood by the door, her hand on the knob as she looked at me. "I love you, Jim. I love you very much and I can't live without you, but if I ruined Frank's life, I would feel guilty."

"You've got yourself to think of, too," I said.

She nodded. "I know, and I've got you to think of. I can't forget that. I should never have let it start."

"No," I said, remembering my thoughts about the memories. "What we've had has been good. It can't be taken from us no matter what happens now."

"I've thought about that," she said, "but in my saner moments I know I've got to make a decision." She stopped, biting her lower lip, then added, "Jim, I don't know how I could go through a week if I didn't have Saturday night to look forward to, but I can't keep coming, either."

She opened the door and left the house. I stood there for a time before I went back to bed, thinking about it. I told myself again that she was the one to make the decision. If she decided not to come here again, I would sell my property and leave Cheyenne.

I could not stay here and know she was in the same town I was in and leave her alone. I would end up going to Frank and bullying him into divorcing her. She wouldn't like it, and if it ruined Frank, she might refuse to marry me. For the only time in my life I wished I had the gift of second sight. I just could not look ahead and see any solution to our problem.

I finished the wood contract on Thursday and spent Friday winding up the odds and ends such as paying off my men and promising them work the next contract I had. Besides that, I had letters to write and several business deals to explore, so I had plenty to do, but on Saturday I couldn't settle down. I fidgeted around all day, wondering if Nancy would come and what decision she had made.

Perhaps I was unduly fearful about it, but I had no real hope — that was all. I would not even try to force her to see it my way. If she came to me, it had to be of her own free will, accepting all the risks there were in making that decision.

She came not long after dark, bright-eyed and eager. As she took my hand and led me into the bedroom, she said, "Frank was home when I got back last Saturday, but he didn't suspect anything. I told him I couldn't go to sleep and had gone out walking. I've done it before, so he wasn't surprised."

The evening was so warm we lay on top of the blankets. She did not go to sleep, but stayed in my arms and pressed her body very hard against mine as she hugged me.

"I've decided, Jim," she said. "All of my married life I've thought of Frank and tried to do exactly what he wanted me to — at least until the night of the storm. I even took the rent money to you because he was too big a coward to face you. He was willing to live in your house, though. I kept thinking it would be better after the church was finished and he'd pay what he owed you, but he hasn't.

"Well, I've thought about it all week, about you saying I had you to think of. Myself, too. I'm going to Denver. I'll divorce Frank. I kept telling you I couldn't do it, but I know I can. I'll write to you and let you know how I'm getting along and where I'm staying if you want to see me."

"Of course I want to see you," I said. "You'll need some money."

"Oh, I'll work," she said. "I couldn't just sit still and do nothing."

"You'll still need money to get started," I said. "If you need more, or if you don't find a job, let me know. Money is one thing I have plenty of."

She sat up on the edge of the bed. "All right," she said. "Give me lots of money and I'll spend it. After we're married I'll spend all of your money."

"Now wait a minute. You don't need to go whole hog." I reached over and patted her stomach. "Have I told you lately what a beautiful body you have?"

"No, not lately," she answered. "You never tell me often enough."

"I'll do better in the future," I promised.

"I'd better get home," she said. "I don't want Frank to find me gone again. He had several calls to make, so he told me he'd be away two or three hours."

I got up and crossed the room to my bureau. I had quite a bit of money left after paying off my men. I opened the top drawer and picked up a roll of bills. I asked, "Will $500 be enough?"

She didn't answer. I heard her heavy breathing. I turned to ask her again, thinking she hadn't heard. I froze, dropping the money back into the drawer. Frank stood in the kitchen doorway, staring at me, his face dark with fury. Hate, too, I guess. I had never seen an expression on his face like the one I saw then.

He was not the Frank Rush I had known for more than a year. He was a madman. A gun in his right hand dangled at his side. I knew he would use it.

"You bastard," he said. "I'm going to kill you."

Nancy was putting on her clothes as fast as she could. I don't think Frank saw her. Maybe he didn't even know she was in the room. I couldn't think of anything I could do except distract him. Then maybe Nancy would be able to slip out of the house. She could go for help. At least she could save her own life.

"You're a sick man, Frank," I said. "Let

me have the gun. Then you come and lie down."

I started walking toward him, one hand extended. He backed into the kitchen. "Don't come any closer," he said. "I'm sick all right. You made me sick. You're a great man in Cheyenne, and all the time you've been committing adultery with my wife. You've bought her. You've got money and property and you contract wood for the army. I trusted you and you steal my wife."

He was in the kitchen now. I saw Nancy slip around the bed to a window and ease up the lower sash. Frank couldn't see her from where he stood, about halfway between the back door and the door into the bedroom. She'd get away.

I took another step toward him, my hand still extended. Then I knew from the expression on his face, the sudden tightening of his lips against his teeth, that nothing could save me. He was ready to pull the trigger.

Still, I had to try. At least I could buy a little more time so Nancy could get farther away from the house. I said, "Give me the gun, Frank. Yon don't want them to hang you."

He fired. I seem to remember a burst of flame, the roar of the gun, and I reeled back, trying to stay upright and knowing I couldn't. I thought he had killed me, that he had blown off the top of my head.

I had a weird feeling I was in two worlds. I was falling as I tried to hold to this world and at the same time I was reaching into another with the other hand. Then there was nothing but blackness.

Chapter XXXIII

Paul Lerner laid the manuscript down. He leaned back in his chair and closed his eyes, thinking it was a strange place for Jim Glenn to end his story. There was much that Glenn had left unsaid. Perhaps that was the reason he had asked Lerner to see Cherry Owens Lind, Nancy Rush and Frank Rush. He would start with Cherry in the morning, he told himself as he rose and went downstairs for supper.

He ate an early breakfast the following morning, then walked to Stead's Livery Stable and rented a rig. He wondered if this Stead was the Bronco Stead that Jim Glenn had mentioned. He didn't ask because Glenn had not said for him to talk to Stead. The less attention he attracted the better.

"Do you know Cherry Lind?" Lerner asked the hostler. "I believe she lives up Crow Creek about five miles from town."

"Mrs. Lind?" the hostler said. "Sure, I

know her. She always leaves her horse here when she comes to town. She lives on the CO ranch. It's marked. You won't have any trouble finding it."

Lerner thanked him and drove away. He took the Crow Creek road out of town, wondering what Cherry Lind would be like. From Jim Glenn's journal he had a clear picture of the three people he was to see, and he could not keep from wondering how true the picture was. He was sure he would not like Cherry and he was equally sure he would like Nancy Rush. Frank was a question mark. It would depend on what the years in prison had done to the man.

It was still early in the morning when he saw an arch across a lane that turned off the road to the right, the big black letters CO showing up clearly at the top of the arch. The buildings were about a quarter of a mile from the road. Lerner studied them carefully as he approached them.

The ranch had the look of a working spread, with its pole corrals and sprawling log barn and slab sheds. Still, it was not like most of the ranches he had seen in Wyoming and Colorado, which had been built strictly for utility and were lived on only by men. A woman's touch was evident in the washing on the line, the grass and flowers inside the fence that surrounded the house, and the white lace curtains at the windows.

He pulled up in front of the house, wrapped the lines around the brake handle and stepped down. As he turned toward the gate, a man yelled, "Hold it."

Lerner stopped, one hand on the gate. The man who strode toward him was more boy than man, probably seventeen or eighteen. He had the long-legged look of a boy who had shot up fast the last year or so, his muscles not having caught up yet with his bones.

"What do you want?" the boy asked.

"I'm Paul Lerner from Denver," Lerner said. "I drove out here to see Mrs. Lind."

"You still haven't said what you want," the boy said impatiently.

"I'm a reporter," Lerner said. "I want to interview her."

"Oh hell," the boy said scornfully. "Now why would you want to interview her? She's just another ranch woman. You can find a hundred of 'em hereabouts."

Lerner hesitated, wondering if the boy was her son. If so, how much would he know about Jim Glenn and his mother's relationship with Glenn. If he did know, his reaction might not be favorable.

"She was one of the early settlers in

Cheyenne," Lerner said carefully. "I understand she ran a restaurant when it was hell
on wheels. I want to talk to her about her
experiences."

The boy scratched an ear, glanced at the
house, then back at Lerner. "I dunno," he
said dubiously. "She's not much on talking
about those times. Besides, she's busy, this
being wash day and all."

Lerner opened the gate. "I can ask her,"
he said.

"I'll call her," the boy said.

He strode past Lerner, stepped up on the
porch and pulled the screen open. He
yelled, "Ma." For a moment there was no
answer. The boy went into the house and
Lerner followed, taking off his hat and
remaining near the door.

The room was furnished with a black
leather couch, one leather chair, several
rockers, and a claw-footed oak stand in the
center of the room. A number of magazines
and catalogs were piled neatly on top of the
stand.

A rag carpet covered the floor. There was
no fireplace. Instead, Lerner noted the big
heater, which would be adequate in the
coldest winter weather. The wallpaper had a
pattern of small red roses against a silver
background. A pronghorn rack hung near

the door. Everything, Lerner saw, was spotlessly clean.

The boy started toward the kitchen, then stopped beside the stand as his mother came into the room. She looked at Lerner, then at the boy, and said, "Well?" Her tone was not a friendly one, and Lerner sensed that he would learn very little from her.

At least he was seeing Cherry Owens Lind. He recalled Glenn's description of her: bright blue eyes, gold-yellow hair with touches of red, and a small enough body for her to be called Watch Fob and Trinket. The description fitted her now as well as it had more than twenty years ago, even to her hair, which was brushed back from her forehead and pinned in a bun at the back of her head.

The only difference would be in the lines in her face. They seemed particularly deep around her eyes. Then he saw that her lips were thin and pressed tightly together. He was reminded of what Nancy Rush had said about Cherry not making a good wife for Glenn.

"This fellow is from Denver," the boy was saying. "He's a reporter. His name's Paul Lerner. He wants to interview you about the early days in Cheyenne when it was hell on wheels."

"I don't remember a thing about those days," she said sharply. "Good day, sir."

She whirled toward the kitchen door, her skirt whipping away from her trim ankles. "Wait," Lerner said. "Jim Glenn asked me to talk to you."

She whirled back to face him, her lips parting, plainly surprised to hear him say that. "Why on earth would Jim ask you to talk to me?" she demanded.

"He's written a journal about the first fifteen months he lived in Cheyenne," Lerner said. "About his early years, too. I suppose an autobiography would be a better word. Anyhow, he asked me to talk to you of the events he tells about. I think he wanted this interview to be checked for authenticity against what he wrote."

She opened her mouth, then closed it without saying a word. Her eyes moved to the boy, who had backed to the front door and now stood motionless, listening. She said sharply, "Bud, did you finish the chores?"

"No, I saw this fellow drive up —"

"All right," his mother said. "You saw him and you brought him in. Now go finish the chores."

He hesitated, not wanting to leave, but after a few seconds he reluctantly turned and walked away.

She waited until the boy left, then asked, "Why did Jim write all of this? Is he trying to justify himself for his affair with the Rush woman?"

"No," Lerner said. "I would not attempt to say what his motives were, except that he feels other people can learn from his mistakes?"

"They should," she said tartly. "He made enough."

"I would guess there is another reason," Lerner went on, "one that is common to many men. All of us have a desire to be immortal. Leaving a book that survives after a man's death is one way to achieve immortality."

"I see," she said with cold contempt. "Yes, Jim Glenn would want to be immortal. I suppose he didn't have anything to say that was complimentary about me."

"On the contrary," Lerner told her. "He had many complimentary things to say about you."

"You're lying," she said. "Have you seen the Rush woman?"

"No, but I will."

"Have you seen Frank Rush, who put Jim in his wheelchair?"

"No, but I plan to see him too."

"You do that," she said. "They'll have plenty to tell you. I have nothing to say."

"But Mrs. Lind —"

"Good day, sir," she said.

Turning, she disappeared through the door. She was still quick-moving, just as Glenn had said she was when she had her restaurant. She had kept her figure too, he saw, her waist so tiny that a man could almost encircle it with his hands.

This time Lerner did not attempt to call her back. There was nothing to do but leave the house, get into the rig, and drive back to Cheyenne. He told himself that Jim Glenn had foreseen how Cherry Owens Lind would perform. She had not mellowed with age. As a matter of fact, he guessed she was more determined, more dominating, more certain of her judgments than she had been as a young woman.

It struck Lerner as interesting that she had not wanted to recall the events that Glenn had related. He decided that the lines around her eyes were evidence of discontent. She had not, he thought, lived a happy life. She probably could not keep from wondering what her life would have been if she had married Jim Glenn.

Thinking about his short interview with her, it occurred to Lerner that she had not asked him to stay for dinner. She had not asked if he would like a cup of coffee. She had not even asked him to sit down. She had not inquired about Jim Glenn, either, although Lerner was sure she had not seen him for years.

Lerner would have to write an epilogue to Glenn's book. Glenn, of course, had known that. Lerner doubted that he had expected Cherry Lind to tell anything new or different, or add to what he had written. He simply wanted Lerner to see her, to get an impression of her.

Well, he had the impression all right, he told himself with wry amusement. His impression was that Cherry was an unhappy and unfriendly person, and Glenn had been lucky not to marry her. This, he realized, was exactly the impression he'd had of her after reading what Glenn had written.

Chapter XXXIV

Lerner returned the rig to the livery stable before noon, ate dinner at his hotel, and walked to Nancy Rush's place on the corner of 16th and Russell. Everything was exactly as he had expected it to be: the white frame house, the picket fence, also painted white, the green lawn and flowers growing close to the front of the house, and the window box with the red geraniums.

As he stepped up on the porch and gave the bell-pull a tug, he pondered something he thought he had discovered. He was convinced that few people change over the years. Given a certain combination of dispositions, ambitions and attitudes, a young person would be the same kind of person in middle life and old age, at least until senility set in.

He mentally admitted that a great traumatic experience, through some strange inner alchemy, might transform a man or woman and give him or her a new direction, but he considered it unlikely to happen. His theory had held up with Cherry Lind. Now he sensed a warmth, a loving care that Nancy Rush gave her home. That, too, was a feeling he had expected to have.

She opened the door and looked at him questioningly. He said, "I'm Paul Lerner. I'm a Denver reporter. Jim Glenn asked me to talk to you."

"Of course," she said. "I should have guessed. I knew you were coming." She held the screen open. "Come in."

He stepped inside and she let the screen close behind him. She shut the door, then motioned to a hat rack on the wall. "Hang your hat up and come on back. I'm busy this afternoon so we'll talk while I work."

He hung his hat on the rack and followed her along the hall to a room that held a cutting table, a dressmaker's dummy, a sewing machine, two chairs, remnants of several pieces of dress goods, and an unfinished red-velvet gown that had been draped across the cutting table.

"This is the working part of the house," she said. "I hope you don't mind visiting in this room."

"Of course not," he said.

"As a matter of fact, I seldom use the

384

parlor," she said. "I spend most of my time in this room, partly because I like to work, but mostly because the parlor is too stiff and formal for me. Sit down." She motioned to a rocking chair. "Go ahead and smoke if you want to. Oh, can I get you a cup of coffee? I have a pot on the stove."

"No, I just got up from dinner," he said as he sat down. He drew a cigar from his pocket and bit off the end. "As you seem to know, Jim Glenn wrote to the editor of the *Rocky Mountain News.* As a result I was sent here. I talked to Mr. Glenn yesterday and he gave me the manuscript of an autobiography he has —"

"I know," she interrupted. "I've read it. Jim wanted you to talk to me about what happened during those first fifteen months he lived in Cheyenne when I knew him. I am not familiar with all the events he relates, but I know about many of them, and I can assure you that, to the best of my knowledge, everything he has written is true."

Lerner watched her as she talked, and he told himself that again his theory was right. Nancy Rush was in her middle forties, but she was still a very attractive woman, with only a trace of gray in her black hair. She had kept her figure, although not as perfectly as Cherry Lind had. She had the same high, proud breasts that Glenn had mentioned, the same nicely proportioned ankles, but the years and perhaps her hours of sitting as she worked on dresses had given her a spread across her buttocks that she probably had not had when Glenn first knew her.

The fault was a minor one. Lerner could understand why Glenn had called her a slim and shining girl. Now she was no longer a girl, but a mature woman, and there was still an air of excitement about her. He saw, too, the self-possessed curve of her lips, and he sensed the outgoing warmth that he was sure Glenn had felt. Cherry Lind had been embittered by life; Nancy Rush had not, and that, Lerner told himself, was a part of the difference between the two women.

Nancy had taken a chair near the cutting table. Now she picked up her needle and thread, replaced her thimble, drew the velvet gown off the cutting table, and began to sew. Lerner watched her for a moment, then said, "If you've read what Mr. Glenn wrote, you know he didn't finish his book. I'll have to, but before I can do it, you'll have to tell me what happened. I'm curious, too, why he didn't finish it."

"He got too sick," she answered. "He intended to finish it. He worked very hard on it the last two years, writing and rewriting and of course trying to recall the events he relates. Recalling some of his feelings, too, which I believe is even harder than recalling events. He was a very busy man up until about two years ago. He bought and sold Cheyenne property and he continued to do a great deal of business with the army.

"He was always fortunate in finding good men to work for him, and he had a great talent for instilling a sense of loyalty in them. He began to fail two years ago. That was when he decided to write this journal or whatever you call it. He should have started sooner. A few weeks ago he told me he couldn't finish it. Just didn't have the strength to hold on to his pencil and paper. Besides that, he said his mind was getting fuzzy.

"That was why he wrote to Alex Dolan, the *News* editor. He had to have help from a qualified person, he said, or the book would never be published. He wanted it published, Mr. Lerner. It's the one thing he wanted above all others. A great deal depends upon you."

"I appreciate that now," Lerner said. "I

didn't when I talked to Dolan in Denver. I saw Mrs. Lind this morning and she asked me why he wrote his autobiography. I said he told me he hoped people would profit from his mistakes, and also that he may have chosen this way to reach for immortality. I told her it was common to all men in one way or another."

"You are very discerning, Mr. Lerner," Nancy said. "That's exactly right. He wanted a wife and children as a young man. Having children, of course, is the way most people seek immortality, but after he was shot he couldn't have children, so he wrote a book."

She sewed for a moment, then looked up and asked cautiously, "How was Cherry?"

"It seemed to me she was unhappy," he answered. "She wouldn't tell me anything."

"I didn't think she would," Nancy said. "Jim didn't think so either, but he wanted you to try. You see — and God forgive me because I'm making a judgment that perhaps I shouldn't make — I firmly believe she would never have accepted Jim's ring in the first place if he hadn't had money and she thought she could get her hands on it by marrying him. She had to have a husband she could control and she knew Jim was a strong man, one she could not control. I think that was why she put off marrying him."

She bit her lower lip and was silent for a time. Then she went on. "As you probably gathered from reading Jim's book, I didn't like Cherry. Part of it was because I was jealous of her, and it was also because I sensed there was this side of her that escaped Jim. She couldn't give or bend. She had to dominate. Life with her would have been hell for Jim. He would never bow to any woman.

"Anyhow, after Ed Burke left her that money she didn't need Jim. She would have found some excuse to have broken the engagement even if she hadn't seen him come out of the Martin house that morning. She ran the restaurant for several more months, then she sold it and bought the CO on Crow Creek. She married one of the cowboys, made him her foreman, and five years later he was dead. She never married again."

He had been rolling the cigar between his finger tips. Now he lighted it. When Nancy stopped talking, he said, "Well, let's go back to what happened the night Jim was shot."

She glanced at him, her expression grave, then went on with her sewing. She said, "You must understand, Mr. Lerner, that I am a bad woman, a woman of loose morals. I betrayed my husband by sleeping with another man. Most people in Cheyenne have forgotten it or never heard the story, but at the time I was the scarlet woman and it would have been very easy for me to have joined the sisterhood on Eighteenth Street. But I knew enough about their lives to be sure I couldn't live that way. I nearly starved, though, before Jim was well enough to be concerned about me and to send for me.

"He gave me money to live on and later he deeded this house to me. I have always enjoyed sewing and I'm quite good at it. In time, I was able to start a dressmaking business. I've made a living over the years and I'll continue to make one, I think. Jim will leave me something, but I won't get much aside from the trust fund he set up for me, which will be administered by one of the local banks."

She did not, Lerner thought, want to answer his question, but it had to be answered if he was to write the epilogue to Glenn's book, and she was the only one who could answer it. He said, "Now about that evening Glenn was shot."

She glanced up again, smiling. "I know. You can't talk to Jim again. You probably haven't heard, but he slipped into a coma this morning. He won't live much longer — a matter of hours, I think. I hope he goes soon. He had always been such a strong man. It's been hard to see him go downhill the way he has the last two years. Up until then he had retained his strength, even though he was held to his wheelchair.

"He saw lots of people and he kept on making money. As I told you, he was involved in a good many business deals and he enjoyed them. He gave much of his money away. You know his father's saying about the sun on the wall. Well, Jim had a feeling he wasn't going to live a long life and he had to be doing whatever he was going to do. Giving money away was something from which he gained great satisfaction, but he was always careful about it. He never gave money to anything or anybody until he had looked into the situation carefully."

Lerner pulled gently on his cigar, waiting patiently until she finished. Then he tried again. "Mrs. Rush, would you tell me —"

"Yes, I will because I'm the only one who can and you have to know," she said. "I'm like everyone, I guess. I put off doing what I don't want to do. This is a painful memory and I don't like to bring it back into my mind. Perhaps it's the real reason Jim didn't finish his book. It was painful to him, too. When you're doing something which you know isn't right and then you're caught at it, the experience is hell.

"Jim and I loved each other and kept on loving each other right up to the moment he lost consciousness. I've told him many times that I would marry him. I started telling him as soon as I had my divorce, which wasn't long after Frank went to prison, but he wouldn't have me. He kept telling me to find another man. I could never convince him that I didn't want any other man. All I wanted to do was to take care of him, but he didn't want me to do that, so I've been able to visit him and that was all."

This time when she stopped Lerner said nothing. He waited, and presently she said, "There is only one thing I would say in criticism of Jim's book. He doesn't give himself enough credit. For instance, he had great physical courage, like the time in the Head Quarters Saloon when the man was going to knife Frank. Jim saved Frank's life at the risk of his own, because the crowd was hostile and it's a miracle those men didn't turn on him and kill him."

She paused again and for a moment he thought she was going to cry, but she went on, her tone firm. "It was the same the night

Frank caught us. I was sitting on the edge of the bed just starting to put my clothes on when I heard something in the kitchen. We usually locked the doors and I don't know why we didn't that night. I looked up and there was Frank with the gun in his hand.

"My heart just quit beating. I thought he was going to kill both of us right then. As soon as I could begin to think straight, I put my clothes on. Jim started talking to Frank, who backed into the kitchen, and I got out through the window. I ran for help. I heard two shots. I came back with a policeman and a doctor.

"Jim was lying on the floor with blood on his forehead. I thought he was dead. Frank just stood there as if he was frozen, still holding the gun in his hand. We lifted Jim to the bed and the doctor saw that one bullet had grazed his head and knocked him out. I don't know how the second bullet could have hit him the way it did, but it struck his spine and that's what has paralyzed him all this time. I don't know what Frank was aiming at, but maybe Jim was turning and falling when that bullet hit him.

"Well, a few people blamed Jim and said Frank had a right by the unwritten law to do what he did, but most folks didn't agree. Jim was better known and better liked than he realized, and the feeling was very strong against Frank. There was even some talk of lynching. When Frank was being tried, Jim insisted that he be carried into the court-room on a stretcher. He wasn't able to be in his wheelchair yet. He asked that Frank be found not guilty, that he did what any man would have done under those circum-stances, but that didn't change the jury's mind. They found Frank guilty and sent him to prison for a long term."

Again she was close to crying when she finished. Lerner waited for a time, and when he saw she was finished talking, he rose. "Thank you, Mrs. Rush. If I'm still in Cheyenne when the funeral's held, would you like for me to go with you?"

She glanced up and nodded. She said in a low tone, "Yes, that would be nice. I'll have to go alone if you don't come for me. You know, I won't even be able to help with the funeral arrangements. Ron Ballard and Ella Evans will do that. They have always been very honest in disliking me."

She went to the door with him. As they walked along the hall, she asked, "Have you talked to Frank?"

"I'll see him tomorrow."

"He's not in prison," she said, "but I think he's still in Laramie. They can tell you at the prison where he is."

Lerner paused in the doorway. "Is there anything in the book you don't want published? Or in what you've told me?"

She shook her head. "No, nothing can hurt me now. Besides, it's all in the record. There's no use for me to deny anything even if I wanted to."

"I'll see you again before I leave Cheyenne," he said.

He walked away, thinking that she had been a lonely woman and would be even more lonely now that Jim Glenn was dead or soon would be. Life had been unjust to her, and yet it had not made her bitter.

Again his theory had proved correct. He had found her to be the kind of woman Jim Glenn had made her out to be. With any kind of luck, her sin, if that was what it had been, would never have become public knowledge. The strange part of the whole business was that Jim Glenn's image in the community had not been tarnished, whereas Nancy had become, as she had said, the scarlet woman, and it would never really change as long as she lived here.

Chapter XXXV

Lerner took a morning train to Laramie. As the train rolled across the summit of Sherman Hill, he thought of what Glenn had written about that hard winter of 1867–8 when there had been so much snow here that construction had been stopped and the crews had wintered in Cheyenne. He thought, too, of the hunger for profit, and how the survey crews had been sent on west in the dead of winter and the construction crews had been ordered out when the ground was still frozen too hard to be worked by pick and shovel.

The profit motive, Lerner reflected, was still one of the most powerful of all human drives, and human nature had certainly not changed during the years that had followed the building of the Union Pacific. But whatever motives had driven the men who built the transcontinental railroad, the actual physical labor of laying the rails still seemed a tremendous accomplishment twenty years after it was done.

One question had been cleared up by Glenn. Previously Lerner had read everything he could lay his hands on about the Vigilance Committees, for a book he hoped to write. He had suspected that there had been some thread connecting the Cheyenne Vigilantes with the earlier organizations in the Montana gold fields and in Denver.

Now he realized that there could be no such connection unless the man Glenn knew as Jess Munro had been in Denver or the Montana mining country and had helped organize those committees as well as the one in Cheyenne. Lerner would never have an answer to that question, but it seemed possible that Munro was involved with all three, particularly since he had admitted having experience with other Vigilance Committees.

Lerner arrived in Laramie before noon. He ate dinner, then hired a cab to take him to the prison. When he arrived he was told that Frank Rush had served his term and had been released several years before, but that he still returned to the prison once a week to work with some of the convicts.

"He's a good man," the official said. "He's done a great deal for several of our prisoners. He's an excellent carpenter. If you're going to give him work, he'll do a good job for you."

"No, I just want to talk to him." Lerner hesitated, then said cautiously, "Jim Glenn asked me to talk to him."

"Glenn?" The official was shocked. "He's the man who was sleeping with Frank's wife, wasn't he? Hell, I don't see why Frank didn't kill the bastard."

"I believe he tried," Lerner said.

"Well, he should have tried harder," the man said. "I consider it a miscarriage of justice, sending Frank here. Any man with red blood in his veins would have done exactly what he did. I'll tell you one thing. If I ever found my wife in bed getting screwed by some bastard like that Glenn fellow, I'd kill him. I can't understand a jury convicting Frank like they done."

That wasn't the way Frank Rush had found Glenn and Nancy when he had entered Glenn's house with his gun, but Lerner saw no purpose in arguing the point. It was evident that the man had a high regard for Frank Rush, and therefore saw the incident from Frank's point of view.

"Could you give me Rush's address?"

"Sure, but when you mention Jim Glenn, Frank will kick your ass right through his front door." The man wrote the address down and handed it to Lerner. "He lives about a block from the depot. It's your funeral, mister."

Lerner thanked him and returned to the cab. The official's reaction was interesting to him and he wondered if his mental picture of Frank Rush would hold up as well as his picture of Cherry Lind and Nancy Rush had. After reading Jim Glenn's book, it seemed to Lerner that Rush had been a very impractical man who had put his career as a preacher above everything else.

The way Lerner looked at it, this was absurd. He had no sympathy for a man who did not have the practical sense to know that his wife should not have to live in a tent all winter. The way Glenn told it, that was the kind of man Rush had been. Still, he must also have been good-natured and kind, with the best of intentions. With Ed Burke, he had saved Glenn's life the night he had been attacked by Bully Bailey and his friends.

He seemed, then, a complex man who registered high on the scale of human values in some areas and very low in others. In trying to probe his own feelings about Frank Rush from what Glenn had written about him, it seemed to Lerner that he was basically a good man, certainly with more good traits than bad.

Perhaps he didn't have any really bad traits. He just had blind spots. The question, of course, was what had prison done to the blind spots. It occurred to Lerner that Rush must still have his good traits or he would not be going out to the prison to work with some of the prisoners.

When Lerner met him and shook hands with him, he was surprised first by Frank Rush's appearance. He could not have been over fifty-five, yet he appeared to be twenty years older. He was a large man, as Glenn had said, and he looked as if he had retained his strength, but he was stooped, his hair was completely white, and he talked very slowly, as if uncertain what the next word would be.

"I got your address from the prison," Lerner said. "I'd like to talk to you for a few minutes if you have the time to spare."

"Come in," Rush said. "I have plenty of time. I have eternity."

The house was a small one with a single bedroom, a kitchen, and a living room. No more. The outside needed paint, the yard had grown up in weeds, and dust on the furniture was so thick a person could print his initials on it. Rush was clean and his clothes were clean, but he had not shaved for several days, his white stubble adding to his appearance of age.

A moment later, after Lerner was seated in the only rocking chair in the living room, Rush said, "You may not know it, but at one time I was a minister. I started a church in Cheyenne. I had even put up a building and had an excellent congregation when a friend and my wife betrayed me. Perhaps you know that was the reason I went to prison."

"Yes, that's why I'm here to talk to you," Lerner said.

He sensed bitterness in the man and he knew then that in this case his theory had failed him. Frank Rush was a changed man from what he had been twenty years ago in Cheyenne. He'd had the traumatic experience that Lerner realized would or at least could change a person. Yet perhaps the theory hadn't failed after all — this was simply the exception that proved the rule.

Rush leaned forward, his big hands spread on his knees. "Just what do you want of me?"

Lerner remembered what the prison official had said and he sensed he could not tell Rush the full truth if he expected to get the man to talk. He said slowly, phrasing each sentence carefully, "I'm a reporter, as I told you when I introduced myself. The editor of the *Rocky Mountain News* is interested in historical incidents. You and your wife and Jim Glenn and Ed Burke and of course many others were among the first settlers in Cheyenne."

Rush nodded. "That's true. So you know about those people?"

"I've made myself familiar with the early history of Cheyenne," Lerner said. "What I want from you is an account of what happened the night you shot Jim Glenn. It may be a painful memory, but —"

"It is a painful memory," Rush interrupted, "but I'll be glad to tell you about it. I don't know what you can do with it. I hope you'll write it for the world to read and know what happened. I've always wanted an opportunity to talk to someone who would make the truth public. I realize now that I look at some things in a different light than I did at that time. You see, I had worked very hard to build up my congregation. As I saw my place in life, it was to help other people. I know now that the way I lived day by day was more important than anything I ever said from the pulpit on Sunday morning."

Lerner nodded agreement. "I'm sure

that's right."

"My wife had never been happy as a preacher's wife," Rush went on. "I should have known that she would not go on even pretending to be my wife, but I loved her and trusted her. I trusted Jim Glenn, too, although I did not see much of him after I quit working for him. You knew I had worked for him as a carpenter?"

"Yes, I know about that," Lerner said.

Rush stared at Lerner as if wondering how the reporter happened to know so much about him. Then he shrugged his muscular shoulders and hurried on. "At this particular time an old lady called Grandma Carruthers was dying. Both my wife and I sat up with her because she had lingered so long her relatives were worn out. The night she died I came home earlier than I had expected to. It was certainly earlier than my wife expected. She was gone when I got home and she did not come in until very late. She said she couldn't sleep, so she had taken a walk.

"Now this was reasonable, because she often had trouble sleeping and she did walk a great deal, but never so late at night. I knew something was going on from her expression. She had often seemed discontented and unhappy, even nervous — but not that night. She was the happiest I'd seen her for months. She was humming a tune when she came into the house — I don't remember what it was. She smiled at me and called a greeting as she went on back to her bedroom. It was such a reversal from the way she had been for so long that I couldn't understand her. I didn't even tell her that Grandma Carruthers had died. Not until the next morning.

"At first I didn't suspect what had happened, but my suspicion grew through the following week because she seemed anxious and impatient and asked me more than once what I was going to do Saturday night. For the first time in our married life I decided to spy on her. I told her I had several calls to make and I'd be gone for two or three hours. I hid outside and followed her when she left the house a few minutes later.

"She took the alley and went into Jim Glenn's house through the back door. I waited until I saw around the edge of the blind that there was a light in his bedroom. I slipped up to the window and found a narrow opening beside the blind, enough to see what they were doing. I could not believe what I saw. At first I was sick, because I loved Nancy and I respected Jim Glenn, but a moment later I realized I had been betrayed, and I became a madman.

"I went back home and found the pistol I had bought for my wife a few months before, when Cheyenne was a very tough town and I was worried about her safety. I returned to Glenn's house and slipped in through the back door. I crossed the kitchen and stood in the doorway and looked at them.

"They had finished what they were doing and were talking. Both of them were naked. When they saw me, my wife started to dress and Glenn came at me telling me to give him my gun. I backed into the kitchen. I found it hard to shoot a man I considered my friend, but he kept coming and then the truth swept over me.

"He had seduced my wife; he had destroyed my home. He was a thoroughly evil man who had given himself to the devil. I shot him twice, the second time as he was falling. I thought I had killed him. I stood staring at him, not believing this was real. It was a terrifying nightmare. Even now, after all these years, when I remember what happened there is a kind of nightmarish fog over it.

"My wife had got out of the house through a window and she came back later with a doctor and a policeman. I hadn't tried to escape. I was arrested. Glenn lived, as you probably know, and I was sent to prison. I was just an ordinary person, a preacher with a small congregation composed mostly of women — but Jim Glenn, you see, was a very important man.

"Glenn had money and property. He had been one of the leaders of the Vigilance Committee, which was common knowledge by that time, and he was doing a contract business with the army at Fort D. A. Russell. I didn't have a chance. I was found guilty and sentenced before the trial ever started. Maybe Glenn paid the jury to find me guilty. He had enough money that he could have done it. I have no proof that he did, but I still cannot understand how a jury could have found me guilty unless something like that was done."

Rush was silent for a moment, his brooding gaze fixed on the floor. He had taken a long time to tell his story, speaking as slowly as he did. Lerner said nothing, but sat watching the expression on Frank Rush's face, the way his hands gripped his knees, the tension that held him, the intensity of his feelings as he dredged his mind for the events that had happened on what had been a terrible night for him.

Again the thought came to Lerner that an act of this kind depends for interpretation upon the point from which anyone looks at it. To Rush there was no justice in the sentence that had been given him; to Glenn the bullet that had put him in a wheelchair was not deserved. Nancy would see it the way Jim Glenn had. She had intended to marry Glenn after she divorced Rush. They would have been happy, Lerner thought, a happiness that an inadequate husband had stolen from them by making Glenn an invalid for life.

Now, thinking about what Rush had said, it occurred to Lerner that no mention had been made of the fact that Glenn had saved Rush's life in the Head Quarters Saloon, that it had been Glenn, not Rush, who had been concerned about Nancy's safety, no mention of the rent he had owed Glenn, of his inadequacy as a husband, although it was possible he didn't even know he had not been a satisfactory husband. Perhaps the jury had not made a just decision, but Lerner questioned whether it was possible for any man or group of men to make a just decision in a case like this.

"That's all I can remember," Rush said finally. "It's in the past now. Whatever mistakes I made cannot be undone. I have not seen either my wife or Glenn since the trial. I don't want to. I tried to make something of my life when I was in prison, and since I was released I have gone back to work with men they thought I could help."

He wiped a hand across his face and began to tremble. "I don't know, Mr. Lerner," he said in a shaky voice. "This is something I cannot make a judgment about. The Lord will have to do that and I know He will. All of my life I have tried to do what the Lord wanted me to do, but sometimes it's been hard to know what He wants. I cannot believe I did wrong when I shot Jim Glenn. It is true that the Lord says vengeance is His, but the only hands the Lord has are our hands. I believe I was serving as the hand of the Lord when I pulled the trigger."

Lerner rose and shook hands with him. "Thank you for talking to me," he said. "You don't object to anything you've said being published?"

"No," Rush said in a tired voice. "I hope it will be published. It's the reason I talked to you. It seems to me that the Lord's part in solving the troubles of the world is never published for people to read, but the devil's side always gets into the newspaper."

When Lerner left the house Rush was still in his chair, a defeated and worn out man, still trying after more than twenty years to justify what he had done as the Lord's work.

On the train returning to Cheyenne, Lerner ran Rush's story back through his mind. He could not escape one fact, which seemed certain to him: if Frank Rush had really worked at being Nancy's husband, she would never have started the affair with Jim Glenn.

When Lerner reached his hotel, he went into the dining room for supper. He sat down at the table with a folded copy of the *Daily Sun,* left by some previous diner, in front of him. He opened the newspaper and saw the headline: JIM "MR. CHEYENNE" GLENN IS DEAD.

CHAPTER XXXVI

Lerner stayed in Cheyenne for the funeral, partly because he wanted to pay his respects to a man he had come to admire, and partly because he wanted to see what Cheyenne would do for one of her most beloved citizens. Also, he wanted to see and talk to Nancy Rush again after interviewing Frank.

He read everything the newspapers said about Jim Glenn. Nothing was derogatory, much was complimentary, some of it too sugar-sweet. Lerner did not catch any glaring errors of fact. A great deal was made of his gifts, along with statements to the effect that many of his gifts were not publicized and therefore not known.

Lerner was amused by the fact that, after having read Glenn's autobiography, he could have told the Cheyenne reporters several exciting events in Glenn's life that they didn't know. His efforts to obtain a trial for Ed Burke, for instance, and his shooting Jess Munro. Nothing was said about Nancy Rush, and Lerner was pleased by that. He had been afraid the old scandal would be dragged out again and attention focused on Nancy, as it had been when the shooting occurred.

He hired a rig and picked Nancy up shortly before one. The funeral was still more than an hour away, but she was ready, so they left her house at once. It was fortunate that they arrived at the Methodist Church early, because even then they had trouble finding seats. Long before the first prayer was prayed, people were standing along the sides and in the back of the sanctuary. Afterwards Lerner heard that hundreds were massed in the street outside the church.

Lerner saw nothing unusual about the funeral. He suspected that Glenn would not have approved of it. The smell of hellfire and brimstone was in the air, and Lerner was reminded of what Glenn had written about his mother's funeral, which he had remembered so well even though he had been only six at the time.

The one thing that made Lerner marvel was the great mass of flowers. Surely there could not have been that many in Cheyenne, he thought. Some must have been sent by train to Cheyenne from Denver.

One other thing surprised him: Nancy did not shed a tear. She sat beside him, her face grave, her hands folded on her lap. He could not keep from thinking what a handsome woman she was, even at a time like this. He wished he could have seen her when she was young and Jim Glenn had first fallen in love with her. Lerner could understand why Glenn had done what he had, but he could not understand how Frank Rush could have neglected her and been so unaware of her needs.

Lerner and Nancy drove to the cemetery with the funeral procession, a very long one. Afterwards the newspapers commented on its being the longest in Cheyenne's history. The graveside service was short, and as people began moving away, Nancy's elbow prodded Lerner in the ribs. He glanced at her and she gave him a bare half-inch nod to two women who had been crying visibly and loudly. They were middle-aged, plump, and looked exactly alike in their black dresses and floppy-brimmed black hats.

Nancy put her mouth to Lerner's ear. "The Martin women," she whispered. "Rosy and Flossie. They moved to Denver and got married and became respectable."

Lerner had to struggle to hold back a

smile. That would be exactly like them, he thought. The chances were they had married well and were making two men very happy.

Lerner still had two hours before train time, and when Nancy asked him to come into the house for a cup of coffee, he accepted. She did not go into the parlor, but again led him back to her sewing room.

One of the things he wanted to settle was the disposal of the earnings that Glenn's book would return in royalties. "We'll get it published somewhere," he told her. "As to how much it will make, your guess is as good as mine. There are sections I will use for the *Rocky Mountain News*. I suggest that I keep what the *News* pays me for my time, and whatever comes in from book publication will go to you."

She was startled. "Why should I have any part of it, Mr. Lerner?"

"This is something I had no chance to ask Jim Glenn," Lerner said. "It may not even have occurred to him that the book might make money, and that if it did some would come to him. A number of things impressed me when I read it, and one of them was the fact that he loved you very much. Whether what you and he did was right or wrong has nothing to do with the fact that he loved you. There is no question about that, so I'm equally sure he would want the royalty money to go to you."

She cried for the first time that day. When she could speak, she said, "You are a very kind man, Mr. Lerner. If you want to give me this money, I will take it and be thankful for it."

Lerner gave her his card. "You'll get it," he said. "If anything comes up or you want to contact me for some reason, write to me at that address. When you come to Denver, look me up. I would be proud to take a woman as beautiful as you to supper."

"I won't forget it," she said.

"I don't want to go into my talk with Frank Rush in detail except to say that he justified himself by claiming his hand was the hand of God when he pulled the trigger that night."

She stared at Lerner blankly for a moment until the full impact of what he had just said got through to her. Then she cried, "Why, he never used to talk that way. He's gone mad."

"I had that feeling," Lerner said. "He's brooded about it for so long and felt for so long that he didn't deserve the prison sentence he received that he isn't completely sane. But the point I wanted to ask you

about is this. He claimed Jim Glenn was an important man in town with money and property, whereas he was a man of no importance, with only a small congregation composed mostly of women. He believes that Glenn bribed the jury to find him guilty."

Nancy bowed her head, struggling with her temper for a time. Then she said, "There is not a word of truth in it. Frank has really lost his mind to even think that. I told you that Jim was carried into the courtroom on a stretcher to plead for Frank, asking that he not be found guilty — but the jury didn't listen."

"I was sure there was no truth to it," Lerner said, "but I wanted you to know what he was thinking."

She looked directly at him. "Just what are you going to say in the epilogue that you will write, Mr. Lerner?"

"I will say as little as I can, just enough so the reader will know that Glenn lived after the shooting and that Rush went to prison," Lerner said. "Perhaps also a few paragraphs about his gifts and what the people of Cheyenne thought of him."

"Don't you forget that that is what you will write." She rose and, walking to a window, stared at the lawn and row of hollyhocks that ran along the edge of her yard. "Jim read the Bible a good deal, particularly during the last two years, when he sensed he didn't have long to live. There is a passage in James that bothered him. It bothers me, too. It goes something like this: 'What is your life? It is a vapour that appeareth for a little time, and then vanisheth away.' Jim used to say it was such a waste if a man's life vanished away. I don't believe it does, Mr. Lerner. Not a life like Jim's. I like to remember what his father said, that there is no death. We keep right on living."

"I believe it," Lerner agreed. "Well, I've got to go or I'll miss my train."

She turned to him and kissed him on the cheek. "Thank you," she said. "Thank you very much."

"What will you do now?"

"I don't know," she said. "I spent a great deal of time with Jim the last two years while he waited to die. Now there doesn't seem to be anything to do that's worth doing."

"You'll find something," he said.

Later, after he had stowed his bag in the rack above the seat, he sat down and leaned his head against the red plush seat in the coach. He heard the train whistle and the bell clang, then felt the jolt of the car as the train began to move.

His mind went back to his talk with Alex Dolan and Dolan asking what Jim Glenn had meant by saying the sun is on the wall. He knew now, of course, and he would tell Dolan, but it would not really mean anything to the editor until he read Glenn's book.

What an extraordinary assignment it had been, Lerner thought, and then the quotation from James came into his mind. He smiled as he remembered what Nancy Rush had said about it. She was right, he told himself. Some lives might be like vapour and vanish away, but Jim Glenn's life would not be one of them.

ABOUT THE AUTHOR

Wayne D. Overholser has won three Golden Spur awards from the Western Writers of America and has a long list of fine Western titles to his credit. He was born in Pomeroy, Washington, and attended the University of Montana, University of Oregon, and the University of Southern California before becoming a public school teacher and principal in various Oregon communities. He began writing for Western pulp magazines in 1936 and within a couple of years was a regular contributor to Street & Smith's *Western Story* and Fiction House's *Lariat Story Magazine*. *Buckaroo's Code* (1948) was his first Western novel and remains one of his best. In the 1950s and 1960s, having retired from academic work to concentrate on writing, he would publish as many as four books a year under his own name or a pseudonym, most prominently as Joseph Wayne. *The Bitter Night, The Lone*

Deputy, and *The Violent Land* are among the finest of the early Overholser titles. He was asked by William MacLeod Raine, that dean among Western writers, to complete his last novel after Raine's death. Some of Overholser's most rewarding novels were actually collaborations with other Western writers: *Colorado Gold* with Chad Merriman and *Showdown at Stony Creek* with Lewis B. Patten. Overholser's Western novels, no matter under what name they have been published, are based on a solid knowledge of the history and customs of the American frontier West, particularly when set in his two favorite Western states, Oregon and Colorado. When it comes to his characters, he writes with skill, an uncommon sensitivity, and a consistently vivid and accurate vision of a way of life unique in human history.

The employees of Thorndike Press hope you have enjoyed this Large Print book. All our Thorndike, Wheeler, and Kennebec Large Print titles are designed for easy reading, and all our books are made to last. Other Thorndike Press Large Print books are available at your library, through selected bookstores, or directly from us.

For information about titles, please call:
(800) 223-1244

or visit our Web site at:
http://gale.cengage.com/thorndike

To share your comments, please write:
Publisher
Thorndike Press
295 Kennedy Memorial Drive
Waterville, ME 04901